Poles Apart?
The Experience of Gender

Poles Apart?

The Experience of Gender

Alistair White

J. M. Dent & Sons Ltd
London

First published 1989
© Alistair White 1989

All rights reserved. No part of this publication
may be reproduced, stored in a retrieval system, or
transmitted, in any form or by any means, electronic,
mechanical, photocopying, recording or otherwise, without
the prior permission of J. M. Dent & Sons Ltd

This book is set in 10/12pt Garamond by
Deltatype, Ellesmere Port
Made in Great Britain by Guernsey Press Co. Ltd,
Guernsey, C. I. for
J. M. Dent & Sons Ltd
91 Clapham High Street, London SW4 7TA

This book is sold subject to the condition that it
may not be resold or otherwise issued except in its
original binding

British Library Cataloguing in Publication Data
White, Alistair
    Poles apart: the experience of gender
    1. Sex roles. Psychosocial aspects
    I. Title
    305.3

ISBN 0–460–12562–1

Contents

1	Between Ourselves	1
2	Are Women and Men Different Kinds of People?	13
3	In the Temple of the Heart	24
4	Freedom, Intimacy and the Self	36
5	Gender and Personality	50
6	Tenderness	64
7	Goodness and Justice	76
8	Mother Nature, Father Time	83
9	Dependence and Independence	97
10	Being an Individual	117
11	The Best of Both Worlds?	136
12	Humanity	143
13	Turning the World In-side Out	153
14	Personal Relationships	160
	References	175
	Index of Names	177
	Index of Subjects	179

1 · Between Ourselves

Why do things go wrong in relationships between men and women, and what is to be done about it? Are women and men poles apart and destined to remain so? It is a brave man who gets up in public to say he thinks he has an answer to these particular chestnuts. But it would also be pointless and irresponsible to write a book about it which was not trying to find one. It is the trying that counts, which is why the question mark is the most important part of the title. But this book does offer something in the way of conclusions, and since it is not a whodunnit there is nothing to be lost by giving away the plot, and I intend to do so in a moment.

First, whether brave or otherwise, it matters that I am a man. Simone de Beauvoir once wrote that 'a man would never set out to write a book on the peculiar situation of the human male', and that 'a man never begins by presenting himself as an individual of a certain sex',* She would clearly be happy to be proved wrong on both counts. But this is a book about gender, which means it is also about the peculiar situation of women. Many will find this most unwelcome: a man cannot in principle know about that, and has no business trying to write about it. Men, they will say, have long held forth on the subject of women and it is time for women to stop listening to them and work it out for themselves. And men always get into and finally take over whatever show is in town, and if that is gender, so be it. As Rik Mayall wisely observed: 'All men are feminists now. It's the only way to pull the chicks.'

There are often good reasons for not listening to people and those people are often men. There are all kinds of ways of using words that have the effect of confining, confounding and intimidating others,

*Full details of authors and works referred to in the text are listed at the end of the book.

and the people who are most practised in many of these arts – rhetoric, abstraction, certainty, convolution – are often men. And people who are denied a voice have a justified wariness of others who seem to like the sound of their own. But it is evident that I do not accept that men should hold their tongue on the question of gender or that they should stick to talking about themselves. Sooner or later women and men are going to have to start listening to each other, and the sooner the better. Is there any hope of it?

At one time feminism thought it had the answer to that: men simply have too much to lose to risk taking women seriously. Free and open communication is impossible where there are powerful vested interests at stake. While they persist, shouting, mystification and closed ears will be the order of the day. But since most feminists do not wish to see all men hang, at some point men will have to be included in the conversation. And this particular response offers nothing to women and men who feel the force of the argument but still aspire to reasonable relationships with each other.

Everyone also knows how difficult it is to disentangle vested interest from unfinished business, and it is both that prevent women and men listening to one another. Many of the most difficult and emotionally charged issues that we have had to deal with in the course of our lives, ones that engage with fears and desires that we otherwise set aside, are bound up in relations with the opposite sex. The ideas and images that we construct of one another and see in one another are bound to bear the marks of their origins, and be filled with ambivalence, contradiction and all manner of issues that remain unsettled. Human beings are not noted for their preparedness to struggle to grasp and appreciate other people's point of view at the best of times, but the chances of women and men getting each other to listen with a reasonably open mind would appear to be rather slim. They may even not be prepared to give each other the satisfaction.

The genuinely world-shaking insights of the best feminist thought are easily drowned by the sound of grinding axes. There is no doubt that many men and many women simply do not understand what is being said. Where what is being said is something about *them*, and they think they do understand it, they often do not believe it or think it does not apply to them. They are often right, but many listen only to what rankles or to the often cruel half-truths, and will not seek out and attend to the other half. Listening, though, is a positive spiral.

Listening to people, just listening, may often be the best way of ignoring them, but when people know they really are being listened to, they are more careful about what they say, more free to entertain confusion, and more disposed to listen themselves. When they feel that nobody is listening to them they either cut themselves off or start shouting. As two ways of not being heard there is little to choose between them. You shout because no-one listens to you when you talk quietly, and then they do not listen to you because you are shouting. Cutting off may well commend itself as the only peaceable solution, and this is something both women and men know a lot about.

Is there any hope of women and men not cutting off without getting into a shouting match? I think there is. Conflict between women and men is, of course, nothing new. Enmity between women and men was even numbered among the punishments for original sin. But the forms and focus of the conflict shift, and there is now an impulse towards change that is more widely felt than many imagine. What will become of it only time will tell – though of course the telling thing will be what each of us does about it.

And so to the rudiments of the plot. While a synopsis may be helpful in some ways, it is also inevitably over-abstract, indigestible and out of keeping with the character of the book as a whole. So I will put it two ways. The second is on the cryptic side, but I will elaborate on that one because it provides a better sense of the gist and the flavour of what is to come. (This is a serious book, but on the definition of an intellectual as someone who can hear the 'William Tell Overture' without thinking of the Lone Ranger, it may be the intellectual who finds it hard going.)

First, then, the abstract synopsis. The principal setting is within the realm of what is called 'personal life'. The conflicts, frustrations and disappointments that women and men have to contend with within this sphere often seem to them to be idiosyncratic or purely private. But these are in fact expressive of tensions and contradictions that run deep into the heart of our kind of society. If there is a villain of the piece it is not males, but the central element of a masculine world-view: a contrast between the realm of the 'personal' and the realm of 'society'. This contrast is rooted in men's experience of life on either side of the fragile wall that divides the public and private worlds in this society, and the manner in which they pass back and forth between them. This gives men something of a common and distinctive outlook on life, something which is as much a way of feeling as of thinking about things. The ideas that men have built upon this foundation make sense in terms of their own experience but they make considerably less sense of women's experience. As things stand, women and men tend to develop clashing and conflicting perspectives on the world, themselves and each other, and end up talking, feeling and living past one another a great deal of the time. The issues this throws up cannot be settled purely in private. A resolution depends on achieving some synthesis of the feminine and masculine perspectives – not simply in thought, but in the way life is lived. What this ultimately entails is reforming the relationship between the public and the private as it is set up in this society and as we live it in our own experience. Or to put it more simply: it is men who are the true romantics, and it may well be up to women to bring them to their senses.

It is now a century and a half since the masculine sentiment flowed through the pen of Lord Byron and wrote: 'Man's love is of man's life a thing apart; 'Tis a Woman's whole existence.' Here was a man hoping to make real a creature of his own imagination. Love was to be, for the man, a thing apart. He had other things to attend to, important things, and she was to wait for him, maybe find ways to occupy herself, make the place look nice or something. When it was time for love, he wanted it to be with someone who was not a part-timer. He sought in woman a being unlike himself, as if from another world, and he hoped to meet her in a realm set apart – away from and untainted by the public affairs of men. To convince himself that woman really was the complete personification of the episodic kind of love that he himself aspired to, he had to reach new heights of egocentrism and self-deception. He had to deny and fail to appreciate many aspects of the woman's point of view, but above all he had not to dwell too long on the fact that he was rendering women literally social outcasts. Even in his prettiest accounts of it, he wanted women to be *outsiders*.

Men have continued to pass back and forth between public and private worlds in such a way that they hope to put the private behind them when they enter the public and the public behind them when they enter the private, and they still depend on women to enable them to do both. And men still hope to meet women on a terrain that feels to them to lie outside society. The more it changes the more it stays the same. But it does change, and has changed – to the point where men now have an interest in women not being prepared to put up with their ways any longer.

The doctrine of separate spheres for women and men said three things, two of them explicitly. It said women and men belong in different spheres, and, just as importantly, it also said these spheres are in fact separate and must be kept separate. What it implied but omitted to say was that women's sphere lay outside society. And so men came to occupy a public space from which women and the concerns associated with women were excluded. But what did they build in this space? Men have collectively collaborated, often unwittingly and often unwillingly, in the construction of a public world from which they hope to flee into the arms of women. It may be erring on the side of melodramatic overstatement to put it this way, but what men now seek in women is refuge from a monster of their own creation.

Individual men do not feel, of course, that this monster is *their* creation – they are simply busy surviving. But to a considerable extent they survive *as men*, and this is how such monsters are nourished and kept alive. Men as well as women relate to social definitions of masculinity and femininity with, as Lynne Segal put it, 'varying degrees of acceptance, ambivalence, tension, conflict, and antagonism'. (It is always easy to think of *other* people as conformists.) No man and no woman is masculine or feminine through and through, as though it were like letters in a stick of seaside rock, or driven into your back with needles like the name of your crime in Kafka's penal colony. But the proof of the pudding is in the eating. Whatever their secret attitude towards it, men tend to cope as men, deal with things in the manner of men. In so doing they develop a greater investment than ever in meeting women on another plane, in a realm beyond society.

But is not the doctrine of separate spheres now dead if not yet buried? Has not the notice on the gateway to society which said 'Men Only' finally been taken down? On the face of it, it seems that increasing numbers of women are throwing off their status as outsiders and encroaching ever deeper into public space. But these gains are largely illusory. It is the public world which has shifted its boundaries and drawn in more women, and even then most remain stranded at its outer edges. The majority of women now work outside the home for most of their lives and this means they earn some money. Because of this women have gained increasing status in one particular public realm in which we are all included: the society of the consumer. Clothes, hair, cosmetics, convenience foods, a million and one things to do with soap and scent – women are now very big business. It is no coincidence that the picture of woman that the more prestigious fashion designers say they design for should come so perilously close to the image of the post-feminist woman.

The more important point here, though, is what they do to earn this money. The vast majority of women work in insecure, low-paid, low-status, menial and routine jobs with no prospects. Even more significant is the nature of these jobs. Virtually all are either direct domestic exports (catering, cleaning, nursing), public expressions of women's traditional domestic concerns (education, health and welfare), routine 'nimble finger' manufacturing jobs, or ancillary positions supporting the main action (secretarial, clerical, and various kinds of 'assistants'). Where working-class girls once went into service they now go into the service industries. What the middle-class woman once did in the home she now does for the state, and the part she played in the 'family' business she now performs for the company.

But perhaps more importantly still, the business of housework and childcare, of all those activities involved in keeping people in good repair, remain in most households the responsibility of women. (I use the word 'responsibility' advisedly. It does not matter how much he helps – though it helps – if the responsibility is still hers.) If she can hold down a job at the same time, then all well and good. (The 'busy mum' depicted in commercials extolling the virtues of various products on the dance-exercise floor is no more liberated than the 'homely mum' – she is just busy doing two jobs.) It is the fact that so many women must be a houseworker and mother first that has made possible the recent huge growth in part-time jobs. The overwhelming proportion of the increase in women's employment in the last twenty years has been in various forms of part-time work. Women take these jobs because they fit in with their domestic obligations; they are, as many women put it, 'convenient'.

The doctrine of separate spheres has, in short, only undergone relatively minor and superficial modifications. The public ship has grown and taken on more female hands, but women remain well away from the bridge, confirmed as first and foremost creatures of the home port. At the same time, the ways in which women are defined as outsiders have become more subtle. You cannot find out about gender simply by studying statistics. It is there in what a man sees when he looks at a woman, what a woman sees when she looks at a man, and what each sees when they look at someone of the same sex as themselves.

Many men would deny to the heavens that they have an interest in keeping women as outsiders, and close their ears forthwith. In this they are aided and abetted by those who insist that what men see when they look at a woman is a mere sexual object to use and abuse as the fancy takes them. In fact men now have an immense investment in seeing in women a quality that is, to them, the very opposite of being an object: a peculiarly modern and masculine notion of what it is to be a 'person'.

Women are already, in a particular sense, 'persons' first. Men confirm women's status as outsiders in the workplace, for example, by seeing and responding to women in a more 'personal' way. Leering, innuendo and other forms of sexual harassment are only some of the ways in which, by responding to something that is not an inherent part of the job or of working relationships, women are judged to be less serious participants. There are much less obvious and in the end more significant ways of doing this, most evident perhaps when men smile at a woman in a situation where they would not have smiled at a man.

Men want to feel that their relationships with women are of a different order to those that characterize life in the public world. The presence of a woman may offer to a man an opportunity to respond more 'personally' than he is able to with other men. This is one of the principal ways in which women today are expelled from society. As the public world takes on an increasingly impersonal character, so man sees woman and steps out of 'role', and so out of this world, however fleetingly, in order to engage with her – a brief exchange, tending towards intimacy, rooted in men's sense that women are what can only be described as more 'personal' kinds of person than men. But what is a brief moment of respite for him, ultimately confirms women's status as first and foremost creatures of the private sphere of personal life.

What happens then when women and men meet in the private sphere? We are, as we shall see, bound to meet as strangers, and pass each other by like ships in the night. Very often it is literally in the night, for the bedroom can seem to the man to be the ultimate terrain beyond society.

Frustration, disillusion and disappointment are not exactly new, but during the course of this century the expectations that women and men have of their personal lives have been steadily rising. People are no longer prepared to countenance what they imagine to have been the distant co-existence that previous generations had to endure. The emergence of the idea of 'psychological problems' is part of this development. It is no coincidence that women figure so prominently in the practice and folklore of psychotherapy or that the therapeutic should have found its way into magazines for women. But men too have been touched by this, and are far more inclined to feel that there may be something amiss in their emotional lives.

Men are becoming ever more acutely conscious of the price they pay for what seems to be an increasingly dubious privilege: finding a niche in the outside world. The price is repeated failures in intimate relationships. (The fact that men often do not act as if intimate relationships were that important is profoundly misleading. People of both sexes harbour longings that they keep to themselves, and silently accuse others of failing to provide for what they feel to be their real needs.) Perhaps most men would dearly like to have their cake and eat it: to be full members and rightful guardians of the public world, and get their emotional needs satisfied at home. But they cannot have the best of both worlds, this is impossible in principle. If men aspire to greater things emotionally, this does not mean they are prepared to make many sacrifices for it – but they would have to. Why?

Firstly because women have their own ideas about being outsiders – though not all women have the same ideas. Women born or educated into that sphere of society where women have long resented being excluded from public life are most likely to think first of gaining access to that world, of participating within it on an equal footing to men. They also, of course, want change in the realm of personal life, but they often imagine that women who seem content to remain within the domestic sphere are not interested in change or in equality. Women from that sphere of society where it has always been much clearer that women's domestic work was both work and necessary are less likely to see employment as a privilege. If they go out to work it is for the money and to escape domestic isolation – not to embark on a bright new future. In between the two are many women who are profoundly ambivalent. But *within* the private sphere, and this is what matters here, women throughout society are looking to renegotiate the terms of endearment.

There is a pressure coming from both women and men to settle those conflicts in the private sphere which impair, obstruct, undermine or even destroy their relationships with one another. But as things stand this is nigh impossible, for two reasons. The first is that most people – women and men – in this society are investing more and more in their personal lives (and not just the vast sums they spend on furnishings, DIY and electrical goods) to such an extent that intimate relationships threaten to collapse under the strain. This huge investment arises as a reaction to the monster – to the ugliness, emptiness, impersonality, anonymity and uncontrollability of the public sphere. Personal life will implode under the pressure unless we trace it to its source, redistribute our energies, and come to make more demands of the public world.

The second obstacle to better relationships in the private sphere is more fundamental and intractable – and it is this that will preoccupy us for the central part of this book. The experience of living as a woman or a man in this society leads each to develop different ways of understanding what personal life is about. The different experience women and men have of the public, the private, and the relationship between them ensures that this is so. The 'idea' of love, of what intimacy is and how it might be achieved, that arises out of women's experience is not the same as that which arises out of men's experience. And this clash of perspectives is not at all confined to intimacy. Women and men also develop different understandings of the nature of the self, of the meaning of tenderness, friendship, individuality, dependence and independence, nature and culture, time, justice, and many more that are fundamental to the ways we think and feel about life. This is how we pass each other by.

But if there are different perspectives on these things, it is masculine perspectives that still dominate in public discourse. In the new form of understanding that has arisen on the basis of the masculine experience, the poet has turned psychologist. In one of his favourite compositions, the modern romantic no longer declaims: 'man's love is of man's life a thing apart; 'tis a woman's whole existence', instead he croons: 'man's *self* is of man's life a thing apart; 'tis a woman's whole existence'. The masculine romantic sentiment now speaks in psychological tongues.

It is the sense that personal life lies outside society that gives rise to the idea that the study of the hearts and minds of individuals is separable from the study of society, and can be established as an independent discipline. This means that the idea of such an independent discipline can only arise in a society divided by gender, because it is in the *masculine* experience that the realm of personal life appears cut off in this particular way. The idea that an individual can be taken out of context and thought about in isolation is the basis of psychology, and this idea is born of the experience of men. (There is a significant complication here which will have to be dealt with at various points in what follows: psychology has an affinity with a middle-class world-view, as well as with a masculine one. You never get gender without class and vice versa.)

Most of the topics that this book is concerned with – the self, personal identity, personality, dependence and independence, individuality, and so on – would appear to be psychology's home ground. But the idea that you can straightforwardly have a psychology *of* gender is profoundly misleading. Gender has crucial implications for what psychology *is*, taking gender seriously involves rethinking what it means to have a psychology of *anything*. In a way there is 'women's psychology' and 'men's psychology', but by that I mean one form of understanding that arises out of the experience of women and one which arises out of the experience of men. We cannot take existing psychological concepts and apply them to women and men, for this would be to see women through the eyes of men and we already know how to do that.

We have to listen to and try to make sense of both women's and men's experience of personal life. It then becomes clear that this is not a sealed off universe in which we are settling or failing to settle issues that are purely between ourselves. As things stand, both women and men in the society have something of a sense that the private sphere is in the world but not of it (though I think their meanings of this are different). Here it seems that at least in principle it is possible to renegotiate the terms of endearment without intrusions from the outside world. But the problems and conflicts that arise in the sphere of personal life derive fundamentally from the nature of personal life in this society, from the place it occupies in relation to the whole. And it occupies a different place for women and men. Men still want the private to be a thing apart, a terrain beyond society, something they can dip in and out of. This is not how it is for women, and the man's idea of love remains as alien to her experience as the sentiments of Lord Byron. I do not think men understand this, nor do I think women understand men's failure to understand.

There are things that women know and understand because they have found them to be so in their own experience, which men do not know or understand because they have a different experience. And the reverse is equally true. Better relations between women and men, and the creation of a society in which women and men are first of all human, both depend on listening to and drawing on both sets of experience. Neither of us is right, and neither of us is wrong.

As we dig deeper into the nature of these conflicting perspectives we will find that we soon come up against some of the load-bearing pillars of our kind of civilization. Personal life turns out to be a microcosm in which we deal with issues that are by no means simply between ourselves. This, in my view, is the genuinely world-shaking insight of the best feminist writing: that the private sphere is not a sealed-off universe set apart from society. The consequences of recognizing this for understanding and changing everyday relations between women and men and society as a whole are immense and wholly positive. But this insight is by no means peculiar to feminism. It is also central to important strands in that tradition of thought which combines the study of what it is to be human with the struggle to create a more human society: humanism. Just as feminism means putting women first by looking at the world from women's point of view and promoting women's interests, so humanism aspires to put human beings first.

Superficially humanism sounds like a simple advance on feminism – but of course the problem with humanism is that it seems a bit like being in favour of oxygen. In fact there is a central core to the kind of humanism I shall speak up for towards the end of the book, which makes it considerably more than that. Nevertheless, there is no doubt that few humanists have taken gender seriously enough. Gender equality is, of course, a humanist goal – but it is the 'of course' that feminism has objected to. Most forms of feminism are ultimately humanist, but they have had enough of the attitude of: 'it goes without saying that women are included'. *Why* have humanists gone on without saying it? Whatever the reason, the consequences have been serious. For in simply assuming that gender equality is, of course, a humanist goal, humanism has blinded itself to the implications of gender for the nature of its own project. The actual inclusion of women changes not only the sex of the participants, but what it is that humanists want to achieve.

If the creation of a more 'human' society means anything, and I think it does, then any vision we might form of it must combine and go beyond the feminine and masculine perspectives. Neither women nor men can provide a model for humanity, it involves incorporating and transcending both the feminine and the masculine into some kind of new synthesis.

The final four chapters are devoted to understanding what this might mean, what it might entail to have the best of both worlds. The central chapters are given over to the exploration of women's and men's experience of personal life, in particular our experience of the self, personality, intimacy and distance, tenderness and vulnerability, morality, time, the relationship between mind and body, dependence and independence, identity and individuality. But we must start by asking what gender is, beginning with what might seem to be the star prize question: are women and men different kinds of people?

First, a final word of caution. The painter Kit Williams once said to me that there is enough in a yard of English hedgerow to last anyone a lifetime, and the same surely applies to the briefest span of human life. And yet it is extraordinary how often writers on gender are criticized for what they leave out, for what they do not say – as if to not-talk about something is to insist that it is not worth talking about. The result is books and articles which often read like completed questionnaires: these are the issues, indicate where you stand by ticking the appropriate box. You will not find the entire countryside crammed into these pages.

And if the seeds of the future are here in the present, they are first and foremost here in the *confusions* of the present. As Franz Kafka observed, the difficulty in telling the truth is that the truth is alive and has a live and changing face. Between ourselves, I am less concerned that you accept my conclusions than that I have helped the face of the familiar to refuse to sit still.

2 · Are Women and Men Different Kinds of People?

> ... to go for a walk with one's eyes open is enough to demonstrate that humanity is divided into two classes of individuals whose clothes, faces, bodies, smiles, gaits, interests and occupations are manifestly different. Perhaps these differences are superficial, perhaps they are destined to disappear. What is certain is that they do most obviously exist. (Simone de Beauvoir)

In the late 1940s, a scanty two-piece swimsuit exploded on to the sun drenched beaches of the playgrounds of the western world. And in the late 1940s, the United States Navy chose a site in the Marshall islands in the Pacific Ocean to test and to demonstrate to the world the growing power of its thermo-nuclear arsenal. Struck by the evident similarities between the devastating effects of the Bomb and the devastating effects of women wearing those scanty two-piece swimsuits, they decided to name the swimsuit after that place, which was called Bikini Atoll.

If this is the masculine imagination, it is not surprising that some regard men as a luxury the world cannot afford. Only a man, it is said, would even think of making such a connection between sexuality and the power to destroy, let alone congratulate himself for his wit. The show of strength and the reduction of women to objects of men's desire – it seems to confirm the most damning indictments of the male of the species.

And yet, were there not many men who could not so easily blot out the recent memory of Hiroshima with the image of a Blonde Bombshell? Were they the exceptions that proved the rule? Diluted versions of masculine concentrate, pale imitations of the Real McCoy? As recently as 1987, a British prime minister (female) could declare that unilateral nuclear disarmament would 'emasculate' the

British Lion. What then of its male proponents? Is everything from pacifism to a vestige of humanity essentially female or feminine?

Many women appear to have concluded precisely that. Men, they say, stand for all those things that set people against one another – violence, mastery, competition, calculation. It's not just that we have to put up with men, we actually stand for the very opposites of these things. We have nurtured amongst ourselves those qualities that serve to connect people with one another, to preserve life, to promote and enhance human well-being. It is women who embody the essential human qualities of empathy and responsiveness to other people's needs, and an openness and receptiveness to others.

Some men have taken all this to heart, and taken up (as David Morgan put it) either a 'confessional' stance – you're right, we men are an ugly proposition – or a 'petitional' one – you're right, but don't be too hard on us, we've got problems too. Others have not taken at all kindly to being deemed the personification of the Hideous. How can I, as a man, accept the charge that all men stand shoulder to shoulder as the common enemy, not only of all women, but of humanity itself? Must we return once again (with Ronald Reagan perhaps) to the eternal struggle between the forces of good, light, life and renewal, and the forces of evil, darkness, death and destruction – only now with the Prince of Darkness and the Princess of Light as the leading protagonists?

The new mythology seems to echo the old in the most fundamental respect: women and men really are two different kinds of people. On the face of it this seems a crazy proposition – on a par with the idea that there are two kinds of people in the world: those who leave the top off the toothpaste tube and those who never fail to screw it firmly back on. Bertrand Russell and Lyndon B. Johnson may both have been male heterosexuals, but, as Gore Vidal once asked, what character traits did *they* have in common? There may be a much simpler answer to the gender question.

Vidal put it this way for the benefit of his *Playboy* readers: ' "What do women want?" Freud once asked, plaintively. Well Sigmund, they want equality with men.' It is not about 'character traits', what matters is the simple fact that eminent philosophers and political leaders, whether pacifists or warmongers, are nearly all men. Wittingly or otherwise, Bertrand Russell and Lyndon Johnson were both parties to those social processes which cast immense obstacles in the way of women ending up where they had done. Amongst those obstacles are a vast armoury of spurious notions about the difference between women and men. Wait, as the French radical feminist Christine Delphy said, until women live on an equal footing with men, and then we'll see whether such differences are real.

Unfortunately the simple answer turns out to be a simplistic one (whatever its merits as political strategy). It is simplistic for many reasons, just two of which matter at this stage (in fact these turn out to be two different ways of saying the same thing). Firstly it is plain that women and men in our kind of society live, in varying degrees, different kinds of lives. It would be a very strange way of understanding what people are about which suggested that living different kinds of lives did not in *some* way make us different kinds of people. I say 'make us', but this is only half of it – we are what life makes of us and what we make of life, in equal measure.

Secondly, there is a fundamental difficulty in separating fact from fiction when it come to human beings. The beliefs we hold about ourselves, about other people and society, themselves play a crucial part in shaping the way we live (though again this is a half-truth: our beliefs shape the way we live and the way we live shapes our beliefs). If we believe that women and men are two different kinds of people, then we can and do, in a sense and to a degree, make it come true.

A general practitioner once told a friend of mine that there were two kinds of people in the world – ferrets and Queen Mothers – and it was his misfortune to be a ferret. A ferret by nature lives frantically, darting this way and that, searching, rummaging, ferreting about excitedly then suddenly bolting down holes in the ground – a disposition conducive to all kinds of ailments in human beings. He should try to be more of a Queen Mother. A Queen Mother glides effortlessly, or remains serenely motionless, weight evenly distributed throughout the body, only the head slowly pivoting, the slightly cupped hand tracing in the air the perfect curve we accept as royalty waving. The GP might, perhaps, just have told him to calm down, but we are more receptive to a vivid metaphor than to any amount of straightforward good advice.

Metaphors are invitations – to consider yourself or some aspect of the world in a certain light, in an 'as if' kind of way (the very opposite of those ways of using words that have the effect of confining people, which I spoke of earlier). Compelling metaphors, if they succeed in bringing into focus some livable vision of another way, may actually draw people closer to it. But our capacity to make imaginative use of metaphor is constantly undermined by a tendency to mistake compelling metaphors for reality itself. When all is said and done, a ferret is a partially trained polecat with yellowish-white fur and pink eyes, and there is only one Queen Mother – the GP clearly did not mean it literally. But it is possible that these might have been intended, or taken, as emblems of actual human types. If a ferret is what you 'are', then there is little you can do but carry on much as before, look on enviously as the Queen Mothers sail by, and curse your way into an early grave.

When metaphors take on the character of 'facts', instead of inviting, they pass sentence. The stories that get told of what it is to be a woman or a man abound with vivid metaphors disguised as truths, and thereby they beguile us into thinking that this is what we are – there's an end to it, like it or lump it. They turn the power of imagination against itself, blunting its capacity seriously to envisage ways in which things might be otherwise. This is so whether we are talking about individuals and the possibility of individual change, or society and the possibility of societal change.

The idea that women and men are different kinds of people is one of the central guiding myths of our kind of civilization. But by 'myth' I do not mean fiction, illusion or delusion. Perhaps we would like to be able to say: that of all the things that are said of women and men, these are the true things and these the false – but life just is not like that. We are imaginative beings and we live by our imaginations. We live by the stories we tell ourselves and each other – they cannot simply be fiction. Our guiding myths and metaphors must be capable of sustaining life – they cannot simply be false.

In an important sense we *are* the imaginative visions of the world and ourselves that we find most compelling – they construct us as much as we construct them. ('Imaginative visions'? As Humpty Dumpty said to Alice: 'When I make a word do a lot of work I always pay it extra' – you will find that I have had to fork out a lot of overtime for these two.) There is nothing 'imaginary' about such imaginative visions – they serve as the foundations of the ways we live our lives. They underpin and are embodied in the ways we act, think and feel, giving shape to our hopes and fears, dreams and nightmares. And they are not constructed out of thin air but grounded in the lives we lead, in our experience of the worlds in which we move.

If our beliefs about people were whimsical or without foundation they would lead us quite a merry dance into oblivion. So, too, if they were entirely idiosyncratic. (We do have our own private myths, but there is also a set of common mythologies. This must be so, because we live in relation to other people, our lives are synchronized together, and without some commonalities life could not go on.) But if we believe in something – really believe in it and not just pay lip-service – we are apt to insist on it, even if this involves denying or distorting all evidence to the contrary. More often this is not necessary, because we are adept at fabricating evidence to confirm our beliefs. And it has to be said that, on occasions, this does indeed involve the use of force.

In one of the opening scenes of Costa-Gavras's film *Missing*, an army jeep pulls up alongside a bus queue, a woman is hauled out into the road to have the legs of her trousers slit with a knife by one of the soldiers, and the scene ends with the words ringing in our ears: 'From now on, women in this country wear dresses.' This is Chile after the right-wing military coup of the 1970s, and what is striking about the scene is that we are not astonished or baffled by it. This is partly because we are not used to seeing gangs of women going around terrorizing the neighbourhood and so – particularly if we are men and often feel terrorized ourselves – scarcely remark on the fact that it is generally men (though not men generally) who do. (If the soldiers had been women, if they had taken out a needle and thread and sewn up the middle of a man's dress – now that would have been surprising.) But we are also not baffled because the fact that a politics based on an appeal to a return to old certainties should insist on such a clarity about gender is, whatever else it might be, perfectly comprehensible. Gender, it seems, is part of the bedrock: there are women and there are men, let us at least be sure about that.

But if the myth survives, it is not only or even principally kept alive by such acts of violent coercion. A great deal of everyday social life is given over, as it were, to fabricating evidence to fit the theory.

We are born either female or male. Gender begins when someone notices what sex you are and makes something of it. You can be sure they will, for sex is loaded with significance. It is enough to make the point to ask: of all the things you might potentially fail to register or remember about someone, when did you ever forget what sex someone was, even after the most fleeting encounter? We notice and remember because, whether we wish it so or not, sex is significant, and it is this significance that is called gender.

We are 'gendered' at birth and throughout our lives remain enmeshed in a system of signs. The signs themselves change, but virtually any object or activity, it seems, can be designated either feminine or masculine: purses, knickers and patterned umbrellas, sewing on buttons and lager and lime; wallets, underpants and black umbrellas, snooker, Real Ale and nuclear physics. (What matters is not whether a man will carry a patterned umbrella, but whether, if he does, he feels the need to make a joke about it or account for it in some other way.) Such gendering of everything under the sun can seem as arbitrary and pointless as it does when learning where to use 'le' and 'la' in French. Mark Twain once gave vent to his irritation with grammatical gender in an essay tactfully entitled 'The Awful German Language'. Mr Twain clearly despaired of a language in which 'a person's mouth, neck, bosom, elbows, fingers, nails, feet, and body are of the male sex . . . a person's nose, lips, shoulders, breasts, hands, and toes are of the female sex; and his hair, ears, eyes, chin, legs, knees, heart and conscience haven't any sex at all'.

But there is method in the madness of gendering in human affairs, it is by no means arbitrary or pointless. It would be misleading to say these signs have a purpose, that they are there for a reason – as though 'the system' was cleverly designed by someone. But the imagery of gender plays a crucial part in holding in place some of the pillars of our form of civilization. This cathedral of ideas has solid foundations.

What are these foundations? One is clearly the subordination of women to men. For the most part, constructions of femininity either paint a picture of women as deficient in various ways, or judge them ideally suited for those kinds of activities which in this society are considered – protestations not withstanding – relatively unimportant. The various meanings of the suffix 'ette' are enough to make the point: it indicates woman (as in usherette), small (as in kitchenette) and imitation (as in flannelette – which is also fluffier than flannel!). But there is much more to it that that.

Life as we know it is everywhere and anywhere saturated with gender, but at the heart of it lies one central principle in the structuring of social life: the division of the world into two apparently distinct spheres of existence – the 'public' world of industry, of the production and circulation of commodities, of economics, politics, education and so on, and the 'private' world of home, family and friends. The roots of gender lie in the separation of the kinds of activities and relationships that make up the public world from those that make up the private, and the polarities of feminine and masculine represent the pulling apart of these spheres.

The so-called doctrine of 'separate spheres' for women and men has, as I made clear earlier, only undergone relatively minor modifications. Men still occupy the heartland of the public world, and the idea still prevails that, in the end, women's first and most powerful affinity is with the realms of domestic life and 'personal' relationships. But the doctrine of separate spheres does not only assert that women are the natural creatures of the private world and men of the public world, it also insists that these spheres are in fact separate. It is not just that, if it comes to the crunch, a woman's place is in the home, but also that a home's place is outside of society. It turns out that calling gender into question poses a threat to the established order that runs far deeper than appears at first sight. It threatens to expose as fraudulent this pillar of our form of civilization, namely the belief that the public and the private are distinct and independent realms of existence. They are not – as we shall see – and gender is the principal means by which the illusion is sustained, and their interconnections obscured.

The simple message at the heart of all these contrasts between the feminine and the masculine is this: there are two kinds of people in the world, women and men, let us at least be clear about that. This conveys a belief that is hard to shake, because to do so is to shake the very foundations of our kind of society. Is this belief pure fiction then? By no means

To be identified as a girl or a boy, a woman or a man, is to bring into play a set of constructions which underpin the ways you will be perceived, acted towards, and yourself expected to act, think and feel. You find yourself being looked on or defined in a certain way, find that others make certain kinds of assumptions about you and demands upon you, subject you to certain kinds of treatment. These hardly need cataloguing, indeed the list seems inexhaustible – but as a woman you are likely to be taken to be less robust than a man, be expected to prefer a tidy house and to like to 'chat' about the day's events; you are more likely to be talked down to, smiled at and ignored, to be associated with ironing, lace and cottage cheese. As a man you are likely to be assumed to know what you're doing, be expected to like fixing things and taking up space; you are more likely to be challenged to physical and verbal combat, to be associated with machinery and a hearty appetite. These are elements of the social identity of woman or man.

Being the *focus* of such things locates you, as it were, in a particular position in social space. (In T. S. Eliot's famous lines: 'the eyes that fix you in a formulated phrase, and when I am formulated, sprawling on a pin, when I am pinned and wriggling on the wall, then how should I begin . . . ?') But they also locate you somewhere more literally, because ultimately all these definitions of the feminine and masculine are *routing slips* that direct you towards different spheres of activity, to those places in society reserved for women and men. A notorious French sociologist (who shall remain nameless) used the word 'interpellation' to describe this routing process. It means 'Hey you! Over there.' Females this way, males that way – there are places where you belong.

To be a woman or a man, then, is first and foremost to inhabit particular positions in the social landscape. But this does *not* mean that women and men are not different kinds of people in any other sense. A history of living under the social identity of woman or man clearly leave its mark in the significances that we as individuals attach to being female or male. Who or what I am to myself includes whatever the fact of my being female or male has come to mean to me – what I have made of it and what it has made of me. But gender does not only affect how we see ourselves: the experience of living as a woman or a man in this society gives us differing perspectives on all manner of things. Indeed, and the point will be central to what follows, the picture we have of ourselves and the picture we have of the world are, as Don Bannister said, 'painted on the same canvas and with the same pigments'.

The metaphor of the landscape is helpful here. In taking up residence in those places that are reserved for women and for men, we are provided with particular vantage points or angles of vision from which to view and come at the world. We thereby gain a particular range of perspectives on life which allow a limited set of possible ways of seeing or envisaging the world and ourselves. We construct our images of the world and ourselves from these perspectives, developing different out-looks because we look-out *from* different places. (Note that the metaphor only works if we keep in mind that we do not look down on the world from a great height or across at it from a great distance. We do not stand – or as Marx had it 'squat' – outside the world and scrutinize it. We are immersed in the world and have to find our bearings within it. We arrived here, as it were, by parachute and without a map.)

We paint our picture of the world, construct our imaginative vision of it, from our own perspective, from where we are in the world. Being a woman or a man is a large part of where we are in this world. But the imaginative visions of the world and ourselves that we come to embrace are not simply 'ideas', or pictures we just hold up in front of ourselves. We are animated and guided by them, by the things we fear, hope for, strive after and avoid, the images we hold of ourselves and other people, the kinds of future we envisage for ourselves, and so on. In a sense, as I said earlier, we *are* the imaginative visions of the world and ourselves that we find most compelling. Marcus Aurelius captured the point to perfection when he said, 'Character is guided by the nature of things most often envisaged. For the soul takes on the colour of its ideas'. Since the kinds of imaginative vision we hold to will depend on where we are and where we have come from, women and men will be animated by different visions, and the feminine and the masculine soul will come to take on different colours.

What happens then when women and men encounter one another? People tend to notice the sex of the person they are with, and most will acknowledge that the presence of a woman feels to them somehow different in kind to the presence of a man. Are we seeing and feeling the different colours of the feminine and masculine souls, or are we painting each other with colours of our own? Our imaginative visions are not imaginary, we do not construct them whimsically out of thin air, but we construct them from our own perspective. We see each other in terms of the ideas we hold of each other, and in this society the ideas that women hold about men and themselves tend to be, in varying degrees, significantly at odds with the ideas that men hold of women and themselves. We can best begin to discover what these ideas are, not by thinking, but by looking. For our beliefs about women and men are there in what a woman sees when she looks at a man, what a man sees when he looks at a woman, and what each sees when they look at someone of the same sex as themselves.

In *Swann's Way*, Marcel Proust wrote, 'Even the simple act which we describe as "seeing someone we know" is to some extent an intellectual process.' (He was here talking about specific individuals, but the same applies to seeing a person of a particular sex.) He went on: 'We pack the physical outline of the person we see with all the notions we have already formed about him . . . In the end they come to fill out so completely the curve of his cheeks, to follow so exactly the line of his nose, they blend so harmoniously in the sound of his voice . . . that each time we see the face or hear the voice it is these notions which we recognize and to which we listen.' My ideas about you are not in my head, I see them in your face and in your movements, I hear them in your voice.* In this society when a man looks at and listens to a woman, to him her soul tends to take on the colour of his ideas. When a woman looks at and listens to a man, to her his soul tends to take on the colour of her ideas.

To understand the experience of gender, then, we must try to grasp 'from within' the imaginative visions that women and men construct of the world, themselves and each other, and to understand how and when these different visions collide or pass each other by. These different perspectives are rooted in the different kinds of lives that women and men, by virtue of being female or male, tend to live in this kind of society. In a sense these do indeed make us different kinds of people, though we are capable of taking up other perspectives, and capable of significant change. But, and here the plot thickens considerably, our imaginative vision of ourselves and each other *includes* an understanding of what it means to be a 'kind of person'.

It might seem that the idea that women and men are different kinds of beings is probably universal, but what *is* 'a kind of being'? Different cultures give rise to different ideas about what that means. Our own culture provides us with an uneasy mixture of ways of understanding this. I suspect that most people today would read the question that forms the title of this chapter – are women and men different kinds of people – as 'do women and men have different kinds of *personality*'. But what is personality? We find it easy enough to understand that there are social definitions of what it is to be a woman or a man, that females and males are seen and acted towards in terms of definitions of what they are 'supposed' to be (both in the sense of what people suppose you to be, and what they insist you

*As the Little Prince remarked, 'if you tell a grown-up you've made a new friend, they never ask about the really important things like "what does his voice sound like?" '.

should be). But there are also social definitions of what it means to be or to have a personality. Person-ality is no less socially defined than feminin-ity or masculin-ity.

The question 'are women and men different kinds of people?', then, is a deceptively simple one. It is by no means self-evident what it is to say 'who you are' or 'what you're like' – 'as a person' – and it may be that women and men have different ways of understanding what this means. (This is crucial if women are indeed seen as more 'personal' kinds of person than men – particularly by men.) The same goes for a whole host of everyday ways of making sense of what people are about. We often use the same words, but the ideas of self, identity, personality, individuality, and autonomy – to name but a few – that arise out of women's experience may not be the same as those that arise out of men's experience. I am persuaded that this is so, that we think, feel and live according to different 'theories' about ourselves and other people. To understand how they are different and why they are different we must return to the changing relationship between public and private, and how the poet turned psychologist.

3 · In the Temple of the Heart

On camp sites up and down the land a familiar scene is repeatedly re-enacted. The family arrives, the tent is unpacked, and he, perhaps with the assistance of his son, sets about erecting the structure. Meanwhile she concerns herself with where everything is going to go inside the tent, who is to sleep where, places for clothing, places for food, where are the toilets, is there hot water? Evening comes and he lights the barbecue, and when the flames have subsided, particularly if there is red meat to be had, presides over the transformation from the raw to the cooked. Here is the same man who at home may well claim not to understand what simmering or gas mark 4 means, but this is not really cooking, this is *fire*.

What is happening here is deeply serious and deals with issues of such profound importance that one is well advised not to tamper with any of its details. It has all the important features of ritual, and what is being enacted or summoned up in this field is Man the Builder of Dwellings, the Erector of Defences against the elements and their mobilization for human purposes, Man the Protector and the Master of Nature; Woman the Home-maker, the orchestrator of provisions for ministering to organic needs – to eat, to sleep, to excrete, to cleanse – Woman the Bosom, creating within the enclave constructed by Man the glow of human warmth.

The parties to this scene might well enjoy poking fun at such a high-flown (just slightly tongue in cheek) version of what they are up to – he is getting cracking, she is getting organized. (Though they know only too well the bitter quarrels which can ensue when the well oiled camping family machine breaks down – the 'silly little things' which spark them off are highly charged.) He may also, perhaps, be less Buffalo Bill than Bungalow Bill on his holidays; she may feel less of an orchestrator than a second fiddle who never actually gets a holiday at all. And when they go to the pub in the evening and gather under the umbrella in the beer garden, the spoils that he brings back from his hunting and gathering expedition may only consist of packets of crisps and an assortment of fizzy drinks. But there are echoes, at the very least, in this little episode of what purport to be answers to the most fundamental questions about our ultimate human nature.

To read the scene as ritual is to see the participants as engaged in a dramatic portrayal of a particular claim about what women and men ultimately are. However ludicrous you might find it, the portrait is instantly recognizable. It is perhaps the most familiar of all the many ideas, images, myths and stories with which our culture abounds that purport to tell us exactly what the difference is between these two kinds of human being. Unhappily, it is also seriously maintained by many who claim to speak with authority on the subject ('science' is, in this society, frequently the carrier of such myths, and often succeeds in persuading others of their veracity).

The commonest variation seeks the roots of gender in our evolutionary past, by drawing a connection between man-the-breadwinner/woman-the-home-maker, and what is taken to be our earliest human origins. Men, it is said, inevitably took on the mantle of Hunter. Women were constrained by the facts of their biology, by pregnancy and lactation, to remain within the confines of the cave while the men strayed far and wide in search of prey and came home for their tea at five o'clock. The truth is unimportant here, what matters is the imagining of it. It is as though one could simply substitute a briefcase for the spear and a suburban semi for the cave and the basic features remain unchanged. Private Woman, Public Man, hasn't it always been the same?

The answer is that it most definitely has not, for 'the public' and 'the private' as we understand them have been with us for little more than two centuries or so. And during this period the nature of both and the relationship between them have undergone changes which have fundamentally transformed relations between women and men. In fact this only scratches the surface, for these developments have shaped our very ways of understanding, not only what women and men are, but what people are, what society is. It is these that have given us our concepts of self, personality, society, economy, individuality, friendship, intimacy, autonomy, and many more that are central to the way we think about ourselves. I say 'we' and 'ourselves', but as we shall see, these things do not mean the same things to women and to men.

Private Woman/Public Man: the form that this idea takes in our imagination is firmly rooted in the doctrine of 'separate spheres' that figured so prominently in the nineteenth century and again in the period following the Second World War. A woman's place is in the home – it is this that is being most widely and vigorously contested today, with results that must leave John Ruskin turning in his grave.

A little over a century ago he proclaimed the true nature of Home to be 'the place of peace; the shelter, not only from all injury, but from all terror, doubt and division. In so far as it is not this, it is not home; so far as the anxieties of the outer life penetrate into it . . . it is then only a part of the outer world which you have roofed over and lighted fire in.' Today, when all is far from quiet on the home front, such a vision of domestic life as a pool of tranquillity, untroubled by anxiety and doubt, conflict and division, would be taken for irony – or fall on very stony ears.

And yet we – women as well as men – are perhaps even more haunted than Ruskin was by the fearful spectre that inspired such a sentiment. If there is a dream of 'community' in which you can step out of your front door and on to the street and still feel 'at home', there is also a nightmare inversion of it: the dreadful possibility that there might be nowhere to go, nowhere to turn to for refuge and respite from the strain of surviving in an alien and inhospitable 'outside' world. We are not enchanted by make-believe worlds of domestic bliss, but as the 'outer' world grows ever more barren, cold, impersonal and impervious, so the need intensifies to make at least some of the fantasy, or some version of it, come true. Are we not lost if we fail to preserve some portion of the world that we can call our own, and keep it privileged? If not a pool of tranquillity then at least a pocket of humanity in an inhuman world. There is a fundamental paradox here which goes a long way towards explaining some of the horror at feminist claims about marriage and the family – among women as well as men. For as the private sphere is exposed as less inherently a place of peace than a site of deep-rooted conflict and just plain misery, so the need to make it rewarding and fulfilling appears to become more urgent. The more it seems that the thing is unworkable, the greater the determination to make it work.

It is clear that Ruskin spoke here from a man's point of view, indeed this is a recital by the Poet Laureate of the masculine sentiment. In the first place, it is not surprising that Victorian men should find such a portrait of the domestic world, and with it of their own kindly patronage, congenial and even uplifting. It is evident that any peace and harmony there might have been depended on the 'true wife' knowing her place, and that place was in the home, subject to His authority. Home is where the heart is, and the true wife's calling is to keep its heart beating. Any other arrangement, they warned, would be a 'perversion of nature' likely to produce 'disorder, insubordination and conflict in families'.

The moral elevation of the private sphere went hand in hand with the confinement of women to it and their active exclusion from public life. Waxing lyrically on the virtues of the true home and the true wife clearly served as a smokescreen behind which men set about imposing the doctrine of separate spheres, and securing and confirming their own status and authority in both. Women had very little say in the matter. But disguised self-interest is not the only meaning of 'a masculine perspective'. Ruskin also spoke here from a man's point of view because what he said articulated the contrast between public and private as it was, and still is for most men – that is, home as the antithesis of work, somewhere to return to from his daily expeditions into the workaday outside world. Like Lord Byron before him, the Victorian poet hoped to meet women in a realm apart, an inner sanctum, sheltered from and untainted by the public affairs of men.

That such a portrait was painted in masculine colours now seems plain as day. Few now dare to step up in public to declare women's participation in public life a perversion of nature, or to depict her domestic existence as one long basking in the glow of womanhood fulfilled. And yet, such a vision of the home as a realm apart, into which the outer world must not be allowed to penetrate, has become more vivid, not less – and not only to men. The paradox is that at the very same time as the challenge to the doctrine of separate spheres for women and men has been gaining in impetus, the two central features of Ruskin's vision have become more compelling and widely felt: the sense of inhabiting a universe divided into two distinct and contrasting worlds has grown stronger, and with it the desire to establish the private sphere as a privileged space with a special character distinct from and superior to the public world outside has intensified. For as the divide has sharpened and the contrast become starker, so the realm of the 'personal' has come to figure ever more prominently in people's sense of what matters most. Indeed, to an extraordinary and unprecedented degree, the sphere of what we now call 'personal life' has come to be seen as the only arena in which people have any hope of realizing their aspirations for a rewarding human existence and for significant human contact.

What has happened during the course of this century is that the image of a world divided into an 'outer' and 'inner' world has become ever more firmly inscribed in our imaginative vision of how things are, and must be, and along with this, the moral elevation of the private has become increasingly marked, amongst women as well as men. Inside/outside – here is the modern variant on the hunter/cave-dweller, one that speaks volumes to contemporary experience and figures prominently in contemporary thought, for example in the theories of psychoanalysis.* But it is profoundly misleading, both in the implication that inner and outer are distinct and independent worlds, and in the sense that it has always been like this. That the world appears to be divided in this way is the principal fruit of a set of economic and cultural developments that have been under way for some two to three hundred years, but which have gathered momentum in the last fifty years or so. Here is a case par excellence of how it is the past that illuminates most clearly the present.

The idea of having pieces of agricultural or textile machinery in your living room would be an appalling prospect to most people today. It seems to conflict with the most basic sense of what a 'living' room is for. Is nothing sacred, nowhere exempt from such intrusions? But in the most practical ways, most people in the seventeenth century would not have been able, even if they thought of trying, to establish and observe such a boundary between work and home.

In pre-industrial Britain the household was the basic 'economic' unit, and this had a crucial bearing on the kinds of imaginative vision

*The metaphor has also moved out of the home. The egocentricity and impatience of so many car drivers seems to have something to do with a sense of being enclosed in a travelling cocoon, in the midst of others but cut off from and almost oblivious to them. The proliferation of covered shopping malls also owes something to a sense of strolling around inside a kind of bubble, shielded from the squalor and chaos of inner city life. It may also be part of the appeal of the Strategic Defence Initiative, for what it suggests is life going on under the ultimate protective canopy, inside a kind of dome, safe and sound within a sealed-off universe.

people could construct of the world and themselves, and on the ways they were able to carve up their lives and understand the nature of their relationships with others. The contrasts that get drawn today between different kinds of work, between work and non-work, and between 'personal' and other kinds of relationships, simply could not arise. A comparison of our own situation with theirs makes it clear that the most basic ways in which we make sense of our own experience are rooted in a particular and different form of organization of social and economic relationships.

Firstly, it is quite evident that the work done by women played a key part in the 'household economy', in the cycle of production and subsistence, in the business of securing a living. This would simply have been taken as read. For those inclined to think of housework as essentially to do with dusting and plumping up cushions, it is salutary to consider the kinds of work performed in the 'home' by women then. Simply feeding and clothing the members of the household often involved 'dairying, cheesemaking, brewing, baking, preserving, pickling, salting meat, spinning yarn, making and mending clothes and many other tasks', and this was on top of the work women did in the fields, in the garden, and in the yard looking after pigs and poultry. Many of these activities, though by no means all, have either disappeared from the majority of households or changed out of all recognition.

But it is not simply a matter of domestic labour being more arduous or extensive than it is today. Most of the work performed by members of the household could, with a little stretch of the imagination, have been called 'domestic'. The activities we might call 'housework' were generally so intertwined with 'production' that they could not sensibly be separated and identified as one thing or the other. If a woman were to make a quantity of cheese, mostly to be stored for later consumption by members of the household, but with a little extra to sell, is this housework or production? Is only the surplus the product of 'economic' activity? It is equally evident that in modern society such activities as preparing food, washing clothes and utensils, keeping things clean and in good repair, looking after children, daily health care, even perhaps emotional succour, are necessary to the maintenance of life. And we know that people who do such things in other people's houses, or in restaurants, laundries, nurseries, and so on, get paid for it. Yet the full-time houseworker is defined today as 'economically inactive'. It is only the public world, where commodities are produced and circulated, where goods and services are bought and sold, that is now officially included in the category of 'the economy'.

Secondly, where most people worked within or in close proximity to the same building in which they slept, relaxed, sang and made love, the contrast to 'work' could not be 'home'. Ruskin's vision of the true home as exempt from the anxieties of the outer world would have been barely comprehensible. What exactly is this 'outer' world we are trying to keep at bay, to prevent from penetrating the 'inner' sanctum? Whatever contrasts might be drawn between 'working' and 'not-working', they were obliged to accommodate them under the one roof. (And so, of course, are we.)

This is closely connected with the third set of contrasts – between differing kinds of relationships with others. Where the organization of relationships within the household is first and foremost a division of labour, what we call 'personal' relationships must be intimately bound up with other kinds, including 'economic' relationships. Literally speaking, 'personal' relations are simply relations between persons, but this is not the way we now understand it. Our society holds up a particular idea and ideal of personal relationships, attaching an extraordinarily high value to their distinctive character in contrast to other kinds of relationships. In fact we are by no means as clear as we might imagine about what we mean by 'personal relationships', about whether, to what extent or how they might be accommodated with other kinds. But just as the members of the household would have found it difficult to say exactly, using our terms, what kind of work they were engaged in at any given moment, so they would have had a hard time trying to answer our questions about the kinds of relationships they had with each other.

Amongst other things, this makes it not surprising that the seventeenth century did not give rise to three distinct sciences of personal, social and economic life – psychology, sociology and economics. How would they decide what their respective subject matter was? Imagine the demarcation disputes. This had to wait for the later emergence of two, apparently distinct, spheres of existence: a private sphere of personal life, and a sphere of 'society', of public life, political life, and economic life. (The operative word is 'apparently', for these are by no means independent realms.) The contrasts that get drawn today between different kinds of work, between work and home, and between various kinds of relationships, arose out of this fundamental reorganization of social and economic life – the 'privatization' of one sphere, and the 'socialization' (publication?) of another.

The members of the household were, so to speak, faced with a new and fundamental question when it ceased to be the basic economic unit: if this is not about securing a living, then what exactly *is* it about? What is it that we do here? In the twentieth century, one of the loudest voices offering an answer to this question says that what we do here is 'relate' to one another. That the private sphere is the site of 'personal relationships' – or even simply 'relationships' – is by no means the only answer to the question of what we do here, but it is one that has taken a firm hold among many groups in modern society, including some of those that have been most engaged by issues of gender. Moreover, this response has an important affinity with other, apparently quite different solutions (like 'here we relax and look after our own'), for they are essentially variations on a common theme, a theme that I shall call 'privatism'.

What this refers to is a number of related trends in modern culture, the central core being the experience I have been trying to invoke from the outset: the sense that the world is divided into two distinct spheres of existence – the 'public' and the 'private'. But this is only part of it, for coupled with this comes the tendency to invest most or even all of one's aspirations for autonomy and for rewarding human relationships in one of these two spheres – the private sphere of personal life.

Privatism is the active repudiation of the public. In becoming privatist, people opt to turn their backs on what they feel to be an impersonal and impenetrable 'outside' world. Where people find their jobs dull and oppressive, or a series of empty routines or even cynically manipulative, where to venture out is to be confronted by a vast and complex interlocking structure, administered or governed by remote or incomprehensible forces, a world in which people want to say 'where am I in all this?', personal life offers itself up as an arena in which the individual *can* make a difference, can shape a corner of the world according to their own design. (It is often literally 'design' – witness the vast sums now spent on home improvements, DIY, furnishings and decor, designer kitchens and so on.) Personal life becomes a personalized controllable space, and an oasis in an emotional desert – or as Christopher Lasch described it, a 'haven in a heartless world'.

Lasch's phrase is more than reminiscent of the less familiar parts of the passage in which Marx described religion as the opium of the people. Religion, for Marx, is the sigh of the oppressed, the soul of soulless circumstances, the heart of a heartless world. In religion people seek respite from the pain, the misery, and the ugliness of real life in a fantasy world of beauty, harmony and contentment. It is significant, then, that Ruskin called the true home 'a sacred place, a vestal temple, a temple of the hearth'. Does that speak to us? Perhaps it does, for there is something in Lasch's suggestion that many people now demand of their personal relationships an almost religious intensity. The difference is that now the sanctuary and respite we seek in the temple of the heart is from the soullessness, the heartlessness and the ugliness of the *public* world, the world 'out-there'.

But putting it this way, talking of 'people', clearly overlooks the differences in the experience of women and men. Privatism retains many of the features that made Ruskin's vision of the true home an essentially masculine perspective on it. Those who emphasize the incidence of domestic violence of the physical kind, for example, are explicitly aiming to debunk the myth that the home is a refuge for women. Privatism also appears to want to deny what women cannot forget – that the home is (also) a workplace. And there is little echo here of so many women's experience of the domestic world, not as a haven, but as a place of confinement.

From pool of tranquillity to pocket of humanity – has one masculine fantasy simply given way to another, in all significant respects indistinguishable from the first? In many ways it has, but it would be a gross over-simplification to see privatism as merely the latest chapter in the never-ending story of the defence of masculine privilege. Many women, too, sound the privatist retreat, and not only the allegedly unenlightened.

In 1981, eighteen years after telling the true wife's tale of frustration, disappointment, emptiness and futility in her immensely influential book *The Feminine Mystique*, Betty Friedan called women back to the values of community and the interpersonal ties of intimacy embodied and embedded in family life. Why should women respond to that? Because the family, she wrote, is 'the symbol of that last area where one has any hope of individual control over one's own destiny, of meeting one's most basic human needs, of nourishing that core of personhood threatened now by vast impersonal institutions and uncontrollable corporate and governmental bureaucracies and the bewildering, accelerating pace of change'. Privatism in a nutshell.

Defeatist talk this most certainly is, but it shows that privatism is not an impulse solely confined to men. Indeed, as we shall see, the privatist vision is lodged at the heart of various forms of the ostensibly raised consciousness of feminist thought – though often in subtle and unexpected ways. Is it possible, then, to say what women and men share and do not share of this privatist outlook? I think it is, but that involves identifying the vital ingredient that renders this vision ultimately a masculine one, and as such the modern heir to Ruskin's fantasy of the true home – namely, psychology.

Privatism puts a word to a set of trends in modern society which have significantly touched the lives of both women and men. It has a number of features, two of which find an important place in the experience of both: the growing sense of inhabiting a world divided into two distinct and contrasting realms of existence, and an increasing investment in what is felt to be the special and superior character of the private sphere of personal life. But what is this special character of the private? Do we share a vision of the 'inner' world? Here we arrive at the parting of the ways, because this inner world is not the same kind of world for women and for men.

One look at just a few of the ways the contrast is drawn between public and private within the privatist outlook makes two things quite clear. Look at the terms on the right and it is not surprising that such a vision of the public world should lead both women and men to invest so much in the private – despite the disenchantments of their experience of the reality – and to come to identify themselves most closely with the private sphere of 'personal' life. Look at the left and it is equally clear that there is something seriously amiss in the portrait they paint of the inner world:

private	public
inside	outside
family	economy
home	work
intimacy	distance
emotional ties	contractual ties

love	money
mutual aid	competition, exploitation
warm	cold
natural	artificial
authentic	inauthentic
spontaneity	conformity
freedom	necessity
self	society
personal	impersonal
subjective	objective
psychology	society, economics, history

No woman would come up with a straightforward contrast between home and work. But all the other contrasts on the list are equally questionable, and question them we shall. What will become clear, as we do so, is that the privatist vision of the private sphere is considerably more in tune with the experience of men than it is with the experience of women.

Despite what we share of the privatist sense and sentiment (and despite the increasing participation of women in certain aspects and regions of public life), it remains true that women and men 'straddle' the public and private worlds in different ways, and have a different experience of each and of the relationship between them. This ensures that the forms that the contrast takes will, in significant respects, be different for each. I want to suggest here that at the heart of the difference lies the contrast between psychology and society. As the private sphere passed from being a unit of production to an emotional fortress, in the masculine perspective it became *desocialized*. As I said in the first chapter, the poet turned psychologist, and the realm apart became a 'psychological' universe.

This is the new romanticism – though quite what it means and why it matters will take some time to become apparent. First we must grasp what a 'psychological' vision of personal life looks like, and the next two chapters are devoted to making this clear – the first on what it means in the privatist vision to 'be yourself', the second on what it means to have a 'personality'. Only then can we ask whether such a vision of personal life is indeed more in tune with the experience of men, but significantly at odds with the experience of women, and see how far this helps in understanding everyday conflicts and misunderstandings between women and men in the private sphere – beginning with the meanings of tenderness and care.

First, though, the experience of self. As I suggested earlier, if Lord Byron were here today he might well have been moved to write, not 'man's *love* is of man's life a thing apart; 'tis a woman's whole existence', but 'man's *self* is of man's life a thing apart; 'tis a woman's whole existence'.

4 · Freedom, Intimacy and the Self

'Free at last, free at last!' – home is the sailor, home from the sea; home is the Self – from Society. Out-there, in the realm of necessity, it's a case of having to, of needs must. By contrast, or so it seems, 'personal life' is where we are or can be free, and relax into the comfort of our own true selves.

The idea that everything that simply has to be done and must therefore take priority goes on in the 'outside' world, stands as one of the great monuments to masculine egocentricity ('androcentrism' as some prefer). No one who has been obliged to assume responsibility for running a household and looking after small children is likely to think of home as the place where you do whatever you like. But more significant is the wider point: life in the outside world can only go on as it does by relying on the work of keeping people in good repair – of what is called 'reproduction' in the wider sense – being done 'behind the scenes', elsewhere and by someone else. It is less a matter of domestic responsibilities intruding on an otherwise leisured existence, than one of ensuring that these things do not intrude into the public world and mess it up. Just as the task of the secretary is to keep the boss's mind tidy and uncluttered by trivial matters, so the houseworkers and childcarers of the land busily keep business business.

There is, in short, something seriously amiss with the idea that the public world is the realm of necessity and the private sphere is the realm of freedom. But there is considerably more to the privatist vision of personal life as the realm of freedom than simple distinctions between what needs to be done and what can wait, and between doing what you have to and doing what you want. This is a world in which you are free, not simply to *please* yourself, but to *be* yourself.

What does this mean – to be yourself? Privatism has given rise to a number of ways of understanding and experiencing 'the self', but its most compelling image is of a core – a 'real' self, an 'inner' self – hidden away or trapped inside layer upon layer of mere 'social' selves. This sense of self, of the structure of the self, has taken a firm hold in modern consciousness, and provides, for example, the basis for the appeal of various doctrines of inwardness – the idea that one may 'find oneself' by looking 'within'. But it also provides the more common ground on which we construct ways of understanding, not only who we are, but what it is to know someone, to be close to someone, the meaning of friendship, of love and of tenderness. I say 'we' – but these understandings are only, at most, partially shared between women and men.

Privatism is, in part, a response to the experience of the public world as an alien territory – not in the sense of being strange and unfamiliar, but in the sense of being a world in which you are unable to 'be yourself'. Life in public, it seems, consists to varying degrees of routine, ritualized and impoverished exchanges between individuals with no real interest in one another 'as persons', where each is obliged to go through the motions, do what is required of them, and live up, or rather down, to other people's meagre expectations. But this is out-there, in 'society'. In-here people should be able simply to be themselves, express themselves openly and fully, and dissolve the distance that 'social' life puts between us – between our selves. Personal life comes to be understood and experienced as life conducted in a kind of cocoon far away from society, or in an enclave within it but not of it. Hence the attraction of romantic love and extra-marital affairs, the heady exhilaration of encounter groups and so on – and hence the disappointment and discouragement which so often follows in their wake.

This is the modern variant on Ruskin's privileged region, into which the outer world must not be allowed to penetrate. But the 'outer world' does and must penetrate the 'inner' world – not because the Englishman now needs a bigger moat round his castle, but because public and private belong to the same world. Society is not 'out-there'. Look down, as it were, from a great height, and it is self-evident that what we call our personal lives are part and parcel of the way life as a whole is organized and lived. Society is clearly the whole thing. But in the privatist vision the world seems to be divided into two distinct spheres – with one claiming to be set apart from and superior to 'society'. And so it is with the self. The self, too, is the whole thing, and yet the privatist feels it to be divided into two distinct aspects, claiming one to be set apart from and superior to the remainder.

In what sense is it possible *not* to be yourself? As George Kelly once remarked: 'A good deal is said these days about being oneself. It is supposed to be healthy to be oneself . . . it is a little hard for me to understand how one could be anything else.' Everything I do is, by definition, something *I* do. So what do I mean by claiming that on occasions I am not being myself? The answer can only be that it is part of my imaginative vision of myself that I insist that some of my doings do not spring from what I call the real me. These things are not to be taken as evidence of what I am *really* like.

(The reasons for this insistence can be less than laudable. For example, it is common enough in public life for people to do what is expected of them and at the same time disclaim responsibility for it by apparently stepping out from behind a 'mask' to say: it isn't really *me* doing this, I have to, it's a requirement of my 'role' that I report this incident, charge you the full fare, turf you out of your home, and so on. We are all faced with situations where there would be a high price to pay for not doing what sticks in the throat, but if we choose to go along, we choose to go along and there is an end to it. 'I' am not simply the things I do in good conscience.)

If I have a sense of a real me it is because I am actively carving up the totality of my experience into self and not-self, into what belongs to the real me and what does not. Now this is precisely, and not incidentally, parallel to the privatist vision of a divided society: in both cases we find a totality divided into two distinct aspects or realms, one claiming not to belong in fact to the totality, but to be set apart from and superior to the remainder. If we ask exactly where it is that you can be this real self, lo and behold it is on the higher plane, in the privileged and set-apart region of the private sphere of personal life.

There is, in other words, within this vision of ourselves, an image of society, and within this vision of society an image of ourselves – the two are mapped on to one another. (As Don Bannister put it, 'your self picture and your world picture are painted on the same canvas and with the same pigments'.) The self, as we tend to think of it, is not the totality of all we do, think, feel and experience, it is carved out from the whole and then separated from it. 'Society', similarly, is not the totality of social life, but a portion of it carved out and then separated from the remainder. You can be your self in your personal life, but not when you cross the great chasm and enter society. (Hence two independent academic disciplines which take each of these phenomena as their object of study – psychology and sociology.)

This privatist vision of an inner, real self would have no power over us were it not such a compelling one. The problem is that it finds its way into many of what have become accepted wisdoms about gender. The first is to do with intimacy.

It has often been said that men's apparent 'incapacity' for intimacy is at the heart of what masculinity is – at least in its modern forms. This is seen as a necessary consequence of the ways men set up a distance around themselves, a kind of exclusion zone within which we can get our bearings and stay in control. Women, it is said, are more open (or more exposed), more able and willing to live in relation to others, to feel and embrace a connectedness with other people.

Variations on this theme have become increasingly popular in recent discussions of gender. There has, for example, been something of a shift in much contemporary feminist writing away from the idea that women are fashioned out of, or hedged in by, demeaning and diminishing definitions of femininity and of a woman's place, towards a conception of men and women as the bearers of particular kinds of values. In what is essentially a revival of the idea of the moral superiority of women so dear to the heart of the Victorian male for whom Ruskin spoke, men are seen as standing for all those things that set people against one another – violence, mastery, competition, calculation – and women as standing for what connects people with one another. Some versions of this view appear to imply that this is rooted in biology; the more plausible alternative suggests that because women are consigned to the tasks of caring for others, they come to embody the human qualities of empathy and responsiveness to other people's needs, an openness and receptiveness to others, and a more direct sensing of other people's feelings and character. Masculinity, on the other hand, is defined in terms of a notion of individual autonomy as separateness, an isolating sense of being distinct from others, an insensitivity to others, and an obliviousness to those feelings in oneself that involve a reaching out to others.

The reasons why such a view should have come to the fore are complex. Some see it as a counsel of defeat on the part of some women – if you feel you cannot change your situation, praise it; if you feel condemned to subordination develop a sense of superiority over your masters. But there is more to it than that. Amongst other things it reflects and reinforces the growing significance in this culture of a very particular idea and ideal of intimacy.

What is 'intimacy'? It would seem to be bound up with being 'close' to someone, with sharing things, with being emotionally involved, but above all with 'knowing' someone, as we would say, 'personally'. Intimate knowledge comes from familiarity (note that if you overstep the mark and attempt unwelcome intimacies you may be accused of being too 'familiar', from the same root as 'family'). Relationships in the pre-industrial household were intimate in this sense – people's lives were so inextricably bound up together that their knowledge of one another was extensive and took in the whole person. But the privatist idea of intimacy also draws heavily on its other meaning – as a verb: to 'intimate' something. In its origins this meant bringing into the open something hidden, revealing something inner, inmost, or within (the meaning of the Latin 'intimus'). To 'intimate' something has now come to be associated with hinting rather than coming right out with it, but the idea of exposure or disclosure remains.

The privatist conception of intimacy combines both these elements, and says that to know someone intimately necessarily entails disclosure, revealing things to one another. What must we reveal to one another if we are to be intimate? Some aspect of our inner selves.

We might now say that we 'only' know someone 'socially' or in the context of 'work', but it would seem odd to say that we *only* knew someone 'personally'. (This equation of personal relationships with intimate relationships is so crucial that I shall take it as the focus of the final chapter to illustrate my view of what a synthesis of the feminine and masculine perspectives might look like.) It is as though first-hand experience of someone doing their job or socializing with acquaintances can only fill in inessential details of the total picture. These are more 'superficial' aspects of a person, they do not belong to the definition of who they essentially are. How do you 'get through' to the 'inner' woman or man? Above all through talk, real talk, intimate talk. Talking not *as* yourself, but *about* yourself.

If a person says they are a 'good friend' of someone, most of us would simply take it as read that this means they talk to each other about themselves – certainly if the description is 'close' friend. But is it so obvious that talking about ourselves will bring us 'closer together' than talking, say, about your job, politics, car engines or fishing tackle? What exactly is this sense of being 'close to' someone, why is it desireable, and how is it achieved? The contrast to close would seem to be distant, but then what exactly is 'distance'? The fact that people who are 'close' often get physically close – lie down together, sit with and by one another, lean towards and touch each other – can make us forget that this is a *metaphor*. The closing of physical distance plays an important part in relationships with our 'nearest and dearest', but it is not what we mean by being 'close'. So what do we mean? (I say 'we', but it is probable that women and men do not mean the *same* thing.) Since we are not talking about literal distance, what are we talking about? How is such 'distance' set up and how is it eliminated or reduced?

We have come to associate being intimate with 'baring your soul', and this commonly entails the divulging of secrets, even confessing to guilty ones. Above all it means talking about your 'innermost' feelings. In the process it feels that a great divide may have been crossed, that a distance has been eliminated or at least reduced, there is a sense of people standing naked before one another. Two inner selves, at first hidden away from each other's view, encounter one another as the outer layers fall away. It is often felt that this kind of 'sharing' is only possible between people who have things in common – that you couldn't be intimate with just anyone. So we might expect good friends to feel they understand one another *because* they feel similarly. Others believe that what separates us from one another will evaporate as we discover together, through the process of self-disclosure, the common ground of our humanity.

Be that as it may, we tend to set great store by this sense of knowing someone 'personally' – of enabling another to 'open up' and feeling free to do likewise. This is why it now seems so lamentable – pitiful, irritating, disappointing, tragic or pathetic – that so many men appear to be unable or unwilling to do this. In many ways this is wide of the mark, because men find ways of being 'intimate' (in this sense) with one another that can easily be missed by an outside observer. Such intimacy between men is often achieved through understatement and through brief but heavily loaded looks, words and gestures. What these speak of more often than not is a common plight, and often what men feel to be the shared tragedies of the masculine condition – that these are *shared* is crucial and often goes unnoticed. Nevertheless, few will deny that men are less inclined to talk easily and openly about their feelings, and in particular to admit to vulnerability, hurt and confusion.

The difficulty is that at the heart of this view of intimacy lies the impossible dream of the private sphere as an emotional oasis, a self-contained universe of feeling and relating. The faith is in an idea and ideal of relationships between 'persons' in a kind of 'pure' sense, one that can only in principle be achieved within the cocoon of personal life. Whereas 'between ourselves' might once have simply meant 'keep what I am about to say under your hat', it comes to mean that when we are intimate we establish a connection that is purely between our *selves*. Intimacy becomes the *abolishing of distance*, of everything that stands between us.

We now feel, for example, that we have come a long way from the suffocating stiffness, formality and distance of relationships in our image of the Victorian family (from pool of tranquillity to pocket of humanity). 'Good' parents* now have 'good' relationships with their children, and this means 'personal' relationships, characterized by intimacy, spontaneity, openness and self-expression. The modern parent wants to *close the distance* between themselves and their children. But such parents, whilst they attempt to turn the home into a pocket of humanity in an alien, impersonal and even hostile world, find that they have also to prepare their children to survive and even flourish in that very world – the same world that they are actively repudiating within the enclave. This creates inevitable contradictions within the family.

As parents they cannot avoid exercising authority and control, but privatist parents do so guiltily, because it feels like a violation of their children, and they do so reluctantly, because to exercise control seems to jeopardize the possibility of having a 'good' relationship with them, and hence of being the kind of parent they so desperately want to be. Ultimately it is bound to be the children who suffer most, for they will inevitably be rewarded for apparently *willing* compliance, because in this way they help their parents avoid feeling guilty. The triumph over the child may thus be total, exactly what they were trying to avoid.

*The following illustration is borrowed from Richard Sennett.

One might think that psychologists and therapists ought to be the most alert to such destructive interchanges – but what is proposed as a solution? Distressingly often it involves placing even *more* emphasis on the need for openness, intimacy and self-expression, when it ought to be clear that it is the fact that these conflict with other issues that gave rise to the problem in the first place.

The moral here is that the privatist view of intimate relations insists on a repudiation of any suggestion that intimate relationships are *structured* in definite and identifiable ways, that society is not only out-there but in-here too. In here we wanted it to be just us, just me and you – persons in a kind of pure sense. But the private sphere of personal life is not an oasis, a sealed-off universe of feeling and 'relating', and wishing cannot make it so.

Still the wishing goes on, and plays a crucial part in the resistance of many to any attempt to introduce society, structure, necessity, into the private sphere. Take off your mucky sociological boots, leave them at the door, and put on your psychological slippers. The most common example of a refusal to do this, to insist on bringing society into the home, relies on the vocabulary of 'role', and talks of the roles of parent, and, crucially, of houseworker and mother. But privatism is not so easily beaten, and often manages, not just to undermine the attempt, but to turn it to its own advantage.

Life in public, according to a common version of the privatist picture of it, consists in the acting out of socially prescribed and predetermined 'roles', in the playing of parts, the donning and doffing of masks suited to particular occasions. What stands in contrast to this mere playing of social roles is being oneself. But this insistence that behind or beneath masks of conformity to socially prescribed roles lies a self – a 'real' self – plays havoc with the use of the concept to demonstrate the fact of necessity in the private sphere.

Sammy Davis Junior is reported as saying: 'As soon as I leave the house I'm on, man, I'm ON!' Imagine if you will the houseworker and mother rising first in the morning to make breakfast for the family and cajole them on their way: 'As soon as I get up in the morning I'm on, sister, I'm ON!' These are two quite different senses of being 'on'. For the showbiz celebrity it means he is accountable to an audience – he is obliged to get in-role as he passes through the front door and on to the stage of the outside world, to animate and make believable the image – as they say, the 'persona' – that people have come to expect. Being 'on' to the houseworker/mother also means that she is accountable, she has certain obligations that others will hold her to. But as she begins to go through the motions of the morning routine, does she undergo a similar transformation and cease to be her-self? She may not be free to do as she pleases, but is she free or not free to be who she is 'really'?

Put it another way: when a traffic warden sticks parking tickets on car windshields, or a bus conductor takes money from passengers, it is clear that she or he does so *as* a traffic warden or *as* a bus conductor. They would not be either obliged or entitled to do so when 'off-duty' or 'out-of-role' – as a private (note) citizen. But when the houseworker/mother puts the kettle on to make the tea in the morning, does she do so 'in-role' or as 'herself'?

What the privatist contrast between self and role is precisely *not* saying is that all the world's a stage. The *whole* world cannot be a stage – this is a metaphor, one which invites you to see *all* social life as drama and its participants as actors. (To see, for example, how listening attentively to someone is akin to playing a part – not in the sense of pretending, but in the sense of taking up a recognizable stance in relation to another: the role of attentive listener.) The privatist vision, on the other hand, sees the *public* world as a *theatre*, and it is an essential part of the idea of theatre that actors and audience alike have *homes* to go to. There is no room, therefore, in this scheme for the idea of roles within the home – home is where you go *not* to play roles.

It is most significant, then, that research into the experience of being a houseworker should turn up the finding that, on being asked to describe themselves, working-class women virtually always had 'I am a housewife', 'I am a mother' at the top of their lists, significantly more frequently than middle-class houseworkers. (We will return to this later, in the chapter on the meaning of being 'an individual'.) Some researchers are visibly dismayed by such replies – no, I'm asking about *you*, not your *roles*. You surely don't mean 'I'-'am'-'a'-'housewife'! What's the matter with these people? They don't seem to know the difference between self and role.

But it is not a question of 'knowing the difference' between self and role, or even of deciding whether there really *is* such a distinction. It is a matter of discovering whether or not people themselves make such a distinction within their imaginative vision of themselves. If they do, the point is to try to understand why it makes sense in terms of their experience of life to do so. I simplify of course, but it may be that the working-class woman has a different theory, one in which you can put the kettle on as yourself and as a mother at one and the same time, or rather, that the issue simply does not arise. I am not at all suggesting that she makes no distinction between doing what she has to and doing what she wants, but that perhaps she does *both* 'as herself'.

In the privatist vision, you can only be yourself in your 'free' time, when you are not playing 'roles'. Since housework is something you are obliged to do, it belongs to the realm of necessity and *therefore* not to the sphere of the self. Ann Oakley makes this clear in the way she talks about the houseworker's 'fictional' autonomy. Despite the fact that the majority of houseworkers in her study said that the best thing about it is that 'you're your own boss', Oakley claims this autonomy is illusory because the houseworker is not free to pursue her '*own*' ends, to do what 'she' wants – not 'as houseworker' but 'as herself'. As houseworker you are not free and therefore you are not yourself. Once again the self is who you are when you are not enacting social roles, and that is who you 'really' are.

In this logic, an answer to the question 'who am I *really*?' cannot include the positions I occupy in the social landscape. There is a difference between – to use a related term – one's 'social' (meaning public) identity, and one's 'personal' identity. As the character played by Albert Finney in the film of *Saturday Night and Sunday Morning* retorted: 'whatever *they* say I am, that's just what I'm not'. Or as William James's crab retorted on hearing itself classed as a crustacean and thus disposed of: 'I am no such thing. I am myself, myself alone.' To the privatist, the ways you are identified publicly by others – your mere 'social identity', from the details on a passport to the work you do or the family you come from – has little if anything to do with your 'personal identity', with who you are to yourself. So when a woman says 'I'm just a housewife', this is commonly taken to mean, not 'I don't have a job as well', or 'housewives aren't very important are they', but – like the famous Monty Python sketch: 'I'm a Merchant Banker, I can't remember my name' – I have no personal identity.

The value of the idea of 'identity' lies in its potential to draw together the personal and the social, to set the question of who am I to myself in the context of who I am to others. But this potential is constantly undermined by the privatist tendency to contrast personal life with public life and to insist that who I am really is a purely personal affair. Having an identity then becomes a pre-eminently subjective matter. It is a good thing, even a sign of 'mental health' to have a strong 'sense' of identity, and it is up to you whether or not you have one.

Here, the idea of knowing 'who you are' comes to mean first and foremost who you are 'as a person', and although literally 'person' is simply another word for a human being, we tend to use it in the sense of person as opposed to social position. A person is someone who merely *occupies* social positions. As a person you are detachable from these positions and can be, as it were, lifted out of them and set down elsewhere. To put it another way, it is what you have left when you take away all of your roles. But if your identity as a person is defined in contrast to your social positions, then how do you discover who you are? Principally by fabricating the evidence to fit your favourite theory.

One of the most striking things about modern culture is the enormous array of things that can be employed as materials out of which to sculpt an image of yourself, to assemble a montage or collage of yourself, as fixtures and fittings to design your own personal interior, or whichever metaphor commends itself. Clothes, hair, pictures, furnishings, music, books, habits, people, places, gestures, conversations, interests, activities – all of these things commonly figure in people's personal lives not simply because they enjoy them (secretly we may be quite unsure whether we like/enjoy them or not), but because they serve the purpose of *self-definition*. As Richard Sennett points out, sexuality too is often burdened with such tasks of self-definition and self-summary. The decision whether or not to choose a particular person as a sexual partner can become a kind of reflexive act – it tells you who you are. As Sennett says, 'he or she becomes a resource of inner development, and loving the other person for his or her difference recedes before a desire to find in another person a definition for oneself'.

The other is not really an 'other' at all, but a mirror in which you hope to see yourself reflected, and some of the most bitter quarrels arise where the other person insists on reflecting back something you do not wish to see. It is very difficult to convince yourself that you really are the 'kind of person' you take (or wish to take) yourself to be if no-one else agrees with you. Very often we resort to extorting evidence from the other person in any way we can. Very often, too, we charge the people we live most closely with with somehow failing to elicit in us aspects of what we take to be ourselves – and go in for some very big sulking. (This gives rise to a particular critique of monogamy according to which no one person could ever elicit all your possible selves.) Our ideas about ourselves and what we want from other people are usually full of contradictions – how many people want a lover who is nurturant and protective, wild and a little dangerous, a good companion and trusted confidante, someone to feel safe with, someone challenging and so on? It is certain that they will not be up to it, but that of course is *their* fault.

In what kind of society do people *need* ritual objects and activities to 'remind' them who they are, and need other people to be mirrors to hold up to themselves? A world in which people decisively separate the personal from the social, and insist that 'who I am really' is *my* business – it is an entirely *subjective* matter. Here we find the common theme running through the privatist vision of freedom, intimacy and the self. Underpinning this form of aspiration to be ourselves and establish an intimacy between ourselves lies a particular opposition: a contrast between 'subjective' and 'objective', one I believe is essentially masculine.

Privatism defines the realm of the personal in contrast to the social. While strictly speaking a 'personal' relationship is simply a relationship between persons and that just means individual human beings, the privatist defines them in contrast to 'social' relationships, the kinds of relationships that characterize 'society' – relationships that take definite indentifiable forms, with pre-established obligations, in which individuals appear to be interchangeable – in short, relationships which come to be seen as 'objective'. I am only free to be me, and we are only free to achieve genuine intimacy between ourselves, if and when we succeed in extricating ourselves from such relationships. Freedom as opposed to necessity, self as opposed to society, personal/intimate relationships as opposed to social ones – the privatist dream is of a realm beyond society in a double sense: not only a realm apart, but a desocialized realm, a purely *subjective* universe.

But is there such a place? If we are guided by the things most often envisaged, then who dreams this dream of personal life and is guided by it? The answer is mostly – though not exclusively – men. The sense of the private sphere as an emotional oasis of feeling and 'relating' in a desert of indifference and impersonal necessity has a resonance in the experience of both women and men. But the fact that there is structure and necessity in the private sphere, that society is not just out-there but in-here too, is far harder for women to deny than for men.

It has, historically, been men who pass back and forth between public and private in such a way that they can hope and expect to be able to put the private behind them when they enter the public, and the public behind them when they enter the private. Most men feel that they are obliged to live out the better part of their waking lives in an impersonal, indifferent and even hostile public world, a world that seems to consist of routine and impoverished exchanges between individuals with no real interest in one another, a world in which feelings and personal qualities are out of place or at best secondary. What men feel they must endure or ignore in public they tend to want to be released from or find restored in private. They dream of another world which is the very opposite of these things – a purely personal private universe.

The opposition between subjective and objective represents, in heightened form, this contrast – one which is rooted in the masculine way of straddling these two worlds. The situation of the full-time houseworker today, on the other hand, has definite affinities with the pre-industrial household, where personal, social and economic life was all of a piece. Home/work, self/role, personal relationships/ social and economic ones, all these things had to be accommodated with one another, not hived off into separate spheres. It is most unlikely that a contrast born of an experience of straddling two worlds will make much sense to one who is obliged to knit them together. There is already some reason to think, then, that the vision of the private sphere of personal life as a subjective universe does indeed speak more to the experience of men than of women – though before we can settle the matter we must look more closely at our experience of personal life and personal relationships.

(It may seem strange to suggest that men may have the more subjective view of personal life, when it is women who are most often said to be the subjective sex. But who is it that says this? Primarily men. Women sometimes retaliate by calling men too objective, but in doing so they are accepting a contrast that arises first and foremost out of the experience of men, for it is the very contrast between subjective and objective that is essentially masculine. As we shall see, there are a number of reasons for thinking this is so.)

Note that if I am right, it is not simply a matter of a woman finding it harder to find or make space in the private sphere to be herself and devote herself to the cultivation of intimate relationships. The suggestion is that women and men's experience of the private sphere, their fears and aspirations of it, their understanding of what personal life is or can be about, may be significantly different in crucial respects. I am persuaded that this is so, that freedom, intimacy and the self actually mean different things to women and men, and it is this that we are about to explore.

First, though, the sense of the private sphere as a subjective universe is only *one half* of the psychological imagination. Modern culture has also given us another psychological concept which, only apparently paradoxically, gives us the exact contrast to a 'subjectified' view of the person – an 'objectified' one: the concept of 'personality'. Far from it being my business who or what I am, how I paint my own self-portrait or arrange my psychological furniture, I am the way I'm made.

The idea that women and men are different kinds of people in the sense of having different kinds of 'personality' is widely held in this society, and not only by those who think this is for the best or simply in the way of things. Such an idea cannot simply be false – if we believe it we can, in a sense and to a degree, make it come true. If this is your favourite theory about yourself, you may well hold yourself to it. But, as we shall see, it is an idea which obscures at least as much as it illuminates.

It obscures in the same way as the subjective view of personal life we have considered so far: by erasing the social. The reason the paradox is only apparent – that we have a subjectified and an objectified view sitting side by side – is that both have something in common. They are both in a very particular sense 'psychological' – that is, psychological *as opposed to* social.

5 · Gender and Personality

The playwright Dennis Potter once said that the difficulty in finding out about yourself is that there are too many clues. But you do not have to be a particularly *good* detective to notice the countless clues that are strewn across your path from the moment of your birth which seem to point ineluctably to the one conclusion: there are two kinds of people in the world and you are one of them. What did we, and do we, make of that?

One thing is clear: when they told you, directly and indirectly, that there were two kinds of people in the world and you were one of them, this was not offered in the spirit of an invitation to entertain a possible way of thinking about yourself or what you might become. You are a boy or a girl, and this is a fact, this is what you *are*. This is evidently a thinly disguised command, but it is one that is curiously difficult to obey. What it decrees is, not that you should act *as if* you were a girl or a boy – there is no 'as if' about it – but that you should be what you somehow already are, '*be* a girl', '*be* a boy'.

This makes gender a very particular kind of invitation. It is, of course, an offer that is difficult to refuse, but the agreement also comes in two distinct clauses. The first is that you will learn to act, think and feel in ways considered fitting for your sex. The second is that you will also learn to convince yourself, and thereby others, that these ways of acting, thinking and feeling are expressive of your feminine or masculine nature. There has been a considerable clamour to get the first clause rewritten or even struck out, but it is the second that is more far-reaching. What it commits you to is a particular understanding of what femininity and masculinity are, what gender is – *a quality of being*, something you 'are'.

One version of clause two has, of course, undergone something of a battering – the idea of nature as inborn. Women, it is said, are not 'naturally' passive, dependent, submissive, sensitive, nurturant or co-operative; men are not 'naturally' active, independent, dominant, emotionally controlled, purposive or competitive – 'socialization' makes them so. These are *acquired* characteristics. Girls and boys, it is said, are 'treated' in different ways, they are shaped and moulded by 'the environment' so that they come to take on feminine and masculine 'characteristics', and become what we recognize as women and men. Gender remains, nonetheless, a quality of being. In acting, thinking and feeling in feminine or masculine ways, we continue to express our (acquired) feminine or masculine natures.

All this makes the question of the relationship between 'gender' and 'personality' far more slippery than appears at first sight, for the belief in gender as a quality of being is only one instance – perhaps the purest case – of a more general belief that runs deep into the foundations of our culture, and which gives rise to the modern concept of 'personality' itself.

There is in this culture a firmly and widely held conviction that what people do and say, the ways they comport themselves, their gestures, even their clothes and possessions, are *signs* that express something, reveal something, about the nature, the essence, of the person who gives them off. This is a belief in 'essential' signs, a belief that Erving Goffman calls 'the doctrine of natural expression'. This belief in essential signs is nowhere more evident than in the ways femininity and masculinity are perceived and experienced. The implication is that in learning to 'be' girls and boys, women and men, we are not simply learning the ways of our sex. We are also learning to apply the doctrine of natural expression to ourselves. And so we learn to be persons with 'personalities' – in this case feminine and masculine ones.

One way this shows itself – and it is only one way – is in the sense we have of femininity and masculinity as different kinds of *presence*. The ways women tend to be depicted in advertisements illustrates this well as regards one particular variety of femininity. (A great deal of what all of us do has the character of commercials, designed to sell ourselves, often *to* ourselves, seen from a certain angle, and in a certain light – and not just when we are engaged in posing.)

As Goffman observes, women are far less often seen in advertisements grasping or manipulating objects than they are seen using their fingers and hands merely to trace the outline of an object, to cradle it, caress it, just barely to touch it. She does not spit on her hands, rub them together, take up some hefty instrument and wield it to bend some part of the world to her will. Very often she is turned inwards, watching herself barely touching herself, immersed or even luxuriating in her own moment-to-moment existence. Whether or not this is an accurate portrait *of* anything is quite another matter, the point is that by such signs we are invited to feel that we are in the presence of Femininity, of some quality which Woman exudes.

John Berger captured well the masculine equivalent when he wrote: 'A man's presence is dependent on the promise of power which he embodies. If the promise is large and credible his presence is striking. If it is small or incredible, he is found to have little presence . . . A man's presence suggests what he is capable of doing to you or for you. His presence may be *fabricated*, in the sense that he pretends to be capable of what he is not. But the pretence is always towards a power which he exercises on others.'

What separates 'the men from the boys' is the art of staging such a masculine presence, and the way it is done is by convincing others that, with them, it just comes naturally. It is part of the 'performance' that it emanates from within, that it is given off like an *aroma*. We who suspected that it would never come off no matter how much we practised were probably right – you have to believe it. But believing it is no easy matter, for we all had to *learn* the signs and how to assemble them to construct a feminine or masculine presence. Inevitably this means that in learning to 'be' a girl or a boy, a woman or a man, we also learn to worry about being exposed as frauds.*

In the course of my own masculine apprenticeship, a schoolteacher once unknowingly conferred on me a great distinction. I, it seemed, was another of those roll-up-bus-ticket-type-boys. Such a boy, as the title suggests, could not refrain from rolling up his bus ticket the moment he got it, but this was a mere sign which pointed towards a deeper and altogether more ugly set of truths: idleness, slovenliness, disrespect, unsavoury habits, perverse inclinations – in short, a pact with disorder. This metaphor spoke to me, for it seemed that we had a shared perception of bus society.

Upstairs/downstairs, two kinds of people. Downstairs they kept their bus tickets in mint condition and were given to much tut-

---

*The evident fascination (which you may or may not share) with drag queens and the like owes something to the threat that they pose to the belief that only a woman can be convincing as a woman and convey a feminine presence.

tutting. Upstairs, the aisle formed a dimension along which people arrayed themselves and which led up to the highest level of the colony, the back seat and the aristocracy of bus society. Here lounged masculine self-confidence, self-possession, an easy defiance of authority, and an awesome capacity to say 'so what?'

What was presumably intended as a warning, I took as an invitation, even a licence, to begin to think of myself as a novice among the brotherhood of the roll-up-bus-ticket-type-boys. I knew it wasn't true – they were something I was not, they had something I didn't, something possibly not unlike what the young Jean Genet saw 'strolling around on the legs of handsome hoodlums'. If I made my way down that (figurative) aisle and staked my claim to a place near the back, it would be as a fake, a fraud, an impersonator. On the other hand, I *had* found bus tickets rolled up in my hands . . . The door was now open, some of it just might be true, or I could make it true, or at the very least make it *look* like it was true. As someone once said, act as if ye had faith and faith will be given unto you. I took up smoking.

I later discovered that what I had done was stake the full weight of all the implications of the difference between belonging on the top deck (near the back) or the bottom deck of a double-decker bus on the fact of smoking cigarettes. I was left, not with an 'addiction' but with a conviction, one not unlike that of the man Tschudi tells of, who was forever in financial difficulties because of an 'inability' to handle money. If only he were better organized, why was he doing this to himself? All he stood to lose, it transpired on lengthy reflection, was 'the freedom of a child playing at the beach'. What he stood to gain in its place was a whole new life as a bourgeois, trivial, dull, blind and rigid follower of rules.

The shared conviction is this: in order to act differently, in my case to give up smoking, in his to fill in his cheque stubs, you have to become a different kind of person. This belief, and the point is crucial, co-exists uneasily with other beliefs – we contradict and confuse ourselves endlessly. But it is not the invention of individuals, it is part of the culturally shared belief in essential signs.

The belief is drawn on most obviously and directly in the context of various forms of 'social deviance'. Homosexuality, for example, no longer refers to certain activities or desires, it has been re-defined as an in-dwelling essence, a quality of being, something you are: 'A Homosexual'. All of us have feelings in relation to members of the same sex that we *could* interpret as sexual feelings. If people tend not to, this is because of what they imagine would be the implications of doing so. In this society, in the main, people take homosexuality and heterosexuality as two clear, well defined, mutually exclusive alternatives. Have feelings or desires towards a member of the same sex which you interpret as 'sexual', and you may begin to ask: am I really, after all, 'a homosexual'? Even a single experience may threaten – or promise – to show you that you are a completely different kind of person from the one you thought you were. Decide to take it up, and it can seem as though this has the character of a *truth* finally revealed. Go over your history, rewrite the story, find signs that you really 'were' homosexual all along.

Sexual orientation is for most people very close to the 'core' of who or what you take yourself to 'be' – it is something you cannot imagine changing easily, if at all. Indeed, we tend to assume that something as deep-rooted and apparently self-evident as this *must* be a fact of our personal nature. 'Being heterosexual' for most people in this society is something they simply 'are'. What this means is that it belongs to those ways I have of understanding myself to which I am most deeply committed. I can hardly imagine being any other way; if these were to change it would seem to me that I had become a different kind of person.

So it is with gender. Picture the small boy watching his sister playing with her dolls' house. Will he let himself appreciate its pleasures and join in, or will he repudiate any suggestion that there is anything there to appreciate? Once schooled in the belief in essential signs, he can no longer avoid asking himself: if I like dolls, if I want to play with dolls and dolls' houses, what would that mean? What kind of person would it make me? I am a boy, and boys know dolls are rubbish. Picture the man who allows himself to envy the feel of sensual delicate fabrics on the skin which women are permitted to enjoy. Best not, or one day, when she's out, I might – just for a minute, can't hurt to try it on . . . I am a man, a heterosexual man, and men like what fishermen and cowboys wear – sandpaper if you like, our bodies are instruments.

The message is clear: first learn the signs. Then act as if you were masculine, and masculinity will be given unto you. Act as if you were feminine, and femininity will be given unto you. Act in ways that signify the other thing, and you threaten to rob yourself of your own nature.

You might call this conviction – that in order to act differently in significant respects you have to become a different kind of person – a belief in 'signatures', a composite of 'sign' and 'nature'. Although the word signature is now associated exclusively with idiosyncratic scrawls on cheque cards and invoices, its sense as a 'mark' potentially goes wider than this. One could once talk of the signature of passion or an early death on a person's face; again, that a herb has yellow flowers has been taken as a signature indicating that it will cure jaundice. This is now an obsolete use of the word, but there is another immensely significant way of putting it which is also something of an anachronism, but which was almost certainly what my schoolteacher had in mind: signs of *character*.

One suspects that most people today would rather have 'personality' than 'character' – though perhaps it would be good to have both. The trouble is (setting aside its sense of being 'a character', a tolerated oddball), that character speaks to us of backbone and respectability, of a well ordered psychic household to the point of self-stupefaction. This makes its offer of integrity somewhat less attractive. But the modern concept of personality has much more in common with this notion of character than is generally appreciated. I say 'concept' of personality, but we are not talking here about some abstract realm of ideas. Such cultural constructions are lived and not merely thought, and this means that, in an important sense, the history of changes in the meaning of words is the history of changes in what people *are*.

Until comparatively recently, the idea of signs *of* character would have seemed more than a little odd, for characters were *themselves* signs. We still talk of graphic 'characters' like letters of the alphabet – in written Chinese the 'characters' themselves mean something in particular. This reflects the origins of the word – in the making of impressions in some material by an instrument, as in engraving. The word character later came to be applied metaphorically to facial features like a 'furrowed' (the mark left by a plough) brow, as we might talk of someone having something 'written all over their face'. It was later still and only gradually that it came to be applied to a person as such, as in 'strength of character', 'character reference', 'character actor' and so on. A 'blemish' on your character came to mean, not that you had suffered some loss of face or diminishment of your reputation, but that *you yourself* were flawed in some way. It is here that we can see the beginnings of the belief in essential signs, for the idea of character moved from the *sign* to the reality *behind* the sign. In place of characters as appearances, the appearances became signs *of* character. Character moved inwards, became written-in and then displayed.

'Personality' is one of a range of cultural constructions which have 'person' as their root. As has often been noted, 'person' has its origin in the Latin word 'persona', which initially meant a mask worn by actors but was later transferred to the part played by the actor. But the Latin 'persona' itself passed beyond a part in a play to a general word for a human being, and when the word 'person' entered the English language in the thirteenth century – through the old French 'persone' – this is what it denoted. 'Personality' – like the Latin 'personalitas' in mediaeval theology – meant simply *the quality of being a person*. It is person-ality that distinguishes us from things and from (other) animals, it consists in those qualities which make us human.

There have, of course, been countless attempts to enumerate such qualities – language, thought, consciousness, imagination, the ability to love, to transform nature, the capacity for hope, for despair, and so on. But it is important that the issue of 'defining' what a person is in these kinds of terms is inseparable from moral and political questions. 'Person' is as much a status as a form of being. We talk, for example, of treating someone 'as a person'. Again, some arguments about the 'rights' of the foetus or of non-human animals hinge on the question of whether or not they give signs of possessing any of those qualities which define 'person-ality' – for example the awareness of pain. More directly to the point here, married women in the nineteenth century had no 'legal personality', which meant that they were unable to enter into contracts in the market place. Legally, that is, married women did not count as 'persons'.

I shall return to this crucial aspect of the meaning of personality later. At this stage the point is that the notion of personality as the quality of being 'a person' is strikingly different from our own way of understanding the term. The modern meaning of personality did not fully emerge until the last century, and when it did it carried two implications: the first is that personality is, not what makes us human, not what we share with all other human beings, but what makes us *different*. Personality thus became individualized. The second is that such differences between us became revelatory of some in-dwelling essence. It is here that the history of character and personality converge – in the doctrine of natural expression, the belief in essential signs. (*Why* this happened is as much to do with changes in the social organization of class as it is with gender, but the point must be left to pass by.)

So far has the idea of personality travelled from the quality of being a person that it can now, in a logical as well as absurd extension, be applied to things. It is, for example, now part of the marketing professional's armoury of self-justifications. Just as the hefty discrepancy between the price of a pound of potatoes and a pound of crisps is to be accounted for in terms of the value that the cutting, frying and flavouring adds to that of the original raw materials, so the cost of packaging and advertising is more than justified by what they add to the pleasure of the experience of consumption. These give a product its 'personality'. Who would eat cornflakes if they weren't made of sunshine? This is a form of fetishism, meaning in this case the sense that in consuming the product you also somehow partake of the qualities with which it has been imbued by the arts of marketing: the 'personality' of Pepsi-Cola and Andrex toilet tissue. But a bank or a washing machine must take care to add a touch of 'character' to its 'personality' – integrity, reliability, solid as a rock – but not too much or it will become stuffy and old-fashioned. Summon the mantle of modern technology.

In more mundane if more consequential ways, a concept of personality founded on a form of fetishism took hold in the nineteenth century, which is still to be found in contemporary psychology. For example, in place of law breakers and criminal acts, 'criminality' arrived on the scene. A criminal became a kind of person, a form of personality, a form, moreover, which inhered in certain body types. Degeneracy was marked on the bodies of its 'victims', and could be detected through a meticulous examination by an expert of, for example, the contours of the cranium. Thus began the practice of 'psychometrics', the measurement of 'personality'.

This usually takes the form of 'rating' people on personality 'traits'. This is done by drawing up a list of pairs of adjectives, positioning individuals at some point along each of these 'dimensions', and compiling the results to yield an accurate portrait of their 'personality'. A trait is commonly represented as a line drawn on a piece of paper with two 'poles' and a scale running between them –

with definitely a ferret, no doubt about it, at one pole, passing through some fairly's and slightly's to the full strength Queen Mother at the other end. (It would be more to the point if they rolled up the piece of paper and suggested that the person put an eye to one end and look down the tube, along the line from one pole to the other.)

This way of understanding personality is central to one of the principal ways in which gender is conceived today: the idea that women and men tend to have different personality traits. It also gives rise to a vision of how things might be different which many find most appealing, the idea and ideal of the 'androgynous' 'personality': the individual who manages somehow to combine, blend or synthesize both feminine and masculine traits. As it happens, the central claim of many exponents of androgyny is that femininity/masculinity is not a single dimension, a 'bi-polar' scale running between two extremes. There are two dimensions – degrees of femininity and degrees of masculinity. The villain of the piece in this scenario is the belief that femininity and masculinity preclude one another. This is not only undesirable, it is actually wrong – all women and all men possess in some measure both feminine and masculine characteristics, and some people 'score' highly on both. But the issue of whether femininity and masculinity should be thought of as two dimensions or one is quite irrelevant here. The question is whether we should think in terms of dimensions or traits at all.

Simply in the interests of calling to mind the traits generally considered to be characteristically feminine and masculine, here is a selection drawn from a number of sources. (For the sake of clarity and simplicity I have taken only one pole, but in each case there is an implied contrast, even if it is only 'not very' or 'not at all'.) I have shuffled the pack, but you should have no difficulty in spotting which are the allegedly feminine traits and which the allegedly masculine: affectionate, competitive, dominant, childlike, gullible, ambitious, sensitive to the needs of others, soft spoken, tender, acts as a leader, flatterable, aggressive, analytical, assertive, gentle, sympathetic, forceful, has leadership qualities, independent, individualistic, warm, yielding, makes decisions easily, unable to separate feelings from ideas, self-reliant, quiet, self-sufficient, conceited about appearance, willing to take risks, hides emotions, objective, easily influenced, excitable in a minor crisis, logical, passive, worldly, feelings easily hurt, adventurous, sneaky, strong need for security.

Whether or not these are the 'right' traits is quite beside the point. Why should we think in terms of dimensions at all? The question this kind of psychology asks is why do individuals respond differently to the same set of circumstances, and the answer is differences in personality. To use a common analogy, heat melts butter but hardens eggs, so the explanation for the melting and the hardening must lie in the nature of butter and egg. Janet Spence is quite explicit on this point: femininity and masculinity are 'psychological *properties*'. This is, of course, a *metaphor*, and it should come as no surprise to find the literature on androgyny littered with metaphors drawn from chemistry. Feminine 'elements' and masculine 'elements', new androgynous 'compounds'. Those drawn to more archaic images look beyond chemistry to a new 'alchemy' to effect a reunion of opposing elements. For them gender is a kind of Fall, a rupture in a primitive unity. Light and dark, positive and negative, eternal and temporal, hot and cold, spirit and matter, mind and body, art and science, war and peace – these are polarities which were once bound together in one body: 'the Primordial Androgyne'.

There are many versions of androgyny, some more fanciful than others – but all aim in some way at combining or synthesizing feminine and masculine characteristics. (The most fanciful treat personality characteristics as disembodied entities that can be juggled and rearranged. It is clear that whatever 'personality' might be, it must be rooted in some way in the actualities of the lives that women and men lead.) All the various conceptions of psychological androgyny depend on having a theory about how and why such characteristics go together, and how they might be rearranged or transformed. But most rely on one particular culturally shared theory of personality.

It runs something like this: 'a person' is not simply an acting, thinking and feeling unit. All the things that a particular individual does, thinks or feels have a kind of coherence to them, they hang together as in some way expressive of their unity as a person. The word 'personality' is intended to describe this coherence, what it is that keeps everything in place, holds the 'bits' together in some kind of relatively consistent, though not necessarily unchangeable, pattern or arrangement. How you act, think and feel depends on 'how you're made' and it seems that women and men are 'made' – by a combination of genetics and 'the environment' – differently.

This concept of personality is a variant on the one I described earlier as fetishist – one which sees one's personality as a kind of in-dwelling essence. What trait psychology does is to see this essence as having a structure, so that change entails shaking something loose, rearranging the elements of which it is composed, introducing new elements and adjusting the pattern to enable them to be assimilated. This is clearly an objectified view of a person – we become complicated objects with certain properties. You act, think and feel as you do because that is the kind of person you are – your behaviour is expressive of your personality.*

Having seen that the psychological imagination houses both a subjective and an objective view of the person, we are now in a position to explore the different experience that women and men have of personal life, and see whether the portrait of the private as a psychological universe is indeed more in tune with the experience of men – beginning with the meanings of tenderness and care. There are two versions of care in the psychological outlook: *feeling* and *personality*. Is this how it is for women, or the story of how the poet changed his instrument but not his tune?

The words love, care and nurturance not only have similar meanings, each of them also refers to four different things. I shall call these the four elements – the earth, fire, air and water as it were of everyday social life: subjective experience (ways of feeling and thinking), personality, activities and relationships. Love, care and nurturance are each used to refer to something you *feel*, a *personality* characteristic (someone who possesses the qualities of nurturance), something you *do* (in Yorkshire people still talk of giving aid and comfort even to a stranger as 'loving' them), and a kind of *relationship* with someone. So you may care for someone by doing things for them, care about them (that is how you feel towards them), the relationship may be a caring one, and you may be said to be very caring.

These particular ways of construing people and situations are common to most people in this culture, and we also have theories about how the four elements are related to one another. Psychologists, amongst others, ask what 'the' relationship is between subjective experience, personality, activity and social relationships – but this is, I believe, a profound error. Different people have *different* theories about how they go together, and these are theories

*The point is not that this is 'wrong', but that you have to *learn* to become a personality in this sense, by learning to live by the theory, by this particular version of the doctrine of natural expression.

they live by and so in an important way make true. Most of us are confused about this, and this is not because we do not think sufficiently clearly – it is life that constantly eludes us.

How the four elements are interconnected, then, depends on the theory you subscribe to. For example, one theory has it that people 'show' they care about someone (the feeling) by the way they act (the doing) towards them. But even this conceals important differences. To some (are these more likely to be men?) it is like joining two things together which are in principle separable: there is on the one hand the feeling, and on the other the question of whether or how you act on it. To others (more likely to be women?) care that is not 'expressed' is not care at all. The connection between feeling and doing is not the kind that can be unplugged.

There are many possible variations, and which makes most sense to you will depend on your life experience. If it is correct that men drive a wedge between subjective and objective, and between the psychological and the social in the ways I have suggested, they will be more likely than women to think, for example, that mothers do what they do for their children because they care (the feeling) and because they are caring (the personal quality). Women will be more likely to see it as all of a piece, and have a sense, not that feelings and personal qualities have nothing to do with it, but that these are embedded in a whole in which caring for children is (also) something you are obliged to *do* in the context of a definite *relationship*. A question of emphasis it may be, but there is a distinct possibility that the ways in which doing, feeling, qualities and relationships are interrelated may be different for women and men.

As I said earlier in the more particular case of the subjective, it may seem odd to suggest that men have the more psychological view of personal life, when it is so often said that women have the closer affinity with psychology. Women appear to be more interested in character, motivation, and human dramas – hence, for example, the large number of women writers of murder mysteries: Dorothy Sayers, Agatha Christie, P. D. James, June Thompson, Margaret Yorke, Ruth Rendell, and many more. But there is good reason to think this is highly misleading. Women, I think, are far less prone to disconnect feeling/thinking and character/personality from the activities and relationships in which they are always embedded. This gives rise to a different kind of psychology, if indeed it is a 'psychology' at all, a more social kind of psychology.

It is crucial that these 'theories' are not ideas in our heads. We live, think and feel by and through them. If the four elements are indeed interrelated in different ways in the imaginative visions women and men construct of the world and themselves, then, in a way, women and men are indeed 'put together' differently – but not as this is normally understood.

Before beginning to explore this possibility, though, an important qualification must be registered: our theories are influenced as much by social class as they are by gender. Gender and class – not to mention age and ethnicity – are only separable in thought in the same way as the four elements. You do not get any of them by themselves, each individual is some permutation of all four. But the meaning and implications of social class are as difficult and complex to grasp as gender, so to understand how the two work together is a massive undertaking. It is gender we are interested in, so the question of class will only be introduced where it is plainly essential to do so (principally in Chapters 8 and 10). The qualifications set out below, then, must simply be borne in mind.

Firstly, middle-class men are not in the same situation as working-class men. One important qualification here is that many middle-class men work in situations where, in a particular sense, 'personality' is crucial. Advertising executives (female as well as male) do not only market products – to 'get on' they must also market themselves. The masculine emphasis on *doing*, on getting the job done, still prevails among working-class men, but self-presentation, credibility and impression management are central features of work and other areas of public life for many middle-class men.

Secondly, psychology has a greater affinity with a middle-class world view, and so some of the things I am going to suggest are masculine may well be shared by some middle-class women. But I think most women will recognize that this masculine psychology conceals, obscures, overlooks, oversimplifies or mystifies important features of their experience of life (as indeed it does of much of men's experience). This is how what is called 'ideology' works. Ideology is rarely lies. Usually what is said has the ring of truth about it, but seems to be exaggerating something or missing something out, twisting it in some way or other. Often there is just a dim sense that there is something wrong here but you cannot quite put your finger on what it is. More often than not we have different and inconsistent ways of understanding the same thing and only one is given public currency.

These qualifications noted, then, let us turn to our experience of tenderness and care, and the celebrated nurturance of the female.

6 · Tenderness

It is not only the very best shampoos that are 'gentle', 'caring', and 'kind' – women too are said to be blessed with such qualities and fine feelings. Women care for people, and they do this because they care. Why do they care? Because they are caring. Here we see combined the two principal ways in which personal life is desocialized, transformed into a purely psychological universe: a world of feelings and personalities.

Taking feeling first. When it is asked in the marriage ceremony, '*Will* you love . . .', this seems to many in our society to be an impossible promise – 'I love you today, but how can I promise to *always* love you?' I speak here not in praise of the institution of marriage, but to say that this takes love to be a *feeling*. The kind of romantic love so often aspired to in our society is a relationship between pure feeling subjects – which is why it blossoms outside the usual routines of everday life, feeding and thriving on the lack of context. Hence the common disillusion when such purely 'personal' relationships take their place in the social order of things, become interwoven with bills, buildings and domestic arrangements. Popular wisdom has it that one 'kind' of love is replaced (if you're lucky/work at it) by another. What is more likely is that love comes to be a way of living with and acting towards someone within a particular form of life, and not a stray feeling that alights upon you and which may equally mysteriously and without warning simply disappear. Other cultures ask *how* to love someone, seeing love as something people *do*. The romantic dreams of finding in reality something which psychology accomplishes in thought: the disconnection of feeling from life.

The idea of personality obscures in the same way – by disconnecting and abstracting, by taking individuals out of context. What you do becomes expressive of 'the way you're made', it reveals your underlying or in-dwelling individual nature. Your doings are signs of who or what you are – 'as a person'. The crudest version of this actually claims that you do what you do *because* of your personality. Why do women 'nurture'? Because they are 'nurturant'. How do we know that women are nurturant? Because they nurture.*

But women are clearly *supposed* to do this, they are *assigned* to the tasks of nurturing others, of caring for and looking after children, and keeping themselves and their menfolk in good repair. The idea that women are ideally suited to such tasks obviously serves to justify such a state of affairs. Note that this does not imply that it is simply a lie put about by men. An individual woman may indeed believe that women nurture because they are nurturant, and that having babies and a husband and ministering to their needs will be the fulfilment of her nature as a woman. This may be built in to her imaginative vision of herself and the future she envisages for herself. But she soon finds out that she is obliged to nurture whether she feels like it or not, and often she does not. If she concludes that not 'feeling maternal' shows that she is unfeminine, or that she has failed in the task of attaining womanhood, and if this is something to which she is deeply committed, she is at risk of falling prey to intense self-doubt, self-denigration, hopelessness and depression.

But most mothers know there is something seriously wrong with the idea that mothering is expressive of your personality, and that it is something you do out of love. You do not change nappies and clear up vomit out of love, or because it comes naturally, but because they need doing and because no-one else will do them. At least in part, it seems to most mothers, mothering is some*thing* you *do*, not some*body* you *are*. It is something you are called upon to do, and very little counts as a legitimate reason not to.

If we recall to mind the four elements – feeling, personality, activities and relationships – it is clear that a psychological view emphasizes the first two at the expense of the others. It is also at the expense of women, of the feminine perspective, because it does most violence to the experience of women. Women are far less prone to

---

*This is about as convincing an 'explanation' as the one in the children's joke which asks: why are elephants large and grey with big ears and a trunk? Answer: because if they were small, white and round they would be aspirins. Why are women nurturant, gentle, caring and kind? Because if they were rough, boorish and insensitive they would be men.

disconnect feeling and character from the activities and relationships in which they are always caught up.

Indeed women are rarely allowed to get away with such disconnecting, or cannot afford to do so. It is still more likely to be men, for example, who feel that it is possible to draw a circle around an intimate encounter and isolate it from the rest of their lives. It is still more likely to be men who feel that they can be many things to many people and insist that what they are to one is none of the others' business. In all sorts of ways women are more obliged to be mindful of the social implications of feeling and the social and economic context of their intimate relationships. This is why it is so misleading to think women more 'romantic' than men. The most important feature of the romantic fantasies written for and read by women is precisely that its character as fantasy is not disguised. It is men who are the true romantics because they are in danger of believing it.

The tendency to divorce ways of feeling and behaving from the context of social relationships can be best brought into relief, I think, by looking at the origins of words like gentle, kind, tender and so on. You may already feel that I am suffering from the delusion that you can find out about life by reading dictionaries. I am not, but the comic Steve Wright had a point when he said that the first time he looked at a dictionary he thought it was a poem – about everything. Amongst other things a good dictionary is a poem about how people have changed.

The word gentle comes from the Latin 'gentilis' meaning of the same family. It came to be associated specifically with coming from a 'good' family, with being high born – hence 'gentlemen' of 'gentle birth'. Is there not a recognizable grain of truth in the idea that 'being gentle' means treating someone in the manner considered appropriate to someone of the same family as yourself? (assuming that thumping people is not considered 'appropriate').

Take 'kind'. Hamlet was less than kind to Claudius the king, but this had nothing to do with how he felt towards him. He was being precise when he described himself as 'a little more than kin, and less than kind' to the king. 'Kin' meant relatives by marriage or blood more distant than father and son. 'Kind' meant of the same sort or 'genus' – as in 'our sort of people'. Hamlet was the king's stepson and so was more than kin, but he was not one of his sort and so was less than kind. Is there not, too, a recognizable grain of truth in the idea that 'being kind' to someone means treating them as one of your own kind?

I say this not to 'prove' anything, but simply to help shift the focus on to the character of social relationships. In fact the word that gets us closest to the heart of all this is not gentleness or kindness but the thing the old song tells the man to try a little of when a young girl gets weary: 'tenderness'. (For love, the song continues, 'is her whole happiness' – not all the poets turned psychologist.) As with love, care and nurturance, we are inclined to think that people *act* tenderly because they *feel* tender, and that some people 'are' more tender than others. I say 'we', but I think this speaks more to the experience of men than women – for reasons I shall explain.

'Tender' comes from the verb to 'tend', unambiguously something you *do*. Someone who tends is 'a tender'. We talk of people who 'mind' children as child-minders – it would be no more odd to talk of people who tend to children (as shepherds tend to sheep) as child-tenders. A child-minder/tender is someone who assumes the responsibility for looking after children – who stays mindful of them and tends to their needs. Tenders acts tender-ly. If you are a tender and you do not tend to others, you are not acting tenderly, like a tender should.

This emphasis on doing, and on the relationship between tender and tended, is quite in keeping with the accounts I have read, heard and shared of women's experience of caring for others. Men, on the other hand, are inclined to think tenderness is first and foremost a *feeling*. That this is so is, I think, made plain by Jules Henry's illuminating analysis of what tenderness means to men, though the impression is that he intended to talk about what it means to *people*. The fact that he is a man is not enough in itself to conclude that he expresses a masculine perspective – if it was then I would have to stop writing this book at once. But there is reason to think that what he has to say about tenderness is indeed a masculine perspective on it.

Tenderness, as Henry understands it, is a *feeling*, and it is one aroused by the apprehension of another's *vulnerability*. The fact that cruelty towards the weak and defenceless strikes us as the most heinous of crimes shows, he believes, that we have set vulnerability at the heart of our ethical sense. It is scarcely, if at all, possible to imagine a set of ethical principles which did not affirm this. There can be *no* good in a world which responds to vulnerability with callousness or indifference, without tenderness. It is vulnerability in others, then, that arouses tenderness in us, and at the same time it awakens our own vulnerability. (The fact that we describe an injured part of the body that is sore to the touch as 'tender' confirms the existence of such a connection in our culture.) Tenderness, in other words, becomes a feeling virtually synonymous with compassion for the helpless.

There is more to the apprehension of another's vulnerability than simply acknowledging that they need something. A baby may patently need feeding, for example, without our sensing their vulnerability. But if we do sense it, this arouses tenderness, and the reason it does so, Henry suggests, is because it awakens in us the sense of our own vulnerability, and with it the vulnerability in all of us, built in to the human condition, part of the common ground of our humanity. The effect of television on people's response to the recent famines in East Africa helps to make the point. What this did was *personify* the victims' plight, by picking out individuals, particularly children, dwelling on expressions in the eyes and on the face. We already knew there was suffering, but these pictures were moving because, through their way of depicting helplessness, innocence and incomprehension, our sense of their profound vulnerability – one we could 'identify with' – was overwhelming.

If the reason vulnerability in others arouses tenderness in us is that it awakens our sense of our own vulnerability, this means that people who live in the delusion of their own strength will not be tender, and will not awaken tenderness in other people. (It presumably also means, though Henry does not say so, that those who are so overwhelmed by the sense of their own vulnerability that they do not see it in other people will not be moved to tenderness either.) It might seem that masculinity includes an *instruction* to live in the delusion of your own strength – to 'be' strong – and some men may well be so deluded, and rarely experience tender feelings. But the instruction is first and foremost to be *seen* to be strong, and there are occasions when you are not obliged to be so. This is why it seems to many women that 'men are real babies when they're ill'. Being ill is one of the few times when men feel relieved of the obligation to appear to be strong, and it is not surprising if they go the whole hog.

If tenderness is the response to sensed vulnerability, and if you are normally obliged to claim to be strong, then you will rarely be responded to with tenderness (women judged as falling on the wrong side of the contrast between carthorse and filly will suffer the same fate). Men will not generally show tenderness towards other men – *except* when they are relieved from making claims about their strength. A soldier dying on the battlefield, for example, is released from this obligation and this enables his friends to respond with tenderness and feel, temporarily, the vulnerability they cannot afford to dwell on.

Every man and boy knows that to be male in this society is still to live under the shadow of an ever-present possibility of being subjected to humiliation, derision and degradation at any sign of vulnerability. (It is not only women who feel themselves to live in a world populated by aggressive, insensitive and uncaring men.) Of all forms of cruelty, humiliation is perhaps the closest to being the opposite of tenderness, in the way it exposes and exploits another's vulnerability. So you must claim strength, and thereby forfeit the possibility of being treated tenderly.

It follows from this that men have an immense and very particular investment in the perception of women as vulnerable. It may be that for most of the time they can only acknowledge their own vulnerability through a tenderness awakened *by someone else's*, and that would have to be, by definition, a non-man – in other words, a child or a woman. If you look at the things that we are said to respond to spontaneously with tenderness – helplessness, vulnerability, weakness, innocence and incomprehension – the striking thing is that we first and foremost attribute these things to infants, but the very same characteristics have long been attributed to women.

(It is also worth noting that although infants are generally depicted as 'innocent' – as free from the hypocrisies, the deceptions, the guile and the manipulativeness of the adult – mothers are often given dire warnings about not 'making a rod for your own back' by 'giving in' to the 'demands' of the infant, and this often implies a deliberate intention on the infant's part to dominate the household. What may be perceived in a child's crying is not vulnerability, but the immense power of the totally unreasonable but unignorable demand. Some mothers even find that they experience their babies as *evil*: there they lie, incessantly crying, accusing the mother of incompetence or hard-heartedness, refusing to be satisfied, damned if they will, you're not getting off the hook that lightly. Likewise, alongside the vision of woman as innocent run innumerable tales of her deceptions, her guile, her manipulativeness, her calculating seductiveness. If there is Mary, there is also Eve and many more like her. Men's images of woman have always included what he fears she may be, as well as what he desires and finds her to be.)

Men's interest in women's vulnerability has on occasions extended to literally crippling them. Men have also clearly conspired in all manner of ways to deprive women of those resources which would make them less vulnerable and more powerful. But men have a special and very particular reason for wanting women to be less powerful than themselves, and this allows a glimpse, I think, of one of the ways in which man-kind feels profoundly threatened by the feminist project of gaining power for women: men are dependent on women's vulnerability for there to be any respite from the strain of denying their own.

But *respite* it is, a temporary thing. Men do not wish to feel tender (and vulnerable) most of the time, and feel they cannot afford to. What men seem to want is to be allowed an intense experience of both – but only as an episode. This is a masculine conception of tenderness because it could not withstand the continuous experience of tendering, of responding to and anticipating other people's needs, that is the lot of so many women. It depends on being able to dip in and out (perilously close to the way some men talk about sex). This is why masculine tenderness so easily slips into sentimentality – how many fathers dearly love their children, but most of all when they're not around? Then you can *feel* love for them without having to *do* anything about it. (It is not only men who are prone to this. Parents of both sexes are given to bouts of sentimentality – often tinged with guilt – when they see their children sleeping, for example.)

Mothers, however, do not tend to babies and small children because they are overwhelmed with compassion for their plight. At times of course mothers are moved by their children's vulnerability, but this is not why they tend to them all their waking hours. The idea that tenderness is a powerful, intense and momentary feeling, disconnected from the activities of tending, positively jars with the unbroken repetition of the process of tending to those who cannot fend for themselves that is the all-day every-day reality of being the mother of young children. However intense, the feeling must pass.

To see tenderness as a passing feeling is both masculine (it fits the kind of experience that is more likely to be that of a man) and it is subjectified (it disconnects feeling from the activities and relationships in which it is caught up). This clearly adds weight to the suggestion that the vision of the private as a subjective universe is indeed more in tune with the experience of men. But we can add yet further weight to this suggestion, because there are other ways in which the masculine view of tenderness is subjectified. To see what these are, we must look more closely at the meaning of vulnerability and its association with tenderness.

What exactly is this 'sense' of another's and one's own 'vulnerability'? There are two points here: firstly, why do we talk of a *sense* of vulnerability? In the days of Harold Wilson, politicians and the press liked to talk of a 'sense of injustice' among particular groups of workers, and this was a problem to be taken seriously. The task was somehow to remove – not actual injustices – but their *sense* of injustice. We were not to get embroiled in the question of whether these injustices were real, it was their perception, their state of mind, that needed to be altered. So are we talking about a subjective sense of vulnerability – a feeling or a state of mind – or actual vulnerabilities?

Secondly, what exactly *is* 'vulnerability'? Vulnerable (from the Latin 'vulnerare': to wound) means susceptible to injury. So what exactly are these potential wounds, to what kinds of injury are we susceptible? In Henry's account they are things we all have in common. The vulnerability he talks of is one we all share, built in to the human condition. Now, as Bob Dylan once said, even the President of the United States must sometimes have to stand naked. Perhaps he does, but he is also one of the most powerful men in the world. No doubt we could be told of some deep tragedy in his life and be moved to compassion – he is, after all, human, one of us, susceptible to death, defeat and despair. But he is a lot less vulnerable in all kinds of ways than countless other human beings.

To dwell on what we all have in common is plainly to let pass the obvious and massive differences between us. Under the aspect of eternity we may all be the same – simply human – but under today's sky we most certainly are not. To talk of the human condition can readily suggest a non-existent equality – as if, for example, South American landowners and peasants, or white and black in South Africa, all participate in the same universal abstraction. The secure and the comfortable are always more struck by what they have in common with the insecure and the uncomfortable than the other way round.

Are women and men equally vulnerable and to the same things?

Plainly not – we cannot be unequal and equally vulnerable. (We will return to this point in Chapter 9, for vulnerability and dependence are closely linked.) To take the obvious example, as things stand, considerably more women than men do not earn, and are not in a position to earn, a living wage. This makes women economically more vulnerable than men. And even if a husband were to give his full-time houseworker-wife his unopened wage packet every week, she would be continuously dependent on his good will and hence vulnerable to its being withdrawn. Again, however harsh and inhospitable a man may experience public space to be, and however fearful he may be in passing through it alone at night (the majority of assaults are against men), no-one can seriously deny that it is far worse for women. These are just two of the many ways in which women *are* more vulnerable than men.

To talk, then, of a 'sense' of vulnerability is subjectified, and it is more likely to be men who dwell on the vulnerabilities that women and men allegedly share. But there is more. What is the opposite of vulnerability? Men are more inclined to see it as *strength*. But what makes some people more susceptible to injury than others is their relative inability to prevent it happening. Men do not get better jobs with higher wages and status because they are 'strong', women are not dependent on the good will of a 'breadwinner' because they are 'weak'. The capacity to control your own destiny goes by the name, not of strength, but of *power*.

It is all too easy to become embroiled in issues of power and gender and never get to say anything else (there is more to gender than power, just as there is more to power than gender). It is impossible to deal adequately with the immensely difficult and highly charged issues this raises here, but equally we cannot let it pass entirely. Let us simply note that a rather different picture emerges if in place of the construct* vulnerability/ strength we substitute inequalities of power, and say that there is in this society a close connection between tenderness and *power*.

Issues of power are always present in intimate relationships, in ways that may not be obvious – particularly to men. Men are often so intent (largely out of habit) on constructing the presence of a person to be reckoned with – not a wimp or a wally, a prat or a dickhead –

*The word 'construct' may need explaining. We think in contrasts and a construct simply identifies exactly what is being contrasted to what.

that they rarely stop to think what effect this might have on the people they are with, particularly on women. They seem barely aware of how extremely intimidating to others it can be to succeed in denying your own vulnerability. At the same time, if most men feel they can only experience their own vulnerability with a woman, then she will seem to him to have the ultimate power – to be able to elicit neediness, and then respond with imperviousness or indifference, to reject or humiliate you at your most exposed. What men feel to be the costs of claiming to be 'strong' play a significant part in enlarging the blind spot that prevents them from seeing how it is for women.

But it is not always easy for either women or men to see how power works in intimate relationships. The ordinary usage of the word power is so narrow that it needs to be said that power is not always mobilized for selfish ends. Power is anywhere that anything happens as a result of what somebody is doing. To have power is simply to be able to make something happen, or contribute to making it happen. To exercise power is to draw on whatever resources may be available to you – from nuclear warheads to a kind word – in order to achieve some end. Helping someone involves the exercise of power – you cannot help someone if you do not have the necessary resources, whether it be time, money or a little encouragement (and whoever has the power to give aid also has the power to withhold or refuse it).

Consider: if someone cries painfully in your presence and it arouses your compassion, the chances are this will be accompanied by an urge to comfort them, and this seems to entail the quite literal abolition of distance. The impulse is to move closer, to touch, possibly to hold, perhaps even to envelop their entire body in your own. This seems only natural – but there may be a price to pay, because it can readily confirm the inequality at the heart of our most intimate exchanges.

Erving Goffman observes that when affection and tenderness are expressed, one person typically takes up a position different from and reciprocal to the other person, establishing a relationship between giver and receiver, protector and protected, embracer and embraced, comforter and comforted, supporter and supported and so on. 'The gentlest, most loving moments', he suggests, 'can hardly be conceived of apart from these asymmetries.' This is not at all to say that such exchanges *cannot* occur between equals, or that members of the same sex do not embrace, or that women do not embrace men. A mutual embrace is not unthinkable, but in *most* embraces in this society someone is being embraced by someone else. The point is perhaps best put as a question rather than an assertion – is there *usually* an answer to the question, who is cuddling whom here? If there is, then why should this be so?

According to Goffman, the reason lies in the immense significance that relationships *modelled* on that of parent to child have in our emotional lives. Indeed he claims that this provides the models for the only ways of 'gentling' the world we know. (The 'proof' of this would perhaps be whether, when a woman cuddles a man, he typically takes up the position of a child, and feels like a little boy. He may not be prepared to do this, and she may not be prepared to take up the complementary position and respond in ways that feel to her like 'mothering' him.)* It is quite evident that parent-child is an unequal relationship, and so to the extent that the expression of affection or tenderness or the giving of comfort is modelled on that relationship, it is inevitable that such inequalities of power will be written into these exchanges. And to the extent that it seems natural in intimate exchanges between adults of different sexes that men encompass and women be encompassed, then women are rendered equivalent to children. As Goffman says, 'male domination is a very special kind, a domination that can be carried right into the gentlest, most loving moments without apparently causing strain'.

What men are inclined to feel as the shared tragedy of the masculine condition – the obligation to deny 'vulnerability' and claim to be 'strong' – has the effect of reproducing inequalities of power that must in the end be to their advantage. Men often deny this and say they envy women, but this is simply trying to have their cake and eat it. There are costs to be sure in occupying positions of power, but you can always give it up. If you do not, then you cannot blame women if they conclude that, as Jock Ewing once told J. R., power is not something you ask for, power is something you take.

This transformation of power inequalities into strength and weakness is just one instance of a masculine psychologized vision of

---

*It is also interesting that when women and men hold hands it is invariably the man's hand that is in front, a position hardly conducive to following or being led. (If you have not noticed this, try it the other way round. The reason it feels awkward may be partly physical, but there is a strong element of leading and following in it as well.) When an adult of either sex holds a child's hand it is the adult's that is in front. So when a woman is with a man she takes up the position that a child takes up in relation to her.

personal life and it is this we shall continue to dwell on. To see tenderness as a feeling, and vulnerability as a 'sense' or a personality characteristic, is to blind oneself to the character of the social relationships in which these are always caught up. At the heart of this, I believe, is the 'dipping in and out' that I spoke of earlier. The desocializing of love, intimacy, tenderness and care, and the desire to meet women in a realm of pure feeling and personal qualities, are rooted in the masculine experience of straddling two worlds – the private and the public – and their interest in defining personal life in stark contrast to their lives in public.

But the different experience that women and men tend to have of these worlds and the relationship between them also crucially affects many other things that are closely related to tenderness and care. One of these is the sense and idea of what is 'moral', and it is this that is the subject of the next chapter. If Aristotle was right, care and morality are inherently connected, for 'between friends there is no need for justice'. Or in the words of Laurie Anderson's 'Oh Superman': 'When Love has gone, there's always Justice. And when Justice has gone, there's always Force. And when Force has gone, there's always . . . '

7 · Goodness and Justice

Being good and feeling bad – a great many women seem to recognize this condition. Being good for a woman tends to be identified with putting other people first, and this implies a contrast: putting yourself first. (As an advertisement for a Bradford newspaper once explained: 'it's what it isn't that makes it what it is'.) This ensures that women in this society will be faced with a particular form of dilemma: being selfish as opposed to being responsible, pleasing yourself versus pleasing others, self-centredness versus self-sacrifice. According to Carol Gilligan, this leads women to develop distinctive ways of thinking about and resolving moral dilemmas. If this is so, if women and men really do have – or rather tend to draw on – differing conceptions of morality, the explanation for this may well be found in our differing relation to the public/private contrast.

Gilligan's work can only be explained by contrasting it with that of another psychologist: Lawrence Kohlberg. In a nutshell, Kohlberg was developing a research tradition begun by Jean Piaget into changes in the ways children and young people think about moral issues and make judgments about right and wrong. His research involved giving them hypothetical dilemmas, asking them what would be the right thing to do in that kind of situation and to explain why – it being the *reasoning* behind their decision that Kohlberg was interested in, not the actual judgment itself. The most commonly quoted example of such a dilemma is one where you have to decide whether Heinz would be right to steal a drug that would save his wife's life from a chemist who demands an extortionate price for it, which Heinz cannot afford.

On the basis of this research Kohlberg concluded that changes in the way children and young people think about moral matters occurred in a particular order, that there were stages in the development of moral reasoning which appeared in a particular sequence. He identified six such stages, which he grouped into three levels: the pre-conventional, conventional, and post-conventional. The reason for calling them that is to put conventional in the middle – children, he suggested, moved towards and then away from thinking about moral issues in conventional terms.*

The fundamental difference between these levels is that moral reasoning becomes more *abstract* – you can formulate general principles which can then be brought to bear on concrete situations; and more *independent* – you can make judgments about what is right without reference to your own wants or needs, and independently of the values of those around you. Something isn't necessarily right or wrong just because most other people think it is.

This is best thought of in terms of a kind of expansion outwards from the self. Initially the child makes judgments in terms of what he wants, whether it's allowed, whether he can get away with it, and so on. Next he thinks of it in terms of agreed standards or rules – lying, stealing, cheating and so on are wrong – everybody says so. In the third phase the individual thinks in terms of moral principles that enable him, for example, actually to *criticize* what most people would say or do, question whether the fact that something is illegal necessarily makes it wrong, and so on. This expansion is a two-stage shift from an *egocentric* to a *societal* to a *universal* moral viewpoint.

Now, you may have noticed that I keep saying 'he'. This is not ignorance or carelessness on my part. One of Kohlberg's most widely read papers is called 'The *Child* as Moral Philosopher', and throughout the paper he talks of the way 'children' reason about moral issues and make moral judgments. But these children he talked to were in fact all *boys* – and this, to put it mildly, makes a difference. Just speculate for the moment that perhaps girls and boys, women and men, think *differently* about moral issues. If this is so, and you

*One of the most widely read of books for young children today – Roald Dahl's *Fantastic Mr Fox* – includes the following conversation: 'Suddenly Badger said, "Doesn't this worry you a tiny bit, Foxy?" "Worry me", said Fox. "What?" "All this . . . this *stealing*." Mr Fox stopped digging and stared at Badger as if he had gone completely dotty. "My dear old furry frump," he said, "do you know anyone in the *whole world* who wouldn't swipe a few chickens if his children were starving to death?" There was a short silence while Badger thought deeply about this. "You are far too respectable," said Mr Fox. "There's nothing wrong with being respectable," Badger said.'

base your stages of development on boys and then see where girls have reached in this progression, then you are *bound* to find more boys than girls at the higher levels. The male would inevitably come out as superior in moral terms because the standard is a masculine one. This has repeatedly been found to be so – on Kohlberg's scale, women come out generally as developmentally inferior to men. Is this because women are a bit retarded, or is it because women are being compared to a standard which defines men as right?

What is this supposed developmental inferiority of women? According to Kohlberg, there is an 'interpersonal bias' in women's moral judgment. In his scheme, a great many women 'freeze', as it were, at stage three. He decides that their moral reasoning falls into what he calls the 'good-boy, good-girl' orientation. Here: 'Good behaviour is that which pleases or helps others and is approved by them'. To get from stage three to stage four, you have to leave behind issues to do with how individuals feel, to do with helping people and pleasing them, and proceed to societal definitions of what is right and wrong in more abstract and general terms. Kohlberg suggests that women may not *need* to make that kind of transition, because most of the moral issues women face are to do with personal relationships, so an interpersonal code is quite adequate.

Gilligan insists that this is a travesty of women's morality. Her research on women's moral reasoning suggested to her that women *also* go through a three-level progression, from an egocentric through a societal to a universal perspective, but that this progression occurs within a quite different conception of what morality is. She suggests that there is a *kind* of truth in the charge that 'women can't keep their emotions out of their judgments' and tend to think in concrete terms. The truth in this is that women's judgments are more closely tied to empathy and compassion, and more concerned with real-life moral conflicts and dilemmas than with hypothetical ones. But this is no reason for classifying women's thinking with that of children. It may be men that are wrong – or perhaps we've *both* got it wrong.

Take the Heinz dilemma. Women are more likely than men to respond to this by thinking about who is going to be *hurt* the most. If Heinz does *not* steal the drug then his wife will die – bad for the wife, and bad for Heinz because he doesn't want to lose her. If he *does* steal the drug, then the chemist will lose some money, and Heinz will probably go to jail – bad for the chemist, bad for Heinz, and bad for

Heinz's wife (who must then presumably acquire the feminine 'prisoner-visiting' personality trait). Which is the lesser, they ask, of these particular evils? But this falls woefully short of the top of Kohlberg's morality tree. The stage six response in his scheme is to ask, which has the greater moral priority – the value of life, or the value of property? The right to live, or the right to possess? By contrast to this, the women's response sounds, to Kohlberg, rather concrete and emotionally laden – they seem to be asking: 'who would I feel sorry for most?', instead of thinking the issue through in terms of abstract universal principles. But this may be an equally 'high-level' response, based on a different conception of morality.

It is this that Gilligan set out to investigate, and she did so by asking women how they made up their minds whether or not to have an abortion. It is important that this was a real-life dilemma, because one significant finding is that women are more likely than men to ask for more information about Kohlberg's dilemmas. The implication is that you need to know all the particulars before you can make a judgment. (A woman magistrate I have spoken to confirms that this is her experience, but I can find no systematic research on the issue.) It may be that men are happier to think in hypothetical terms than women, and to pass judgment on the basis of a thumbnail sketch of a dilemma.

As Kohlberg did with his male subjects, Gilligan concluded that there were three levels of moral reasoning in the women's accounts. The first level centres on the woman's own needs. Here the women would simply say, 'I had an abortion because I didn't want the baby.' If there was any difficulty in reaching a decision it was because of conflicting wants: 'Having the baby would have been a good opportunity to get married and leave home, but it would have restricted my freedom.' This is a conflict, but not a moral conflict.

At the second level the decision becomes a difficult one in a different sense. Here the women would say, 'You have to think about other people, not just yourself' – about the effects of having or not having an abortion on the child, on the father, on the woman's own parents and so on. Here is the beginnings of a morality of 'responsibility'. But here being responsible means doing right by *other* people. Being moral, being 'good', means *self-sacrifice*, ignoring your own wants or needs. To think about yourself is seen as *selfish*.

If you look at the attributes generally considered to be desirable in a woman it is not surprising that women come to identify being good with self-sacrifice: tact, gentleness, awareness of the feelings of others, an easy expression of 'tender' feelings, and so on. The point is not whether this is true, whether women are or are not 'good', but that being good for a girl or a woman means care of, concern for, and sensitivity to others. Remember the adage: 'it's nice to be important, but it's more important to be nice'. Note that if you *are* good in this way you get marked down as deficient in moral development – too conventional, too emotional, too involved. (As Dr Gillespie was always telling Dr Kildare, you must not get personally or emotionally involved with your patients – it clouds your judgment.)

According to Gilligan, it is in their care and concern for others that women are judged and judge themselves. So at the second level, what is most moral is what causes the least harm. If there were an ideal solution to such conflicts, it would be one where no-one got hurt. But there is a price to pay, because that no-one does not include *you*. If your own needs and wants are selfish, then you are obviously not being good if you take them into account. But if what is right means no-one getting hurt, how can it be right to make a decision that hurts you? When women permit themselves to take this seriously, Gilligan suggests, this sets up a tension which must be resolved. This can only be done by rethinking the contrast between selfishness and responsibility.

Is there a way you can look after yourself without being selfish, be responsible without sacrificing yourself? At the third level, women develop a universal morality of care and responsibility, where what is moral is not merely to respect the *rights* of others, but to care about what happens to people. This *includes* yourself. One reason why this is the basis of a genuinely universal moral principle is that it enables you to criticize convention. Laws which prevent abortion *may* be wrong if they cause too much human damage. (Note that the third level would not necessarily think abortion was legitimate.)

There is no need to get into the question of whether this talk of 'stages', of 'progression' and 'higher levels' is an appropriate way of talking about ethics. The point is simply this: Kohlberg takes a conception of morality and of moral reasoning that seems to fit what boys and young men have to say, and then uses it as a standard by which *both* males and females are judged. Gilligan might have been forgiven for playing him at his own game and judging the male wanting – he doesn't care enough, he is too detached, doesn't empathize enough, and ignores the *consequences* of moral choices by focusing on the *logic* of the choice. In fact she does not. While others conclude that this feminine morality is superior to the masculine and should replace it forthwith, Gilligan aspires to some kind of positive synthesis of the best of both moralities, calling for a 'dialogue' between fairness and care. (The final four chapters here will be devoted to considering what having the best of both worlds might entail, not only with respect to morality, but to the feminine and masculine perspectives generally.)

There is, I think, something in this idea of two conceptions of the moral, and they are ones which make sense in terms of the differing experience that women and men have of the public, the private, and the relationship between them. Kohlberg's masculine morality is built up within a picture of an expanding world – from the self, going 'outward' into society, and then looking down on this society from a higher universal plane. Gilligan's feminine morality is built up within the one world, constructed out of the raw materials of personal relationships and the dilemmas these throw up.

Note that what is *not* being said is that women are fit for making moral decisions in the concrete face-to-face situations that arise in personal life but are hopeless when it comes to 'wider' issues. Gilligan's claim that women's higher-level moral sense is a universal one is absolutely crucial. It has long been a justification for denying minorities and subordinate groups a significant part in the political process that they are less 'universal'. British politicians still talk (though perhaps more quietly now) of 'the Asian vote' – as if being of Asian origin meant you had no interest in anything that did not specifically affect your own kind, and that means others of Asian origin. The same is said of 'women's votes'. It also arises in connection with questions like whether there should be 'women's programmes' on television. Programmes made and presented by women perhaps – but *for* women? What are women interested in – only things to do with women?

What *is* being suggested is that men may be more likely than women to look on human affairs in an abstract, detached and distant manner, and it is this I want to pursue further. Many have claimed that this gives rise to a masculine form of rationality and objectivity that could be the death of all of us. Be that as it may, men do seem more inclined to disengage, to detach themselves from the here and now in all its concrete particularities, and take off into the realm of the abstract. Men have the 'capacity' to do this because the female sex is in our kind of society assigned to those kinds of activities and relationships which keep you rooted in the immediate. This has immense consequences for the forms of thought that prevail in and dominate the public world. It is gender that has given us, amongst other things, the opposition between mind and body, culture and nature, and our ways of experiencing time. It is the ways these figure in the everyday experience of women and men that is the subject of the next chapter.

8 · Mother Nature, Father Time

The best shampoos are not only gentle, caring and kind – they are also 'natural'. So are McVities' biscuits, hand-made pottery and homeopathic medicine. Here is the latest edition of a new kind of portrait of Ruskin's true home which began to come to the fore in the first half of this century: the surburban dream of city homes in country lanes. The best of both worlds, the marriage of town and country, the rural and the cosmopolitan. Homes (with just a hint of the country cottage) with gardens. Back to nature (naychoor as Ivor Cutler sings it) – but only half-way, near enough for the breadwinner to return from his daily expeditions and relax, not only into the comfort of his own true self, but into a little piece of the countryside.

Today's women are too wise to the fast one pulled on their mothers to become part of a national Ideal Homes Exhibition. Who was going to make the home-baked bread and the home-made jam, fill the house with flowers and do the farmhouse cooking? The housewife. The gaff would seem to be blown on this one – the little woman has become a lot more worldly. And women are also far too important as consumers to let such small steps towards self- sufficiency go too far. The masters of the marketing arts have found the answer: convenience products with Natural Ingredients! Tell me Simon, do we make convenience foods natural by taking something out or putting something in? How about crisps made from unpeeled potatoes? Would they buy that one? Save a lot of peeling.

What did Ruskin call the 'true home'? A place of peace. It was so easy to paint this portrait in the colours of the countryside. Flowers both pretty *and* (mildly) wild. The tranquillity of the meadow, cows mooing, baa-lambs frolicking, hedgehogs in little gingham aprons scurrying about – ah, naychoor, naychoor. It began to be said that we are at our most *human* when we feel ourselves to be at one with naychoor. But naychoor is not nature. It is not a cruel and threatening place, indifferent, impervious, beset with earthquakes and volcanoes, extremes of heat and cold, storms and swamps, plague, disease and famine. These are the ingredients of nature, but they are not what we want in our muesli.

This sentimental vision of the natural is a peculiarly modern variation on a much older theme. Some vision of the domestic world – and with it of women – as being closer to the order of nature, recurs throughout human history and is to be found in many different cultures. But what is most striking is that both have more usually been seen as *dangerously* close to nature.

We humans organize ourselves and live in relation to the world of nature – it is set over and against us as a source of both sustenance and threat. But we are clearly also *part* of nature. We are embodied beings, and bodies eat, excrete, and produce secretions, they engage in sexual activity, some of them menstruate, get pregnant and produce offspring. All of these things have tended to be associated with women. It is usually women who prepare and cook food, it is still, even in the most supposedly enlightened homes, women who clean the toilet. Sexuality might seem to be the odd one out, but the myth has it that Man is 'called back' to his animal nature by women's bodies – men, it declares, are only sometimes sexual beings, women always so.

It might seem that women in this mythology *are* nature, but that would not be strictly accurate. Women are assigned to the daily *control* and management of the natural. Take cooking, for example. Speeded up rotting it may ultimately be, but the transformation from the raw to the cooked epitomizes the ways in which human beings work on nature to bend it to their needs and it is women who have usually been charged with this task. Note, too, that in eating there seems to be a felt danger of our descending to the bestial, and so eating becomes generally a social act accompanied by great ceremony. Food and/or drink are associated with most social occasions and often provide the focus of them. And it is not only 'respectable' people who insist on 'table manners' – few people would now spit on the carpet or blow their noses into their clothes while sitting at the table. There is nothing more bodily than phlegm, and hence such habits seem disgustingly 'uncivilized'. Language above all would seem to set us apart from nature, indeed Samuel

Beckett maintained that the only truly dramatic thing in the whole world is the fact that out of the most earthy and material of things – that rubbery and slimy thing the mouth – comes what is least material and most 'spiritual': language. But it is generally women who teach children to talk. Illness calls us back to the body, but hygiene and daily health care belong to women.

Taken together the activities of 'reproduction' lie on what is seen to be the borderline between nature and culture. Women have long been obliged to live on this frontier. But, the story goes, they are in danger thereby of being tainted by it or being absorbed into it – they get too close to nature for comfort. Women become peculiarly ill-fitted to the task of 'culture-building', because this entails rising decisively above the natural order. Men become the carriers of civilization and must be protected from the threat of being called back to the realm of unreason. (It is no coincidence, I suggest, that the director of such romantic fables as *Close Encounters of the Third Kind* and *E.T.* should also have given us *Jaws*. The shark is the epitome of terrifying unreason – though the psychoanalyst might mutter something about vaginas with teeth.)

The myth plainly confirms the assignment of women and men to different spheres of activity. But, equally importantly, it also confirms the idea that these *activities* are necessarily distinct and must be kept separate. Somehow the contrast between nature and culture becomes itself 'natural', it could not be any other way. And since the affairs of the body are conducted in private in this society, public and private must be distinct and kept separate. But myths are not simply false. As things stand, women and men have a different engagement with these 'borderline' activities and this difference makes its presence felt in some of our most basic everyday ways of experiencing the world and ourselves. I shall single out two of these here: 'the' relationship between mind and body, and our experience of time.

This morning I was sitting in a garden, thinking. A garden is a private space, and a little piece of nature – more often naychoor – tamed and ordered to varying degrees, a pool of tranquillity in a turbulent world. Alone in such places, the mind is apt to wander. This particular mind had wandered into wondering about this wandering, ruminating on what the difference might be between daydreaming and abstract thought – as two ways of being mentally transported out of the here and now – and wondering whether women and men characteristically engage in different kinds of flights of mind. Then a wind blew up and I thought about nothing at all for several minutes. I then set to thinking about why the wind in the trees seems to fix you in the present, almost transport you *into* the here and now. It had to be drawn to my attention by a woman that there was one thing I most definitely was not thinking: good drying weather!

In one of Fay Weldon's novels there is a line which runs: 'Down among the women . . . If we look upwards, it's not towards the stars or the ineffable, it's to dust the tops of the windows.' The ability – if that is what it is – to disengage mentally, depends on not having to deal with what is under your nose. *Having* to? Do you *have* to see the dust and not the stars, *must* you think about the effects of the wind on wet clothes and not make philosophy of it? Even Fay Weldon adds 'we have only ourselves to blame'.

It is often said that women keep the house clean and tidy because if they do not there will be hell to pay when He gets home. But he may well say that he does not notice whether the house is clean and tidy or not. He thinks he is quite happy in what she calls a tip or a pigsty. He is very adept at picking his way across a room littered with objects without even noticing they are there. He thinks she is *obsessed* with cleaning and clearing – haven't you anything better to think about?

We are not in the business of taking sides here – rethinking gender cannot be a matter of judging one gender through the eyes of the other. The point is this: women are not simply assigned to the *activities* of housework and childcare, but to the *responsibility* for them. Such responsibility literally focuses the mind. When it comes to the business of domestic order, the minds of most women are focused on the one thought: 'if I don't deal with this no-one else will'. But the more important point is that someone else *might* – He might – but only if it is pointed out to him that it needs doing. Women are obliged to *notice* and it is when men feel relieved of such an obligation that they are enabled to rise above such things and see them as mundane and trivial matters. The significance of this becomes clear when we think about women and men, not individually, but collectively.

I said earlier that the houseworkers and mothers of the land busily keep business business by ensuring that these matters are prevented from intruding into the public world and messing it up. The same applies to what is taken in this society to·be the higher forms of thinking. It is women who 'liberate' men from time and place and enable them to take off into the realm of the abstract. Providing for this liberation, as Dorothy Smith says, 'is a woman who keeps house for him, bears and cares for his children, washes his clothes, looks after him when he is sick and generally provides for the logistics of his bodily existence'. Of course men are also always bodily present somewhere and sometime. In Smith's words again, he is always in a place where things *smell*, where the irrelevant birds fly away in front of the window, where he has indigestion. But these are things to be put out of your mind if you are to keep your mind on the job.

The people who manage and govern the various spheres of the public realm in our kind of society are usually men, and they operate primarily through an abstract, conceptual mode of consciousness.* They can only do so because the logistics of their bodily existence are catered for elsewhere and by someone else. The minds of men whose work involves this abstract conceptual mode of consciousness are constantly under threat from the intrusions of the bodily, of the immediate, in all its concrete particularities. You need to become *absorbed* in this mode of consciousness, and you cannot be so absorbed if you have to focus your interests on what is, sometimes literally, under your nose.

To talk of men as being 'liberated' in this way means only that these forms of thought depend on the gender division of labour, not that they really are 'higher'. (There are plenty of men who demonstrate all too clearly that it is possible to be so 'rational' that virtually everything passes you by.) Taking gender seriously involves rethinking a whole set of contrasts, and abstract versus concrete is surely one of them. The issue is too complex to develop fully, but one aspect is especially relevant here.

While writing this book I have been haunted by a kind of recurring daydream in which sometimes a woman and sometimes a man suddenly appears out of nowhere to say in a fiercely challenging tone: What's all this about 'women' and 'men'? *Look* at me, look me in the eye. What do you see? 'A' woman? 'A' man? There is, it seems, an abstract kind of way of thinking about people that cannot withstand the vivid presence of any single individual. What good is a way of understanding 'people', 'women', 'men', that starts to burble and mumble when faced with, or rather confronted by, the immediate

*This mental (as opposed to manual) work of white-collar workers is, of course, regarded by many manual workers as 'cissy', as in some way 'effeminate'. It is not 'Real Work'.

living reality of each one? People in general are always people in particular, and would not 'sexism' (and racism) just simply disappear if we only looked at one another and saw beyond woman and man (black person, white person)?

This challenge was central to the resurgence of feminism in the 1960s and 1970s. The women's movement was the most alert to certain features of those times that are now more widely acknowledged. Among these were an extraordinary intolerance of others and an easy dismissal of the vast majority of the population. These were said to be open and tolerant times, but in the main they were not. This was the era that gave us Norman Normal and Mr Nowhere Man, little grey people, complete nobodies. Switched-on people could easily sustain such arrogant or sometimes patronizing delusions because they had very little to do with switched-off people. And if 'ordinary' people took exception to this air of superiority and mockery, it was, of course, because they were bigots.

Women began to notice that the political, mystic and mere stylistic forms that this took had one thing in common: they were dominated by men. Whether the talk was about Sounds, The Revolution, or the Divine Light, most of the talking was done by men. Perhaps, they wondered, this outlook is distinctively a masculine one. Perhaps it is women who are actually more open to others, open in the way that is necessary for other people to come alive to each other, and which is incompatible with such categorizing and thus disposing of. It was not *only* women who felt the force of this. An influential text published in 1958 by Rollo May called *Existence*, for example, identified as the central dilemma in the practice of psychotherapy the fact that every theory or conceptual system seems inadequate and beside the point when you permit yourself to feel the presence of the individual client. On the other hand, without some guiding set of ideas about people you simply do not know what to do or how to pass on the fruits of your experience.

This dilemma is an inevitable consequence of the way the contrast between abstract and concrete is drawn in this society – but it cannot be resolved purely in thought. Resolving the dilemma entails reordering the social reality in which such oppositions are rooted. Abstract as opposed to concrete, mind as opposed to body, subject as opposed to object – these dualisms that run so deep in western thought have their source in a society divided simultaneously into two spheres of activity and along lines of gender: one which keeps you rooted in the immediate with all its concrete particularities, and another in which you are obliged to disengage, to dwell in a detached and abstract mode of consciousness.

All of us participate in both spheres and in both kinds of activity, but the different ways in which women and men tend to straddle these two worlds ensures that our experiences of the relationship between the mental and the bodily, between subjective and objective, and between abstract and concrete are bound to be different. Those women, for example, who engage in the kind of work in the public sphere that involves the abstract conceptual mode of consciousness, but also take prime responsibility for housework and childcare, find themselves painfully caught between the two. They must cross a kind of daily chasm, and the result, as Smith says, is a 'bifurcation', a splitting of consciousness: abstract conceptual activity on the one side, the world of concrete practical activities on the other. In this second world, 'the particularities of persons in their full organic immediacy are inescapable', in the first you must actively distance yourself from such things. There are the seeds in this tension of a possible resolution, but as the gap between private and public widens and the contrast grows starker, the tension mounts and becomes ever more painful. Perhaps we might all learn to bifurcate equally, but this would simply exacerbate the problem.

Our different ways of straddling the public and private worlds also show themselves in our experience of time. Time may appear to be a very abstract subject, something to make philosophy of when you have time on your hands. In fact, though, our different ways of living in time go a long way towards explaining the distinctive conflicts and frustrations that many women experience in their domestic lives, in particular, the dread of 'stagnation'.

Women and men in our society tend to live in different kinds of time. Kinds of time? How many 'kinds' are there? I will say for the sake of simplicity that there are two. Names are not important, but call the first 'linear' time. This is where, to put it crudely, it is not just one damned thing after another – there appears to be a thread running through and linking events at different 'points' in time. When you make plans for the future, embark on a 'project', feel you are in the process of moving away from something and towards something else, when there is some sense of progress, advance, development or unfolding, where you feel you may be 'getting somewhere', your experience is underpinned by a linear sense of time.

Higher education works as a good illustration of what this means. People enter higher education knowing that there is a qualification to be had at the end of it. A particular qualification sets you up to follow a limited range of paths in the future. These paths may well take the form of 'careers', with increments, promotions, rungs to climb. Even if the qualification seems to you to be the lesser part of it, you may see education as a process of self-improvement, which also suggests a forward movement. The course itself progresses from year to year, and within each year there is a syllabus or programme to follow. Each day is situated at a point in the process of working through the course from start to finish. You are supposed to read books and concentrate on following the argument. You must write essays which have a beginning, a middle and an end, and a 'sense of direction'. Higher education is a process of being schooled in linear time.

By contrast, it is of the essence of housework that you are getting nowhere (fast) and there will be nothing lasting to show for it. It is said that 'a woman's work is never done', but this does not mean simply that there is always something to do, it means there is never a sense of *completion*. Housework is a process of constantly re-doing that which has just been un-done. Washing something just makes it like it was before it got dirty; eating the meals you make for them just keeps people going – and they will be hungry again soon; and domestic order is forever becoming domestic chaos and must be perpetually repaired. Many of the tasks themselves are repetitive – it is not insignificant that so many women dislike ironing more than any other job.

Housework is 'reproduction', it reproduces what was there before. Time becomes 'cyclical' – day in/day out, year in/year out, on and on, round and round, endless repetition – a quality that is intensified by the common practice of constructing and following weekly and daily routines and schedules. But at the same time, when combined with childcare, the rhythms of such cycles are anything but smooth, they are always fragmented and uncertain.

Mothers are constantly thinking ahead, trying to anticipate the needs or demands of small children and structure the day accordingly. If you can work out when the child is most likely to be hungry, tired, restless and so on, then you can try to arrange things so that you are ready and available (if not always willing) to be called on at a time which fits in with your other obligations. But children are not machines and do not run on clockwork, so you are always liable to be interrupted, to have to break off and deal with the child. The sense of *discontinuity* this can engender is aggravated by young children's rapid mood changes. For someone who is used to dealing only with other adults, the way in which episodes of intense rage or distress in a child can quickly give way to contentment or excitement – and vice versa – can be quite mystifying and disturbingly hard to follow. In time the mother can become equally changeable, and come to feel that she is like a tape recorder constantly erasing what has just happened, as well as continually making contingency plans to deal with what *may* be about to happen.

Though the metaphor is military, many women use a telling expression to describe such an experience of domestic life: 'fighting a losing battle'. This battle is an essentially *defensive* one: it is like digging a hole in the desert which fills up again with sand at the same pace as the digging, or baling out water from a leaking boat just quickly enough to keep it afloat. As it happens, the metaphor that speaks most to me likens it to the circus act in which someone tries to keep as many plates as possible spinning on the top of vertical poles – the difference being that he gets to take them off at the end of the performance. Housework is perpetual plate-spinning and you can never say you have 'done' it. The hope is that not too many plates start to wobble at once, and that occasionally they will all spin together sweetly and merrily for a while – but you had better keep an eye on them.

In a word, housework is a process of *containment*. And few mothers can seriously deny that the same is to some extent true of looking after young children. But many mothers would be extremely reluctant to accept that this is what childcare is essentially about – containment. Many, but by no means all. It is here that another dimension must be introduced into the discussion. It will no longer do to talk about 'women' and 'mothers' in general.

We have been looking thus far at the commonalities and differences between women and men, but not all women share a common situation or a common experience. The most significant differences between women that are relevant here are to do with what is usually called social or socio-economic class. Class is every bit as complex an issue as gender so it is impossible to deal with this properly, let alone consider in detail how they interact. But here the interaction is crucial, and so I must first say what I intend by the terms working-class and middle-class.

One of the central problems is that different classes have different ideas about what class is. 'Middle' is not usually thought of as the opposite of 'working', and the reason these terms are used is important. It is the middlers that originally called themselves middle – but what were they in the middle *of*? They were the middle *orders* – this was not 'class' but *rank*. The opposite of working was not-working, the working-class defined themselves in contrast to the idle privileged, those who had no need to work. 'Class' in this case was an economic category. The confusion in popular consciousness over the meaning of class has its roots in these two different conceptions – one defined in terms of status, the other in terms of economic position.

What matters for present purposes is that people's experience of life is rooted in a particular pattern of activities and social relationships. Regardless of the ultimate basis of class, it makes sense to talk of two distinctive types of pattern. The question is not whether any particular individual really is or is not working-class or middle-class, but whether the activities and relationships they are engaged in conform more closely to the middle-class or working-class type. I shall use the term middle-class here to refer to people who have a significant connection with certain kinds of occupations, and that includes the wives, husbands, cohabitants and children of people who work in such occupations. What kinds? Career-structured occupations – ones that pay salaries and not wages, have some form of possible progression built into them, which also usually involve making relatively consequential decisions, a degree of autonomy and perhaps some control over the allocation of resources and/or people. This is all that is necessary for what follows.

The sense of forward movement inherent in the idea of career stands in clear contrast to the experience of people who either stay in the same job for most or all of their working lives, with no incremental increases in income, no prospects of promotion and so on, or who simply move 'sideways' from one job to another. Careers are also more likely to involve activities that take the form of projects, sometimes very long-term ones. Since careers are associated most with middle-class males, it would seem that linear time is primarily both middle-class and masculine. But the experience of middle-class *women* who do not themselves have careers is also significantly affected by goals, projects and aspirations which imply linear time, and I will single out three examples of the ways in which this is so. This is immensely significant, and goes a long way, I think, to making sense of some of the most intense conflicts and frustrations that many middle-class women experience in their domestic lives.

First, an illuminating study of the experience of motherhood by Mary Boulton found a clear class difference in mothers' attitudes towards playing with their children. Working-class mothers tended to see play as an end in itself. If they played with their children it was an opportunity to enjoy being with them. They were also more likely to see their children as 'company' and often kept them up late if there was no other adult there. Middle-class mothers, on the other hand, thought that children need to play and ought to play, it is an important part of their 'development'. Playing with your child is something you ought to do whether you feel like it or not. It is a responsibility, even a duty, and you should set aside time for it even if you do not enjoy it.

The idea that children 'develop', that childhood is a 'preparation' for adulthood is a relatively recent one, and in its origins is distinctively middle-class. It first arose out of a concern to teach children the skills of literacy and numeracy necessary to work within and eventually take over the family business. In time, the children of middle-class parents increasingly became middle-class adults through the educational process – this is how boys gained access to career-structured occupations, and how girls gained access to men with career-structured occupations. All this is too complex and too important to deal with so briefly, the point here is that the middle-class mother's attitude towards play is part of an overall notion of child development which is most meaningful to middle-class people. And it is an example of a domestic activity that is very much oriented towards the future. You 'invest' time and energy in the ways you bring up your children, to yield returns which will only come much later.

This introduces a more linear form of time into the middle-class household, but it does not by any means replace containment. All parents resort at times to tactics of containment, whether bribery, bullying, 'letting them get on with it', or 'laying down the law' – but it is mainly the middle-class mother who feels *guilty* about this, feels it to be a betrayal of her principles, an abdication of her responsibilities to the child's future, or even evidence of her failure as a mother.

Second, more middle-class than working-class people are inclined to think of their stay on this earth as a kind of 'project' in itself. This includes ideas of self-development and 'personal growth'. It also includes that of self-advancement, of 'getting on'. The wives of men with careers may be very much concerned with the advancement of the 'living standards' of the family as a whole, and expect to be moving on from one stepping stone to the next. Of course many working-class people also want to 'better' themselves, perhaps by becoming 'respectable' or simply 'comfortable', but this does not imply the same notion of continual progression.

Third, and this is very much connected with the question of 'being an individual' which we will consider shortly, there is the matter of what you do in your 'free time'. It appears that the middle-class mother is far more likely to want 'time to *myself* to do what *I* want to do'. This time to yourself is unbroken time, free from interruptions, free from the obligation to respond to others' demands. Obviously all mothers want time to put their feet up and relax, but the middle-class mother is more likely to value this unbroken free time (if she can get it) as an opportunity to engage in *projects* of various kinds. She thinks about evening classes, learning to draw or service the car, reading novels, taking something up, getting involved in something. This means something I do 'as myself' and 'for myself', but the middle-class mother's desire to find or rediscover a lost sense of 'individuality' also seems to be bound up with finding room for a sense of *linear time* – something with an aim, the possibility of achieving something, a sense of not *stagnating* – in a world dominated by discontinuity and repetition, by the cyclical but fragmented rhythms of housework and childcare.

The experience of domestic life as a defensive process of containment is strikingly in tune with the dominant themes of working-class culture as a whole. Routine manual labour is much the same in the home and in the factory, but more widely there is a common sense, not of progression, of getting somewhere, but of surviving, of taking each day as it comes. By contrast, the middle-class household is beset by clashing and conflicting kinds of time, and it is no wonder if the middle-class houseworker and mother feels confused and torn apart.

I oversimplify of course, but if there are two kinds of time, two genders and two social classes, then the experience of middle-class men with careers is diametrically opposed to that of working-class houseworkers and mothers. Middle-class women in the domestic sphere are caught suspended somewhere between the two. Many are schooled in linear time in higher education (first year, second year, third year, and now ... ?) only to find that it has left them disastrously ill-prepared for domestic life.

We can now join together the nature/culture contrast with this discussion of time, explain something of the elevation of naychoor, and add a significant qualification to the story so far. It is not only the more abstract forms of thought distanced from the immediate and the organic that have been associated with culture, culture has also been linked with the idea of *progress*. One of the reasons the domestic world, and with it women, was seen as dangerously close to nature was that it appeared to be unchanging and hence backward, threatening to stand in the way of progress. Men felt the need to be liberated from these concerns in order to get on with building the future.

The world is still changing, but – and here is the twist – where is the belief in progress, the faith in the future? The world appears to be either lurching forwards out of control, or whirring away like a giant mechanism that works according to its own laws (or perhaps both). As people lose faith in progress, they begin to lose faith in linear time altogether, even in the idea of history itself. One way this shows itself is in the 'therapeutic' idea, so popular in the 1960s and early 1970s, that one should strive to 'live fully in the moment'. Some said then that the hardest thing in the world is simply 'to be, now'. This was taken as going against the grain of the modern world – in fact the precise opposite is true.

Christopher Lasch suggests that one of the central characteristics of modern culture is the waning of historical time. History is now what happened in the *past*. People's memories become shorter. As has often been said, the news reports *incidents* without situating them in any historical context. As for the future, few people today give a hoot about 'delayed gratification' – the current credit boom is testament enough to that (to what great heights of consumerism will the children of the indulgent credit-card using parent aspire when they grow up?). There is an intense fear of ageing and the decay of the body. All these speak of a society that is neither past- nor future- oriented, but whose prevailing passion is to live in and for the present.

The siege mentality of privatism at the latter end of the twentieth century has little time for the linear. And given what 'culture' – the public world – appears to have become, we no longer straightforwardly value culture over nature. Hence the natural ingredients. Hence the extraordinary concern with everything *bodily* – particularly health and fitness. There is a receptive audience waiting to hear – if it has not done so already – the feminist assault on the abstract, disembodied mind of the male, with its daft ideas about thinking and living in straight lines.

9 · Dependence and Independence

F. Scott Fitzgerald once said through one of the characters in *Tender is the Night* that the trouble with being dependent is that other people may turn out not to be dependable. The moral is: be careful who you rely on. But it is far more usual in this society for dependence to be seen as a *failing*, something shameful and reprehensible. It is associated with being weak, pathetic and clinging, with not having a mind of your own, with being helpless, with expecting other people to look after you, protect you, and put things right when they go wrong. Such dependence, it is said, is more characteristic of women. Just as men are said to be sadly lacking in the capacity for intimacy, so women are seen as suffering from a equivalent deficiency: an incapacity for 'independence' or 'autonomy'. There is a great deal that is seriously misleading in such talk of dependence and independence and the ways they figure in the experience of women and men. Once again it is the tendency to think in 'psychological' terms – to dwell on 'personalities' and subjective experience – that obscures far more than it illuminates.

To begin with, men are by no means as 'independent' as they are made out to be. It was always nonsense that women are dithery, fragile and passive beings, incapable of doing or thinking anything for or by themselves. But it is still said that men are the opposite of these things: decisive, self-reliant and resolute beings who know what they are doing and know where they are going. One way of putting a word to such half-fiction (at least), which has become highly influential in the psychology of gender, identifies masculinity with the principle of 'agency'. This is a word with multiple meanings, but here it means something like purposiveness, mastery and control, acting upon the world to make things happen. The idea that men are animated by such a principle is not without foundation, but it paints a grossly distorted picture of our experience of modern life.

Who today can put their hands to their hearts and say, with the Victorian poet: 'I am the Captain of my Ship, I am the Master of My Soul', steering an unerring course through the hazardous waters of the Gulf of Life? Which is more in evidence today, a firm belief in progress or a lack of faith in the future? You'll be a Man, said Rudyard Kipling, if you can trust yourself when all men doubt you, wait and not be tired of waiting, hold on when there is nothing in you except the will which says 'hold on'; if neither foes nor loving friends can hurt you, if all men count with you, but none too much; if you can fill the unforgiving minute with sixty seconds of distance run – what a sorry sight the modern male must be to Mr Kipling's ghost.

Most of today's men can probably recall those proud and desolate words: 'Look – I did it all by myself.' Doing it by yourself, not being 'helpless', trying your hardest – these are still more prized in a boy than a girl. But are men really as self-reliant, as 'independent' as they are so often said to be? We live in a world in which most people in paid employment have no control over what they do or make, or how they do or make it; we are encouraged in most things to acknowledge our own ignorance and to appeal to the authority of the expert; the economy seems to work itself and might collapse at a moment's notice; we could find ourselves on the brink of nuclear annihilation over incomprehensible events in faraway places; the political process appears remote and alien, the public world looms over us as an immense and faceless bureaucratic structure – and yet men are said to be independent and autonomous? In this society both women and men are vulnerable and dependent. That women have even *less* control over their lives than men has been allowed to obscure that fact.

The idea that men are the embodiment of the principle of agency is no longer tenable. The principle has been dying a lingering death over the better part of this century, and there is one particularly significant realm in which this can be shown to be so. Even in the realm of ideas, it is said, beating paths through forests is the masculine way of dealing with things. The masculine mind gives us 'linear' forms of thought of various kinds, most importantly the ideas of 'chains' of events, the links being relationships of cause and effect. The operative question (the man's question?) is 'what will happen if I do this?' This presumes that you will be able to specify exactly what it is that you are doing, be in a position to do it, and be able to identify a definite, distinct and specific outcome. Such confidence is, however, notably lacking in many areas of modern thought.

The usual opposite of 'agency' is 'communion' – a much sunnier contrast to masculine purpose than feminine ditheriness. This emphasizes, not independence, but interdependence, the essential connectedness of things and of people. On the level of ideas this would presumably give rise to, for example, the idea of an ecological system where intervention in one sphere has an effect on, and reverberates throughout, the whole system. Again, instead of those forms of 'scientific' medicine which appear to want to wage war on people's bodies with carefully targeted surgical or chemical strikes, you would get holistic forms of medicine like homeopathy, and notions like overall 'well-being'. Essentially what communion says is that everything and everyone is ultimately related to everything and everyone else. Out of a recognition of this, the hope is, comes an emphasis on harmony and even peace in our time.

The striking thing is that these more holistic forms of thought have clearly been gaining ground in our society. When the modern mind looks out on the world and asks 'what will happen if I do this?' the answer is likely to be either 'bugger all' or 'who knows?' Just as I, as a child of the times, look through my notebooks and scribblings, covered with circles and arrows linking this with that and protest – this is impossible, everything is connected to everything else, where do you start?,* so the modern mind surveys 'the system' and protests: this is impossible, everything is connected to everything else, if you wanted to intervene in this, change it in some way, where on earth would you start? (Hence, amongst other things, the near-universal insistence on setting things in 'context'. Along with its sister 'diversity', context is one of the watchwords of our times.)

In a world which appears to take the form of a vast and interlocking system governed by remote and incomprehensible forces, we have, then, to think twice about the equation of men and masculinity with single-minded purpose, autonomy, and self-reliance. But there is much more to it than this. As agency recedes into the fog of history, other things have been emerging to take its place in the masculine

*Some take this as a cue to pass off as thinking an unstructured assemblage of thoughts and images – like the person who went to a Swiss clinic which specialized in removing all the bones from people's bodies in search of the ultimate relaxation.

soul. Along with 'communion', 'context' and 'system', the most important is the privatist mentality. That this is so becomes clear, I think, if we consider the popular but only superficially persuasive idea that dependence is actually a good and beneficial thing. The trouble with men, many now say, is that they do not allow themselves to be dependent. Would we not all benefit if men were able, as Orbach and Eichenbaum put it, to express their 'dependency needs'?

We are dependent on all the things we need, that is, on all the things we could not readily do without. This makes the idea of 'dependency needs' rather mystifying – if we need something we are dependent on it, if we are dependent on it we need it. It would take forever to list all the things we are dependent on if we want to sustain a particular way of life: money, legs, electricity, hope, clocks, kind words, indigestion tablets, rain, cement, musical instruments, contraceptives – we could do without all of these things, but there would have to be some changes made.

We are all dependent, then, on all manner of things. But it is quite clear that those who praise dependency and speak of dependency needs have a particular form of dependence in mind – the kind of emotional support that entails intimacy. Why is this considered so important?

Faced with an undependable, incomprehensible and impenetrable 'outside' world, a desperate search begins to find some reliable corner of the world over which we *can* exercise some control. Hence, in the knowledge of their lack of control over the public world, people turn to home improvements, DIY, growing their own vegetables, making their own bread. In the knowledge that our dependence on oil may be the death of us, that you apparently can't do much about the threat of nuclear war or the pollution of the earth and the sky, people change their diets, take up jogging and give up smoking. Faced, in other words, with our lack of control over the public world and our lives within it, we seek autonomy where we think we may actually be able to find it: in the private sphere of what we call our 'personal' lives. And faced with what seems to be a distinct lack of humanity in the public world, we like to feel that we have fought a successful rearguard action and created *pockets* of humanity in our own backyards – in our homes, with our families, and with our close friends.

The very idea of 'rewarding human relationships' has in this society come to mean, exclusively, relationships involving intimacy to be sought in our 'personal' lives, and at the same time 'dependency' – whether a good thing or a bad thing – has come also to be associated with personal relationships. But even *within* the category of what we call our personal relationships we are dependent on other people for many things. These may (or may not) include having someone to moan to or slag other people off with, someone to let go and have a good time with, someone to share good news with, someone to confide secrets in, someone to seek advice or reassurance from, someone to do battle with, to go on holiday with, and so on and on. People are usually judged to be dependent on something – say alcohol – if doing without it is a cause of discomfort, and not to have anyone who fits these bills may well be a source of acute discomfort. In a shrinking private world, people tend to invest more and more of these kinds of 'needs' or 'dependencies' in fewer and fewer people. And as we narrow the distribution of our dependencies on others, so we make ourselves more vulnerable. We begin to approach the condition of the so-called 'alcoholic' in the way we put all our eggs in one basket. Just as the alcoholic always 'turns to' the one thing – drinking – so many today turn to just one person or a small handful of others when they feel the need for something only people can provide. This makes us increasingly vulnerable.

But it is not just a matter of a huge over-investment in the private sphere – this tendency turns out to be yet another instance of how personal life comes to be understood in purely 'psychological' terms. We are now prone to think of dependency as a kind of personal condition or characteristic, but to sustain this idea entails ignoring or denying a great deal of our experience of life. This begins to become clear, I think, when we consider relationships between women and men, not as individuals, but collectively.

The organization of life in the public world depends, to repeat the point, on the work of keeping people in good repair – the work of 'reproduction' in its wider sense – being carried out elsewhere and by someone else. Men collectively are dependent on women collectively. It is only in the light of this that the significance of commonplace experiences of individuals becomes clear. The vast number of women with children who have part-time jobs know only too well that you have to ensure that the job fits in with your domestic commitments. Employed women also know that children get sick sometimes, generally without notice, and it is usually no simple matter to arrange for the father to take time off work to look after them.

There is no need to labour the point: men depend on women as much as women depend on men, but it is women's dependency on men that is more firmly inscribed in everyday talk – particularly, of course, amongst men. If we look at it in this way we can see how dependence is not a personal condition, but a feature of the *relationship* between women and men. And perhaps the most straightforward way that the relational aspect of dependence and independence is obscured is to be found again in the idea of personality – the idea that dependence and independence are 'personality characteristics'.

You cannot simply 'be' dependent or independent – we are all dependent *on* some things, and by the same token independent *of* others.* The idea, then, that people are either one thing or the other, for example that independence and dependence are 'traits' – or that independence/dependence is 'a' trait, a continuum running between two poles – must be grossly misleading. But traits are just one example of the modern idea of personality as a personalized in-dwelling essence, a quality of being.

When, for example, a heavy drinker is persuaded to 'accept' that he or she is 'an alcoholic', this generally replaces one deception with another. The deception you give up is that you are not dependent on alcohol. Pay attention and you will notice how often you turn to drink, how terrible you feel without it and so on, acknowledge that alcohol has become indispensable. You drink too much, and that is something *you do*. But 'an alcoholic' is not something you *do* – it is something you *are*. The paradox is that the acceptance of this is supposed to help you begin to change – but how do you change what you 'are'? By stopping drinking of course.

If calling yourself an alcoholic works for you, it is because you can now no longer evade the issue, and because you have made a commitment to change that you may well hold yourself to – particularly if you have identified yourself as such to other people. But if you take the theory literally it may well not work at all. What it says is not that 'alcoholic' is the word we use to describe someone

---

*Women are often unable to act independently, not because they are dependent, but because other people (particularly children) are depending on *them*.

who drinks too much, but that if you drink too much it is *because* you are an alcoholic – drinking corresponds to something in your nature.

People's theories about themselves (in all sorts of respects) sometimes make change easy, sometimes very difficult and there are grave dangers in this idea of personality. But you must also ignore or deny a great deal of your experience in order to sustain it. Amongst other things you must not notice that the way you behave tends to depend on *who you are with*. And this is a large part of what gender is about. People tend to act differently with and towards one another depending on the sex of each.

Among the characteristics commonly associated with independence are: taking initiatives, being assertive, being capable, practical and resourceful – but everyone acts in all of these ways some of the time. (If you take the initiative and put the kettle on to make yourself a cup of tea, you are asserting your want of one and showing yourself to be capable, practical and resourceful.) So when is it that women are submissive, deferential, incapable and impractical? First and foremost, it is when they are with men.

You cannot 'be' submissive or deferential – you submit or defer *to* someone. The plain fact of the matter is that women are far more often obliged to defer to men than the other way round. And when women and girls are together, does anyone imagine that nothing gets done because women do not take initiatives? It is when women and girls are with men and boys that they are not supposed to 'take the lead'. And it is not true that women are not *supposed* to be practical and resourceful – only when they are with men. On their own, particularly as houseworkers and mothers, it is a matter of necessity. It is said that women learn a great deal from their mothers. If so it must be extremely difficult for the daughters of the many women who have virtually sole responsibility for the organization of the household, and also work full time outside the home, to see their mothers as dithery and helpless.

Again, it is said that women are not 'supposed' to be competitive, but women have just as much *reason* to compete with each other as men do. An unequal society thrives on competition in its lower orders, and just as men compete for reasonable jobs with a reasonable income and working conditions, so women's economic dependency sets them at odds with each other and in competition for men – and hence a reasonable 'job' with a reasonable 'income' and working conditions. No-one can seriously deny that women have a habit of looking each other up and down, weighing each other up, and are often hostile to attractive women, particularly if they seem to be using feminine wiles and taking in gullible, naive men. Far from not being supposed to compete, women are expected to do all this. It is *men* that women are not supposed to compete with.

Proponents of various ideas of blending or synthesizing feminine and masculine 'characteristics' – the idea of the 'androgynous personality' for example – have a bit of a problem here. Women *already* combine taking initiatives, being assertive, being capable, practical and resourceful, with being deferential, submissive, docile and incapable. The trick is knowing *when* to be these things, and this usually means – as with the example of holding hands – changing your tune according to your company.

A great deal of women's alleged dependence derives simply from being discouraged from *showing* their capability when with men, and encouraged to take up a dependent position. Who drives the car has long been a bone of contention among many, and there clearly have been significant changes here. But sit by the side of the road for a few hours in many parts of the country and count how often a woman is driving when there is a man in the car and the results are not encouraging (except when they are going to the pub of course.) Even where she does drive, there may well have been arguments about it – as silly and as highly charged as those on the campsite. Many men feel extremely uncomfortable when not in control of the vehicle they are in, yet this is just one instance of a kind of experience that women have had to get used to.

But women have not only been discouraged from displaying their competence or capability in the presence of men, they have also been encouraged to display *in*competence and *in*capability. These signs (or characters) are then commonly read into their personality (or character), as if they were expressive of what a woman is. The most obvious of such signs are to do with physical appearance.

'There is no task that would make me look nice that I would consider as not worthwhile' – so said a regular winner of Butlin's Glamorous Granny competitions. Here was a very determined woman – she knew what she was about and would not be deflected. The tone was defiant, she did not care what other people thought. A bit of a character, they might have said, and the impression was of a character with a strong 'independent' streak.

And yet, of course, to 'look nice' you are dependent on the judgment of an audience. In this case they were real judges and she always won – but what about next time? Like actors and celebrities, a glamorous granny is only as good as her last appearance. But, much more importantly, looking 'glamorous' – indeed many of the ways women have of 'looking nice' – involve displays of incapability. Whatever you may in fact be capable of, the look is of someone distinctly ill-equipped to *do* anything at all.

Throughout history, women have often been virtually immobilized by having some part of their bodies – waist, abdomen, breast, neck or feet – tightly constrained, supposedly to improve their 'figure'. From the Burmese neck ring and the Chinese bound foot to steel-ribbed corsets and whalebone stays, as Susan Brownmiller says: 'Each device of beautification restricted her freedom and weakened her strength: each provided a feminine obstacle course through which she endeavoured to move with artificial grace.'

It is important that such discomforts tended to be restricted to women of high social standing. The bound foot, as Brownmiller explains, 'originated in the rarefied atmosphere of a decadent upper class where the physical labour of women was not required, and it became an enviable symbol of luxury, leisure and refinement'. Women did not merely suffer this, they wore it as a badge of rank, a sign of superior position in society. One reason this matters is that it involved looking down your nose at people who *did* have to work, and this is why there is more to the aggression that many women rightly perceive today in the calls and whistles of working men than men treating women as sexual objects. This (also) has its roots in the long experience that working-class men (and women) have had of being looked down on in contempt by elegant upper-class women, and such disdain or even disgust of the coarse and vulgar working man has by no means disappeared from the culture of the privileged. Although men undoubtedly do encourage women to decorate and adorn themselves in such ways – principally by finding them attractive when they do (often then proceeding to chastize them for being narcissistic) – many men today have at times a gnawing suspicion that 'feminine' women are trying to make them feel like unwashed animals.

Nevertheless, it is crucial that such emblems of privilege involved displays of incapability. As Brownmiller says, the bound foot 'imposed an ingenious handicap upon a routine, functional act and reduced the female's competence to deal with the world around her, rendering that world a more perilous place and the imbalanced woman a more dependent, fearful creature. It rendered a man more competent and steady – in other words, more masculine – by simple contrast'.

Such displays of incapability which – by simple contrast – render the man more apparently capable, are still very much with us. Borrowed though they may be from upper-class mannerisms, the movements and gestures most commonly considered feminine generally still have this character. As old-style glamour and frivolity give way to the new 'post-feminist woman' and the homely housewife gives way to the 'busy mum', so some of the details change and the displays of incapability become less obvious and marked. But when most women try to make themselves look 'nice' they still very much shift in this direction.

Still, despite all this, to emphasize relationships and talk of displays does not mean that there is nothing in the idea of personality, that it is complete nonsense. A history of living under the social identity of woman or man leaves its mark in the significances that we as individuals attach to being female or male – what we have made of it and what it has made of us. To the extent that we are successfully schooled in the doctrine of natural expression, the belief in essential signs, we come to see such displays of capability and incapability in others and ourselves as revelatory of an in-dwelling essence, of the 'kind of person' you are in this sense. Faced then with something unfamiliar, the famous declaration of the legendary Yosser Hughes – 'I can do that' – may, or may not, spring to mind.

The word that springs most to mind to capture this is 'confidence'. Confidence is a particularly clear example of a psychologized concept, one that speaks only of personalities and subjective experience. If I say 'I can', then I am 'feeling confident' and/or showing what a confident person I am. We will turn to this in a moment – first though, I have talked so far only of dependence and of women. What about men and independence?

Here I want to single out one particular and highly instructive popular wisdom about masculine independence which has become enshrined in certain academic psychological theories. This is the idea that boys *struggle* to achieve masculinity, but girls have merely to unfold. In the commonest variation on this theme, boys learn to become men by 'repressing' their 'feminine aspects'. What are these feminine things that boys must learn to tear themselves away from? A burning desire to hold tupperware parties or sell cosmetics from door to door? To express a natural concern with the positioning of the nipple or the curve of the calf? To become a dinner-lady or clean the toilet? No – the 'femininity' that boys must allegedly repudiate is something 'inside' themselves.

It is most significant that while it seems to make sense to talk of men repudiating their femininity, it is rarely said that women must learn to repudiate or repress their masculinity. Why should this be so? The main answer lies, I think, in the relationship between nature and culture I spoke of earlier. Men have long identified themselves with culture and civilization, and women with the natural order. Culture/civilization, it seems, is permanently under threat, and if men are its carriers, then they must keep their distance from nature, beware being called back to their animal roots. Human society is here depicted as a ceaseless struggle to rise and stay risen above the natural order, an awesome responsibility bestowed on men. Women get it easy, all they have to do is what comes naturally.

But growing up as a girl and as a boy *both* entail (in a particular sense) the 'repression' of something, though in neither case is it simply something natural. We learn what to 'be' and what *not* to 'be' together at the same time – it is what we are not that makes us what we are, and vice versa. These are two sides of the same coin, one marked yes, the other marked no.

Many writers who talk of the process of 'becoming' masculine as a struggle in which boys strive to repudiate or repress their 'feminine side' find support for this idea in the popularity among boys between around seven and eleven of the *Beano*'s Dennis the Menace.* On the contrary, what these stories show is that we have *first* to build up a picture of what we should *not* be, of what it *is* that we are supposed to say no to.

---

*Antony Easthope provides a useful analysis of the content of these stories, but unfortunately explains it in this way: 'Dennis is the masculine side of a boy, the side which challenges law and the father but accepts symbolic castration, imaged as beating on the buttocks. Walter represents the feminine side which loves the father and submits to him.'

The central theme of these stories is 'Menaces' *vs* 'Softies', the principal characters being Dennis (the Menace) and Walter (the Softie). Walter is a right wally. He squeals, he swoons and faints, he likes flowers and perfume, he has a poodle called Foo Foo. He makes cakes and plays the violin, and thinks Dennis is Horrid. Walter is a Very Soft Boy. Dennis is a prankster with spiky hair, a gravelly voice and a dog called Gnasher. To him flowers and perfume are like a crucifix to a vampire. He is virtually uncontrollable and constantly in trouble for his mischievous antics and crazy schemes. Dennis is a Real Boy, Walter is a cissy and a wimp.

(It has to be said that this is as much to do with class as gender. Walter is explicitly middle-class, he is even on one occasion sent to a School for Gentlemen where he learns to walk around with a book on his head. Dennis's hilarity and contempt is that of the manual labourer at those who don't know what graft is – the reason they historically took up the term *working* class.)

There is no doubt that the reader is being presented with a contrast – Dennis is everything Walter is not, and vice versa. But it is *both* sides of the contrast, the two alternative images, that are being constructed and elaborated. You cannot struggle towards manhood by repudiating Walter until you know who Walter *is*. Perhaps then you might say that you become and stay masculine by, as it were, sitting on Walter, by repressing 'the Walter in you'. But Walter is as much a creature of the imagination as Dennis. It is only when combined with the doctrine of natural expression that to act or feel like Dennis or Walter is to express your masculine or feminine 'sides'. Only then does acting like Dennis 'prove' your masculinity, and the inclination to act like Walter becomes a secret, shameful part of your nature that you decide to keep to yourself.

Repudiating your own 'feminine' or 'masculine' possibilities is not a matter of fighting against some force that is resistable with difficulty. For example, while it is true that girls and women are discouraged from expressing anger in the more physical ways that get called 'aggressive' (possibly the only way in which women occasionally *are* said to repress their 'masculine aspects'), we are far too ready to take literally the metaphor of anger that depicts it as like a head of steam, as if we were pressure-cookers with different size weights. You 'repress' something when you cannot face the implications of beginning to accept it. What psychoanalysis sees as 'driving forces' are aspects of your experience that you would rather not confront or see too clearly, because if you do it may be very difficult for you not to do something about it, with potential consequences you would rather not countenance. You may 'repress' a loathing of your husband or wife, for example, because if you become too aware of it, dwell on it and see no realistic alternative, it might make it very difficult to stay with them. So if you cannot envisage a livable life down the road of a girl who is easily moved to anger or a boy who is easily moved to tears, you may try to erase that road from your map.

Both girls and boys, then, must build up a picture of what it is they are supposed to embrace and repudiate, and growing up as a girl is no less of a struggle than growing up as a boy. But there are also two further problems with this idea of femininity and masculinity as in-dwelling essences.,

Firstly, is the boy supposed to repudiate *femininity* or *girls*? There is very little sign of Beano-age boys being any less scornful in their attitude towards girls than they ever were. Girls are rubbish. Why, what's wrong with them? Everything. They're awful, I can't stand them. What do you think girls think about boys? The same probably. Don't know. Don't want to know.

Boys still play mostly with other boys and girls with other girls. Each have their eyes as much on what the other is doing as on their own activities, and generally insist on rendering unto boys the things that are boys' and rendering unto girls the things that are girls'. This is less a matter of repressing some aspect of your self than of a 'territory' being carved up into two parts, each being the proper sphere of one gender. (This kind of 'gender apartheid' prepares them well to absorb quickly and effortlessly the doctrine of separate spheres for women and men, and different kinds of jobs in the occupational sphere.) Sometimes the spatial metaphor can be taken literally – it is no coincidence that the activity which tends to take up most space in the school playground is largely restricted to boys: football. Here girls and Walters are literally and physically pushed to the margins. This idea of carving up the available territory also makes sense of the fact that girls and boys in single-sex secondary schools are far more likely to choose subjects considered appropriate to the opposite sex than they are in mixed sex schools. When there is only one sex present, it seems, the need for polarization diminishes.

But, and this is the second point, it is by no means clear that what boys are supposed to repudiate 'in themselves' *are* characteristics of girls. Walter is, after all, a *boy*, and to describe him as 'cissy' or even 'effeminate' does not necessarily imply that he is like a girl. (My daughter who is eight and reads the *Beano* is of the opinion that Walter is 'mm, well, I suppose, a bit like a girl, but really it's about making Walter look stupid'.) Many men, I think, suffer from a serious confusion about the connection between what *women* are actually like and what a man is supposed to be *not*-like. This confusion is echoed by many writers on gender, who simply assume that the two are one and the same thing: men repudiate 'femininity'.

This is often the case – men often do repudiate the same things 'in' themselves as they see in women. *But this is women seen through their own eyes.* It is worth developing an example of this to make the point clear, and the example I shall take is the way many adult men tend to deal with requests for 'support'. (I say 'requests', but I suspect that many men experience these as *demands* and not requests at all.)

Most males in this society are schooled, to varying degrees, in a particular construct: asking for help versus doing it 'all by myself'. To turn to another is often, to a man, to 'ask for help' which means you are saying you cannot do it 'all by yourself'. And so when women seek 'support' or express doubt and confusion, in many cases men feel that they are supposed to *do* something about it, whether or not this is what is being asked. Here is a case par excellence of how we paint our pictures of ourselves and others on the same canvas and with the same pigments, of how your soul takes on the colour of my ideas.

He may respond in terms of what he understands to be 'trying to help' – by actually doing something 'helpful', or else by making suggestions, offering advice, 'helpfully' analysing her dilemma for her and so on. On the other hand, he may feel that this is *her* problem and it is not for him to sort out *for* her (as he sees it). If he takes himself to be an Enlightened One, he may even feel that 'not-helping' is encouraging 'autonomy' in her. To her, both responses may seem totally inappropriate, for neither feel like being 'supportive'. She does not want 'help', nor does she want to do it 'all by herself' – these are the masculine alternatives. She may want simply to be heard and to be recognized. She may say that what she wants is 'reassurance', but the man may feel that to reassure her would be to *agree* with her, to accept that what she says is 'right'. (One of the ways men repeatedly undermine other people's confidence in their ability to think for themselves is by 'correcting' them – as though saying something with conviction somehow prevents you from ever deciding you were wrong.)

It is because men often work with such a contrast between doing something 'all by yourself' and admitting that you cannot by asking for help, that they often see women as 'being helpless'. This does not mean that femininity includes an instruction to be helpless, except perhaps when you are 'asked' to conform to masculine assumptions. It is every bit as feminine to be bemused by the contrast, to feel that there is something wrong here, even if you cannot quite put your finger on what it is. Men's definitions of masculinity and femininity may, in short, be quite different from women's definitions of femininity and masculinity.

We clearly miss a great deal by seeing femininity and masculinity as in-dwelling essences. Any attempt to understand the ways dependence and independence figure in the lives of women and men that thinks in these terms must be seriously misleading. But perhaps the clearest example of how such things are obscured by being psychologized is to be found in the way people talk about 'confidence'. To psychologize, I have suggested, is to disconnect personalities and subjective experiences from the activities and relationships in which they are caught up - the idea of confidence tends to do both. It is said that some people are more confident than others, they 'have' more confidence. It is also said that confidence is a feeling, and that if you do not feel confident you cannot act in a confident manner.

Of all the things that are said to 'give you confidence', high 'self-esteem' is generally regarded as the most important – indeed some regard confidence and self-esteem as synonymous. Perhaps the first clue that there is something amiss here is to be found in the extraordinarily patronizing idea of doing something for someone else 'to boost their self-esteem'. The wives of the oil barons in *Dallas* (the television programme) once decided to build a shelter for homeless people, saying that it would do wonders for these people's self-esteem to have a roof over their heads. People who are to all intents and purposes treated as if they were worth nothing, are to be given charitable donations to their sense of self-worth.

Just as to talk of a 'sense' of vulnerability diverts attention away from the features of a person's social situation which make them actually more susceptible to various kinds of potential injury or loss, so to talk of a 'sense' of your own worth or high self-esteem shifts the focus on to you 'as a person' and away from your social position. There plainly must be some connection between 'self' esteem and the esteem you are held in by others, in other words 'social' esteem.

'Women tend to have low self-esteem' has a rather different ring to it from 'women tend to be held in low esteem'. Your 'worth' comes to be a judgment you make of yourself. It is terribly unfortunate if you think poorly of yourself, but all is not lost if we can think of ways to give you an injection of self-esteem and boost your confidence. But there is only one way to 'help' another person feel 'good' about themselves and that is to value them and treat them with respect. You can only, for example, make someone 'feel' your equal by treating them as an equal. This is not the same as treating them 'as if' they were your equal – if you do not believe it you cannot do it.

To talk of a 'sense' of worth, equality, vulnerability and so on, tends to give the impression that these are purely subjective matters, detachable from the kinds of relationships you have with others. This is also the case with other things that are said to 'give you confidence' – for example, the way you look. Many women say that they do not dress up and put on make-up in order to attract men, but because it increases their confidence. But confidence is not something inside your head. To feel confident is to believe that you will be able to deal with the situations you are likely to be confronted with. Confidence, in other words, is a matter of anticipation.

We all live in anticipation – if not necessarily in hope. We anticipate situations, not so much by predicting what is likely to happen, as by setting ourselves up to deal with them in the ways we know how. Everyone needs to have a means of getting their bearings in the company of others, particularly others with whom you are unfamiliar. At that moment when you walk in the room or across the floor and they look at you, you may hope that the time you spent attending to your appearance has provided a convincing answer to that question in their eyes and got you off to a good start.

(In order to become even more convincing you may enrol on one of those courses which are designed to break social life down into step-by-step 'skills' to be taught, practised and perfected: dining skills, self-presentation skills, descending the theatre staircase with high heels and a long dress without looking down skills, how to degrade yourself in public skills and so on.)

Appearances, in other words, are one way in which people – men as well as women – attempt to exercise some *control* over other people's impressions and judgments. The way you look will 'give you confidence' if you have found that it works. But this makes the capacity to make yourself look good a resource you may draw upon in the exercise of power. The same goes for a sharp wit or the gift of the gab, or for being knowledgeable and articulate. Such things give you confidence because they enable you to have an impact, to exert an influence over what happens.

One reason why men appear more confident than women is that there are all sorts of ways of having an impact that pass without comment when engaged in by males. Men are, for example, far more likely to interrupt or contradict other people, not because they are or feel confident, but because they confidently expect to get away with it – so much so that they may barely notice that they do it. Not all men manage to carry this off or even want to, but those who can and do carry it off are most often men. Women do not usually get away with it *because* they are women. Confidence, in short, is believing that you have the resources necessary to make a difference, to exert an influence, to deal capably with whatever is likely to come your way.

Consider, in the light of this, the idea that women are more prone to depression because they 'lack confidence'. What do you do when things go wrong? One thing you *can* do when things go wrong is give up. You give up because you get a sinking feeling that no matter what you do, things are going to turn out badly, so there is no point in trying. It is this *sinking* feeling we call depression, and sometimes people stay sunk.

Many psychologists of varying theoretical persuasion have long argued that people's beliefs about the world and themselves play a very significant part in determining whether or not they become depressed. If you have a poor sense of your own worth and a bleak picture of the future, then you are more vulnerable to depression when things go wrong in your life. But these beliefs tend to be depicted as something in your head that you would do well to be rid of. By contrast, however, a celebrated study of depression amongst women living in Camberwell in the 1970s came to the less than startling conclusion (which nonetheless needed to be confirmed) that if you live in substandard housing with barely enough money to live on, have a sick relative to look after and three small children to take care of, are tied to the house and rarely get out, and if then your husband gets made redundant, they turn off the electricity and threaten to evict you, and you have no-one to confide in about your troubles, you will be more likely than most to become depressed.*

This is, of course, a rather crude and oversimplified version of their findings, but the basic point is clear: such things are hardly 'all in the mind'. Nevertheless, the people who carried out this study – George Brown and Tirril Harris – suggested that there is something else involved: low self-esteem. Depression, they believe, is a profound and generalized state of *hopelessness*, but it is one that people with low self-esteem are more prone to lapse into. Getting depressed then lowers your self-esteem still further, and so on down in a vicious spiral. But, and I think it is a big but, the authors admit that the women themselves more often talked of lacking *confidence*, and this is instructively ambiguous.

If confidence is the belief that you have the resources to enable you to make a difference, then it is not surprising that these women lacked confidence. What *can* you do about such things? A sense of hopelessness in such circumstances is not a subjective feeling somehow visited upon you, it may be based on a quite realistic appraisal of your situation. Dorothy Rowe suggests that one of the beliefs that people who build 'for themselves' a prison of depression tend to live by is that 'only bad things happened to me in the past and only bad things will happen to me in the future'. This can be perilously close to the truth and there may be precious little you can do about it but try to look on the bright side (if you can find one). This must be at least part of what the women meant – but they probably meant something else as well.

One of the central features in most 'cases' of severe depression is self-blame and self-deprecation. Though people who are profoundly depressed find doing anything an effort, it is rarely an empty, quiet condition. It is a noisy and agitated one, filled with dark thoughts and

*It is working-class houseworkers and mothers in this society that suffer the highest recorded incidence of depression. This is a clear instance of how disadvantaged groups are both subjected to the most adverse social and economic circumstances *and* denied the resources necessary to deal capably with such 'stress'. Then, to add insult to injury, they are told that being depressed under such circumstances is either an illness or a personal disposition.

accusations, many of these levelled against yourself. Something like low self-esteem may well play a part in becoming depressed, but the important feature of this is that it involves blaming *yourself* when things go wrong. These things don't happen to everyone, why do they happen to me? Other people seem to be able to cope, why can't I? Answer: it's my fault, there must be something the matter with me.

In a psychological universe people look first and foremost for explanations of 'success/failure', coping/not coping in terms of *individuals*. If a small minority of working-class children make it through the educational system, for example, this is taken to mean that *any* working-class child can do likewise. But just as any individual can withdraw all their money from the bank but not everyone simultaneously, so any individual person from a working-class background can end up with a top job, but clearly not all of them – otherwise everyone would be in a top job, or the children of those in top jobs now would all end up in the factory or on the dole. Yet it is not only the champions of the enterprise culture who believe that it is up to individuals whether or not they make a 'success' of their lives. Many ordinary people think they have no-one and nothing to blame but themselves if they fail to make the most of their 'opportunities'.

All this makes depression a political issue. To many this will sound crazy: what has being unhappy got to do with politics? But politics is about having the power to shape your own and other people's lives. The capacity to determine your own destiny, to bring about changes in your situation, in short to have some control over your own life, is a political matter. And there is a word for it, a word often used interchangeably with independence: 'autonomy'.

Autonomy means two things: free-standing and self-governing. It is the *first* that tends to be emphasized in psychological talk, and it is this that will take us into the next chapter: people who have a 'sense of autonomy' feel themselves to be 'individuals'. (Note how, yet again, we find that little word 'sense' tacked on to the front.) But we are none of us autonomous individuals in either of these senses. None of us are free-standing, self-contained individuals, running our own lives independently of others. As George Bernard Shaw once put it: 'Independence? That's middle-class blasphemy. We are all dependent on one another, every soul of us on earth.'

We are interdependent and interconnected. But if this is so, what happens to the idea that we are all 'individuals'? Are some, perhaps, more individual than others? Are men, perhaps, more individual than women?

10 · Being an Individual

In a culture steeped in psychological forms of thought, the idea – widely accepted in sociology – that 'the individual' is a modern invention, seems barely comprehensible: what *do* they mean? It seems to be enough to point to yourself – maybe do a little twirl – and anyone in their right mind would have to agree. I am an individual, it's obvious isn't it? Well no it isn't.

That twirling entity you are pointing to is 'your' *body*. The skin clearly establishes a kind of boundary marking out where you, as a physical being, end and the world begins. But it is far less clear where you begin and end as a person, indeed it is not certain that we are, as persons, separate bounded entities at all. When John Donne (nearly) wrote that no-one is an island entire unto themselves, he did not mean that we are islands connected, as it were, by bridges, ferries, air-links and telecommunication systems. (Remembering the first line and forgetting the second has enabled the metaphor to be recast in the spirit of the times.) Everyone, he went on, is a piece of the continent – our interconnectedness is such that we are not islands at all.

When Margaret Thatcher made her now famous pronouncement – 'There is no such thing as society. There are individual men and women and there are families' – she was expressing in extreme form a belief widely shared in this society that individuals are self-evidently and indisputably *real*. 'Society', on the other hand, seems to be at best an intangible and abstract entity, at worst a delusion – perhaps one that 'social-ists' wish to *make* real and impose on us all. But it is a feature of the kind of society we live in that this is the way it often appears to us. This is not intended to imply that *society* is more real and the individual is a kind of illusion – neither is more or less real than the other.

Society is not something beyond individuals, separate from *us*, but neither is it all of us simply added together. Each of us lives in relation to other people, and these relationships take particular forms. That our relationships with others take particular forms is what it means to say that society is 'structured'. The fact that people are seen and acted towards differently on the basis of their sex is one of the ways in which society is structured. But so too is the fact that we are often and in various ways seen and acted towards 'as individuals'. We tend to think of being treated as an individual as the very opposite of being treated in accordance with your position in society. But being an individual *is* a position in society. To be treated as an individual is just as much part and parcel of a social relationship as being treated as 'a' something or other (or rather an individual *is* 'a' something or other).

To put it another way, we find it easy enough to understand that there are social definitions of what it is to be a woman or a man, that females and males are seen and acted towards in terms of definitions of what they are (in both senses) 'supposed' to be (as in what people 'suppose' you to be, and what they insist you should be). But the same goes for 'being an individual'. Individual-ity is no less socially defined than feminin-ity and masculin-ity. The fact that women and men have different bodies does not tell us what femininity or masculinity are, what it means to be a woman or a man. Likewise with individuality. The fact that we each have our own separate bodies does not tell us what it means to be an individual.

So we cannot talk of a 'sense' of being an individual without considering what it means in this society to be an individual. Like a sense of worth or vulnerability, it is necessarily bound up with the kinds of relationships in which you are and have been involved. From the moment of our birth we are caught up in a network of relationships, and these are the 'womb', as it were, out of which we emerge, not as bodies but as persons. You will not emerge as a person who has a sense of being an individual unless you participate in relationships in which you are regarded and treated *as* an individual. This means that we have to ask what people tend to mean by a 'sense' of being or not being an individual, *and* look at the ways in which people are regarded and treated as an individual in this society, and consider both of these together. First, then, what is generally meant by this *sense* of being an individual?

When talked about in an abstract way it seems to have three basic elements. The first is a sense of *separateness*, of being 'free-standing'

– as someone said, every tub must stand on its own bottom. But two tubs may be identical (like 'individual pork pies'). By contrast, being an individual usually implies – and this is the second element – *uniqueness*, having your own singular 'personal' 'identity'. (Note that whereas to 'personalize', say, a plant would once have been to attribute human qualities to it – perhaps to talk to it or try not to hurt its feelings – we now have, for example, 'personalized' golf balls, meaning, not that it is cruel and sadistic to whack them with a golf club, but that they are distinguishable from everyone else's golf balls.)

But there is a third element, because you should also have a sense of wholeness or *unity*. To have a strong sense of your own identity as a unique and separate person entails not only knowing 'who you are' (as in ident*ify*) but also being in some sense all of a piece (as in ident*ical*). Here we come close to the origins of the word 'individual' in the Latin 'dividere' (to divide): 'in-dividual' meant 'in-divisible'. A whole is more than the sum of its parts, and so to the extent that the elements of your character or experience seem unconnected and lacking in any internal coherence, to the extent that you appear chaotic or fragmented as a person, you would not be said to be 'an' individual.

This seems straightforward enough, but if we begin to look, not at the abstract definition of being an individual, but at the realities of the ways in which people are or are not regarded and treated as individuals, the picture becomes increasingly complex. In a moment we will begin to explore each of the three elements in turn, but first it is important to see how easy it is to lapse into a simplistic and one-dimensional way of understanding the process of becoming an individual, most evident in the idea of 'individuation'.

Most of us began to emerge as a person within the society of the family (Ms Thatcher contradicts herself in denying 'society' but talking of 'families'), and it is in the nature of this society that your position as a daughter or son entails being treated to a certain extent and in certain ways as an individual. Children are given and usually called by their own names (in other institutions you can simply shout nurse, fag, constable, or even 'hey, you' and so on). Parents have also become increasingly attentive to differences between their children and prepared to cater for such differences in all sorts of ways. These constitute the child as a *unique* individual. If children are also given their own toys, perhaps their own bedroom, their own pocket money and so on, if they are expected to make choices, be responsible, amuse themselves and the like, then to this extent they are also constituted as *separate* individuals. As children get older, they are usually increasingly regarded and treated within the family as distinctive and distinct, unique and separate individuals.

A similar process occurs outside the family. As small children, Emma and Paul remain 'our' Emma and Paul, and others outside the family tend to accept this and identify them with their family. To this extent they are not treated as entirely separate individuals 'in their own right' – they are so and so's children. Nevertheless, as they get older they are increasingly obliged to act on their own behalf without reference to their parents – the most significant early development being, of course, starting school – and they are increasingly seen by others as individuals independently of their families.

All of this is extremely variable, and there are some highly significant gender and social class differences in every aspect of it. Girls tend to be seen as more bound up with the family, they are more closely supervised (particularly in their teens), less frequently and firmly instructed to stand on their own two feet, and so on. Middle-class parents are more likely to have the resources (including space) to give children things and privacy, more likely to discipline according to the motto of 'liberty without licence' (do what you like, within limits – whose limits? – reasonable limits – whose reason? – as long as you behave responsibly – who is responsible for deciding what behaving responsibly is? and so on), their lives are less likely to be caught up in a network of kin, and their children in turn are more likely to move too far away from home (often via further education) to be thought of by others with reference to their relatives and their background and so on.

But the danger in this way of telling the story is that it can seem to imply that any differences between people are simply a matter of *degree*. The underlying metaphor would seem to be something like watching an indistinct and embedded image gradually emerging, becoming more definite and more prominent until it stands out clearly as a figure against a background, and then actually becoming three-dimensional so you can pluck it out of the picture and put it down somewhere. It has its own distinctive character, its own unity and its own independent existence. Here the passage from childhood to adulthood is depicted as a gradual process of 'individuation' and it is simply a question of how far down that road you have travelled.

This is analogous to the kind of uni-directional developmental sequence described by Kohlberg, and every bit as misleading. As we saw in the case of moral development, there is one story to tell from a feminine perspective and another from a masculine perspective.

Take first the sense of unity – a crucial part of what is usually meant by having a strong sense of your own identity. It is by no means clear that people have always had 'identities' in the way we tend to understand it, but there is good reason to think that women and men today tend to assemble their 'personal identities' in different ways and according to different principles.

Here I shall take up and add something to an idea suggested by Miller Mair: the idea of a 'community of selves'. This is not, I hasten to point out, the modern privatist notion of relationships between pure selves. The idea is that it can be illuminating to consider each individual, not as 'a' self, but as a community of selves. I have been very conscious of this metaphor in writing this book, and have often found it instructive to ask myself: who's been sitting in my chair today? Me obviously (or perhaps not so obviously, David Cooper once ended a book by saying 'my next book will be different – it will not be by me'), but it makes sense to ask *which* me on this occasion? (Perhaps the way that you are reading it, the very fact that you are reading it, the attitude you are taking towards it and so on involves one of your own repertoire of possible selves? Who is sitting in your chair?)

The idea of a community of selves suggests that we try thinking of ourselves as housing a multiplicity of selves which, as it were, live together and relate to one another in as complicated a set of ways as those that exist between actual individuals. Perhaps they argue, sulk, criticize, bear grudges, or accuse one another of being unreasonable. Perhaps they seek and provide comfort and support for one another, stick together and defend each other in the face of 'outsiders'. Maybe one (as happens in many families) is given the responsibility for settling conflicts, keeping everyone together and so on. Sometimes, as it were, we bring a self out of the cupboard on occasions to stop it feeling forgotten or neglected – perhaps 'mischief' must be given a turn when 'think of the consequences' has been getting all its own way.

Many of these 'guest appearances' have an essentially *ritual* character, which is why the campsite story was not entirely tongue in

cheek. When people come together and enact various institu-
tionalized rituals and ceremonies they are involved in some
confirmation of existing societal arrangements, an affirmation of
who we (allegedly) are – the family Christmas, the party conference,
a coronation, an election. But it is a feature of our kind of society that
individuals use their own personal rituals and ceremonies to confirm
existing 'psychological arrangements' and affirm something of who
they are as persons. Because holidays are a break from everyday
routines they abound in ritual invocations of what are felt to be
denied but cherished aspects of self – hence, for instance, the urge
common amongst men to turn their backs temporarily on the safety
and comforts of civilization and return to the wild.

It is important that you cannot discern from the outside how
someone arranges, as it were, their psychological furniture. On
Abersoch beach, for instance, I see young executives and estate
agents at play – but what do they see? I suspect that they see
themselves as sailors and windsurfers, caged in their offices for most
of the year, finally released into their natural habitat. I imagine they
have photographs on the walls of their urban zoo picturing
themselves in their wetsuits to remind themselves of how they look
when they are being themselves. We must inquire, as it were, within.
Nevertheless, it is by no means simply *my* business how I construct
my imaginative vision of myself, my personal identity. The different
kinds of society in which we move, the different kinds of social
relationships in which we are caught up, play a crucial part in this.

The fact that individuals today tend to think it is up to *them* how
they orchestrate the various aspects of their lives and selves is itself a
feature of modern society. Take the question of whether engaging in
extramarital sexual affairs or going out to work is seen as having a
bearing on a woman's 'fitness' as a mother. That women are now
more able than they were a century ago to ask 'what has that got to do
with whether or not I am a good mother?' is not simply to do with the
changing situation of women. It is part of a general shift in the kinds
of connections that are drawn between what someone does in one
context or area of their lives and what they do in another, and
between their relationship with one person and their relationship
with someone else.

A distinction proposed by Ferdinand Tonnies between two forms
of social organization – 'community', and 'society' or 'association' –
is extremely helpful in understanding this change and how it affects

our sense of identity. I will be drawing on this distinction in a number of contexts in what follows, and since this is the first it must be made clear now. It may be useful to begin with a rather crude version of the contrast between the two.

As they say of 'close-knit communities', everyone knows who you are, and 'who you are' is all of a piece. Everybody knows everybody else's business, so you will have a hard time keeping relationships or parts of your life separate from one another. By contrast, in the society of the city, nobody gives a damn what you do, and herein lies what seem to be the benefits as well as the costs of living an urban life: nobody cares, so you can do what you like. As Peter Berger says of the third world visitor to the United States, for those who come to the city from a rural community, its anonymity is linked with a particular kind of freedom. To be responded to as an individual, without reference to your family, can be a liberating experience as well as a disorienting one. (Note how many women who face the apparently awesome prospect of adding a shift on the assembly line to their obligations as houseworkers and mothers often say that it is good to be somewhere you are not simply treated as somebody's wife, or somebody's mother – you can just be you, 'one of the girls'.)

To be more precise now, the distinction between 'community' and 'society' lies in the kinds of relationships that characterize them. Most actual societies include some mixture of both kinds of relationships. Unfortunately this makes for a problem of terminology, for if 'a society' has within it both 'community' and 'society', we are going to get muddled over what 'society' means. It is largely for this reason that many writers retain Tonnies' own terms in the original German, and speak of 'gemeinschaft' ('community') and 'gesellschaft' ('society'). Instead I will put the English words in inverted commas and add the German in brackets if there is any room for doubt.

Tonnies likened 'community' to a living organism and 'society' to a mechanical aggregate. In 'community', he suggested, people remain united in spite of what separates them, whilst in 'society' people remain separated despite what unites them. Relationships in 'community' tend to be direct (face-to-face/person-to-person), multi-faceted (you know the same person in a number of contexts), and continuous (they persist over long periods of time). A high degree of mutuality is built in to such relationships, indeed a community is, in its original meaning, literally an individual. A community is a unity, *indivisible* into distinct and separate persons each with their own singular interests.

'Society' is much closer to being an association of individuals each pursuing their own private ends. In 'society' individuals often relate to one another indirectly, or if directly only in partial ways, for limited purposes in specific contexts. In 'society' people's lives are filled with passing encounters with strangers – shop assistants, meter readers, bank clerks, estate agents, and with more extended relationships which relate only to parts of their lives – schoolteachers, workmates, doctors, and so on. Central to society is the contract, a form of social tie where the rights and obligations it involves apply only to the issues it explicitly deals with. Business associates and employers may well know nothing at all about what gets called your 'private life', and you may be entitled to refuse to discuss it.

It might seem that our society has increasingly taken the form of 'society', but this would be misleading. Rather we have seen a sharpening divide between a public world of relations of association and a private world of 'community' relations. Modern society is characterized by a polarization, a starkening of a contrast between two worlds. As the public world has become more fragmented and 'impersonal', taken more the form of 'association', so the principles of 'community' have become elevated to an immense significance, representing for most people the principles of an ideal form of life. Tonnies' phrase has a new resonance: 'One goes into society (gesellschaft) as one goes into a strange country.'

The point here is that the more the kind of world in which you move approximates to 'society', the more it seems to be up to *you* whether or not you can be a mother, a lover, an employee and so on. It is a feature of 'society' that you can be many things to many people, and insist that what you are to one is none of the others' business. This is not an entirely clear-cut matter. (Not all politicians, for instance, are able to survive the exposure of various kinds of misdemeanour by claiming that their private lives have no bearing on their capacity to hold high office.) But while in general the public world has, increasingly, taken the form of relations of association, the private sphere retains many of the features of 'community'. In some parts of modern society the mother shares more with Profumo, Jeremy Thorpe, or Gary ('I do not want to be the issue') Hart than with many others one could mention. Here it remains true that having affairs, going out to work, even turning up to collect your children from school in fashionable clothes and make-up are seen as reflecting on your fitness to mother.

This puts the idea of a 'community' of selves in a new and interesting light. Am I, in fact, a *'community'* (gemeinschaft) of selves, or a *'society'*, an *association* (gesellschaft) of selves? We are all, I think, both, but in mixtures of differing proportions. Men are more likely to be engaged in a struggle to create a community out of an association, for them the problem is *fragmentation*. Many women, on the other hand, feel burdened and oppressed by their *community* of selves and and have fantasies of release – not unlike the youth of Tuscany waiting for the day they can escape from the claustrophobia of what seems to the urban tourist to be their rural communal idyll to the car factory in Milan. The problem for many women is not fragmentation but *unity*. Consider each of these problems in turn.

'Housewife' and 'mother' are, in a particular and significant sense, 'total' identities. What this means and the issues it raises are well aired in other contexts. In a recent TV soap opera, for example, a young man asked his mother whether he could invite a gay friend round to tea. Yes of course, she replied, but . . . what do they eat? An identity is total where it is assumed that, although it may be defined in terms of only one criterion, it has a bearing on all other aspects of an individual's life. This is most commonly assumed in the case of various forms of social deviance. Rather than having, amongst other things, broken a social rule – by being deaf for example – you are assumed to be a certain kind of person: a deaf person, a blind person, a homosexual, a criminal and so on. Housewife and mother are also total identities in this sense. Others, mainly those who have no experience of it of course, often assume that working in the home and bearing children somehow transforms you as a person, eliminates any other aspects not to do with these things, and makes you virtually indistinguishable from all other houseworkers and mothers. This position has more in common with social deviance than might be imagined.

When total labels are applied to people, they are generally identified as *outsiders*. Hence for example that most total of identities: 'mental illness'. If you are judged mentally ill this is seen as having a bearing on everything you think, feel and do, and you are irredeemably different from 'us'. (The manner of this keeping at arms' length may be changing somewhat, but you will still metaphorically be taken 'round the bend' in the road that curves around and behind the row of trees so positioned as to hide the asylum/psychiatric hospital from public view.) The total character of deviant identities –you are this through and through – assists the process whereby individuals are either cast outside of everyday society, or gradually edged to the margins of it. So it is with women – you are a different kind of person and belong outside society. The significance of this for the overall theme of this book will be plain enough: it is not only that a woman's place is (ultimately) in the home, but the home's place is outside society.

(It is also most significant that the response of many groups labelled as outsiders in this way is to give as bad as they get. Rather than saying, for example, that the category 'homosexual' covers an assortment of people with as little in common as the category 'heterosexual', individuals who take lovers of the same sex often refer to heterosexuals as 'straights' and sometimes affirm, not just their common position as a besieged minority, but their common identity as homosexuals. Amongst other things this helps others see homosexuals – like women and ethnic minorities – as less universal in their outlook. This is why, for example, the mass media are happy to talk of 'the gay community'. Similarly, people in the armed forces tend to lay great store on the concept of 'civilians', and of 'civvy street'. It is different out there, we service people have both a common bond and a common identity – as outsiders. So it is with certain varieties of feminism. Rather than saying that there is a presumption of diversity amongst men but a more unitary definition of women, some talk of Men – like straights and civilians – as a unitary category, and of women as sharing, not a common lot, but a common identity.)

The idea that a sense of unity is a good and healthy thing takes on rather a different colour in this light. But if unity is the *problem* in the private sphere, it seems to be a *solution* in the public realm. The problem for those who migrate between one sphere of the public realm and another, and back and forth between public and private realms seems to be one of *fragmentation*.

People who straddle the public and private worlds in the way typical of men (not only men of course) are faced with the problem of how to weave together the various threads of their lives and selves. Some public identities also have a total character to them – for example being a doctor or a priest/vicar. A doctor is likely to be consulted about medical matters at any time (but may be permitted, for example, to smoke). Members of the clergy must be seen to act in accordance with their espoused beliefs all the time – you do not get time off from that. But for most people modern society (which includes 'society') is segmented and fragmented and creates the possibility of a profound sense of personal incoherence. Some people succeed in subsuming the various elements of their lives under a single unifying theme, and it is significant that psychologists are often well placed to do this. A psychotherapist who is also a teacher and a parent, for example, may find it relatively easy to elaborate a common core to all of these – by developing, say, a client, student and child-centred philosophy – and thereby feel a strong sense of *continuity* in their lives. (I suspect this is why Carl Rogers feels that psychotherapists can be 'themselves' in their 'role'.) Others, of course, are more struck by the disparity between their public and private lives and opt for the most obvious privatist solution – a carving up of the self into private bits and public bits, usually elevating the private bits to the status of the 'real me', my 'real' self.

The upshot, then, is this: to the extent that women and men straddle the public and private worlds in different ways, we are likely to assemble our personal identities according to different principles. The ways in which problems of unity and fragmentation figure in our experience will depend on the kinds of relationships, and the pattern of such relationships, in which we live out our lives. It is clearly not enough to say that being an individual involves a strong sense of a unitary identity.

Likewise, the idea of having your own independent existence as a *unique* and *separate* free-standing individual very easily takes on an abstract character and loses any capacity to make sense of our actual experience of life. If being an individual means having a sense of your own 'separateness', then it is important to ask: to what extent do you feel that you are in fact *separable* from the other people in your life? Take each in turn – or rather, classify a little or it might take for ever. What about the person on the till in the supermarket? How long would you queue to get the same one each time? The electricity meter reader may actually come into your home, but does it pain you if it is a different person from last time? Would it pain the meter reader if you moved house and into someone else's patch? If you work outside the home, what about your workmates or colleagues? Even if you hate your job it might be a wrench to leave the people you have worked with and they might be sorry to see you go, but it is generally not an overriding consideration. If you have parents living but not with you, what about them? And getting even closer to home in more ways than one, what about the people you live with?

Everyday language serves us well here, for we are least separable from the people we are most 'attached' to. But the perhaps surprising conclusion then is that we seem to be at our *least* 'individual', in this respect, in the private sphere of personal life. We are most commonly regarded as individuals in *this* sense in the public sphere. In public you move from place to place and expect other people to take you as they find you. These are contexts in which you feel yourself to be the least embedded, and it is not much of a wrench to tear yourself away. And yet this seems to fly in the face of the sense that you are at your *most* individual in your 'personal' life. What do we mean by that? We mean, I think, that here we are regarded as a *unique* and irreplaceable person. Life in public often seems 'impersonal' because you are treated as a member of a category, identified as 'a' meter reader, receptionist, customer, claimant, patient and so on. You merely happen to be the one occupying this position at the time. In our personal life, it seems, other people see us as ourselves, as a singular person, the very opposite of being treated as a number.

This means that it is no good saying that a sense of being an individual includes a sense of separateness *and* uniqueness. We are pre-eminently one thing in the public realm and the other in private. Looking across at the private from the vantage point of the public it seems as if it would be good to get away to where I will be treated as myself, myself alone. Looking across at the public from the vantage point of the private, it seems it would be good to disentangle myself and get away to where I can be . . . myself, myself alone? These are two senses of being yourself: the first emphasizing uniqueness, the second separateness from others.

So what, in the light of this, are we making of the sense that so many women clearly have that becoming a wife and a mother entails a 'loss of individuality'? 'I married too young, before I had time to discover my own identity' is a common enough regret. Likewise, in the study of motherhood by Mary Boulton I referred to earlier, many mothers felt that exclusive responsibility for child care and super-vision all but destroyed any sense of 'personal autonomy' they might have had and replaced 'their identity as individuals with their identity as mothers'. What do they mean? The answer is less obvious and more significant than it might perhaps appear.

One meaning of the sense of a lack of *separateness* is plain enough – your identity as a mother becomes all-embracing simply because there is little opportunity to do anything else. You become, in this particular sense, 'just' a housewife and mother, you cannot separate yourself from these obligations. Hence the common (though far from universal) lament that you never get any time 'to yourself', to do 'what *you* want to do'. (Women are often said to be 'psychologically' committed to domesticity where it might be more appropriate to talk of their domestic *commitments*.)

But the issue runs deeper than this. To be addressed as Missis constitutes you as Mister's wife and this is not just a manner of speaking. (As someone once said, a wife does not take her husband's name, he takes hers.) Things have clearly changed since the eighteenth-century judgment that 'the husband and wife are one person in law; that is, the very being or legal existence of the woman is suspended during the marriage', but married women are still not treated as separate individuals by law and social policy. This both reflects and reinforces the many ways in everyday life that women have not been regarded and treated as individuals in their own right. Indeed, to be a woman has itself long been defined both relative to men and in negative contrast to men.

As Simone de Beauvoir put it: 'The terms masculine and feminine are used symmetrically only as a matter of form . . . In actuality the relation of the two sexes is not quite like that of two electrical poles, for man represents both the positive and the neutral, as is indicated by the common use of *man* to designate human beings in general.' In most quarters it remains true that a man can speak without being taken to speak *as* a man – women begin from the position of being seen as a woman first and human second. But being a woman is commonly defined not simply in contrast to a man, but negatively, as a kind of non-man. Femininity is frequently defined in terms of the characteristics women are allegedly deficient in – decisiveness, self-reliance, assertiveness, rationality, objectivity, resilience, courage, capability and so on. Indeed Aristotle simply declared that: 'The female is a female by virtue of a certain *lack* of qualities.'

It is clear for these reasons, then, why women in general, and houseworker-wives and mothers in particular, should feel the lack of a sense of being a free-standing separate individual. This is presumably a large part of what is intended when it is said that 'girls are taught not to be individuals but to see themselves as future wives and mothers'. But there is a serious difficulty with this opposition between being an individual and being a wife/houseworker/mother which relates back to the question of the relationship between self and role. One can become, the story goes, 'just' these roles, not in the sense of their filling up all your *time*, but in the sense of your self becoming absorbed into and taken over by them to the point where you cease to be an individual.

The way many women put this is to say that in becoming a mother you lose your identity as an individual and replace it with an identity as a mother, that you no longer have an identity 'of your own'. The difficulty is that 'mother' *is* an identity of your own, it is uniquely yours. And unlike other singular positions – like Prime Minister for example – you are not simply keeping the place warm, as it were, until the next one comes along. You and your position are not separable in this way. The distinctive character of the society of the family is that it consists of *social positions occupied by unique individuals*. The contrast we generally draw between the two (between a position and its occupant, between self and role) makes sense in the public realm, but does it apply here? In the public world you might feel that you are reduced to being a cog in a machine or a faceless functionary, readily replaceable and even disposable. But a woman who feels that she has been reduced to being somebody's wife and somebody's mother is always someone in particular's wife and someone in particular's mother. And her children and husband would probably mind a great deal if they got up one morning to find someone different doing her job.* Each member of a family occupies a particular position in relation to each of the others, but none is readily replaceable and some not at all.

This is one major reason why people defend the family so fiercely. The variable meanings of the word 'belong' make this clear. So much has been said about how the marriage contract, in ways that are only slowly receding, historically rendered women the property of their husbands – that she came to 'belong to' him – that the other meanings of belonging have been overlooked. You can feel you 'belong with' someone and that you belong somewhere, without the implication of

---

*Both women and men often insist on this uniqueness, for example, by being reluctant to use child minders. Many mothers have an immense investment in being the only person who is capable of mothering their own child.

possession. (You can belong to, for example, a golf club without being owned by it.) A woman in the home is not just a domestic servant conned into thinking she is someone special, in some sense she does indeed belong there as an individual.

It is most significant, then, that Boulton observes that it was mothers she considered to be 'middle-class' who 'always' talked of a sense of losing their individuality. The mothers Boulton describes as working-class expressed similar frustrations about being mentally, physically and emotionally drained by their children's demands, about never really being 'off', but did not talk of losing individuality or lacking an identity of their own. Indeed it was Boulton's impression that these women felt that they *expressed* their individuality through mothering.

There is clearly some dispute here about whether or not you are being an individual when you act as a mother, and this is of immense consequence. I suggested earlier that the privatist impulse is rooted, amongst other things, in the feeling that people have when they stand in the middle of a public space and look about them, or look up from the assembly line or office desk and want to say 'where am I in all this?' The middle-class houseworker and mother, it seems, looks up from the ironing or a wounded knee and also wants to say (or maybe scream) 'where am I in all this?' But who exactly is this 'I'? Are women who do *not* say this somehow lacking in a sense of individuality or even a sense of self?

There seem to be different theories at work here. In the working-class woman's theory, it seems that you can be a mother and be yourself at the same time. Where middle-class houseworkers and mothers are inclined to distinguish between *self* and *role*, the working-class woman may distinguish simply between *work* and *leisure* – you are not just your 'self' in your 'free' time. For the middle-class mother you are no longer an individual if you spend most of your time responding to others' needs, and fulfilling your obligations as a mother. You are only an individual when you are off duty.

Virtually all mothers of young children talk of being exhausted by other people's constant demands, but there is something distinctive about the middle-class woman's experience of a loss of individuality. This is, I think, to be found in the complaint most often voiced amongst middle-class mothers that I referred to earlier – that you get little or no time 'to yourself', to 'do what *you* want to do'. It is this that Ann Oakley means when, despite the fact that the majority of houseworkers in her study said that the best thing about it is that 'you're your own boss', she insists that the houseworker's autonomy is 'fictional'. The implication is this: to be an individual is to have your own individual purposes, goals and projects and the liberty to pursue them – in other words, the central principles of the political and ethical philosophy known as 'individualism'.

This would have been unthinkable to the vast majority of people in this society before the eighteenth century. About this time, a particular idea of the relationship between individual and society began to take hold in the popular imagination. It began to seem that individuals went out into society in pursuit of their own 'private' purposes. Engaging with other people became a means towards achieving your own individual ends. Individuals were able to imagine themselves as separate from 'society', this world out-there into which they ventured to participate in a network of relationships which brought individuals together and co-ordinated their activities as individuals. It became a world with which the individual was confronted, a world of external necessity. The seeds of privatism were now sown.

For the vast majority of the population this going forth into society was to find work, to sell what was increasingly the only thing they had: their labour. With the development of industrial society, more and more people were drawn into working outside the household. You went *out* to work. But, and it is a very big but, it was increasingly men who appeared as individuals in the market-place, ready and able to enter into a contract of employment as an individual, and this depended on the work of women. Individual men had to be able to turn up at the factory gates each morning fed, clothed, healthy and able-bodied, and without being hindered by other commitments and responsibilities. It was women who ensured that this was so. Employers had to rely on this too, and so the work women did in the domestic sphere was actually *an integral part* of the factory system. Women did not set out to look after their menfolk, or to keep the business of childcare and running a household from intruding into the public realm, for the benefit of the man's employers. But their work was nonetheless indispensable to the employer.

The general point is this: just as a theatre audience only sees what happens on-stage, it is easy to be oblivious of the work which must go on 'behind the scenes' to enable individuals to go forth into society in pursuit of their private purposes. For men to be 'separate' individuals, to be free to go out and earn a living, they had to have someone to look after them and their children, and be freed of obligations in the domestic sphere.

Within the domestic sphere, however, relationships retained something of their previous quality, and continue to retain it to some degree to this day. There, the central characteristics of 'community' (gemeinschaft) prevailed: mutuality and 'personalistic'* ties. A high degree of mutuality is built in to such relationships, for a 'community' is precisely not composed of distinct individual persons each with their own singular interests. It is in part the declining significance of kinship relations that signals the rise of 'society' (gesellschaft), but it remains true in modern society that in the context of family and friends, individuals do not merely associate with one another to further their own individual interests. Here it is not acceptable to try to rip each other off like used car merchants. We are supposed to feel each other's needs as our own, or at least look out for one another and come to each other's aid. As more and more people come to draw a tighter and ever-contracting circle around those they think of as 'us', so mutuality fades correspondingly deeper into oblivion, to be replaced by individual self-interest. But within this circle it remains.

I have already mentioned one reason why so many people are deeply committed to the family – the sense of 'belonging' – and mutual aid is, then, another.† But it is the nature of 'personalistic' ties that is perhaps the most crucial here. In contrast to the modern privatist conception of personal relationships which defines them as

---

*I use the term 'personalistic' rather than 'personal' to avoid the modern connotations of the latter described in the next paragraph.

†Let us not, of course, romanticize 'community'. At the head of the pre-industrial household stood a patriarch. As Tonnies himself said, the desire to aid and protect 'is closely connected with the pleasure of possession and the enjoyment of one's power'. There is a great deal of misguided nostalgia and sentimentality in that word comm-unity. People may have remained united in spite of what separates them, but that unity was increasingly preserved at the price of the woman's silence.

relations between persons in a kind of pure sense, a defining feature of 'community' is that it involves specific unique individuals in face-to-face relationships that are also quite evidently social and economic. The organization of relations within the household in pre-industrial Britain, for example, was first and foremost a division of labour. But these relationships were still quite definitely between individual persons who knew each other 'intimately' and were emotionally attached to one another. It is peculiar to modern society that people come to feel that social and economic relationships can interfere with personal ones.

In the light of this, we can return to the experience of domestic life, and what we find is that, just as I suggested that the middle-class woman in the domestic sphere is caught suspended between two kinds of time, she is also caught up in clashing and contradictory senses of what it is to be an individual. The experience of the working-class mother fits closely the description of relations in 'community': personalistic ties do not seem to undermine her individuality by denying her a unique or separate identity. Into the middle-class woman's world, however, comes a notion of separateness tied to private purposes which makes her feel she is not being herself when she acts as a mother, and a notion of uniqueness that says you are not yourself when you occupy a definite social position.

It is now quite clear that what it means to be 'an individual' cannot be clarified without exploring in some detail the realities of the relationships in which people are involved in their day-to-day lives. Women and men are characteristically involved in different *kinds* of relationships that entail being treated 'as an individual' in quite different kinds of ways. As with the feminine and masculine moralities, *neither* can set the standard for what being an individual 'really' means. As things stand, men are more likely than women to live out a large portion of their lives in contexts where they are regarded as separate but anonymous individuals, and women are more likely to live out theirs in contexts where they are regarded as unique (in a highly particular sense) individuals firmly locked into a pre-emptive and all-consuming total identity.

Is it possible to have the best of both worlds? For both women and men to become 'individuals' in a sense which combines the best of what we know into some synthesis which may go beyond what either of us knows? What the discussion up to this point means for the future, and what we should do about the present, will be the subject of the remaining chapters.

11 · The Best of Both Worlds?

One thing is abundantly clear: the problems that individual women and men encounter in their personal lives are neither idiosyncratic nor purely private. If we experience conflict in our relationships with one another here, if we talk and live past one another a good deal of the time, it is because of our differing experience of life on either side of the fragile wall between private and public and the relationship between the two territories it divides. Our different and conflicting outlooks – as much ways of feeling as of seeing things – are born of these differing experiences. You might say, though the metaphor must not be taken too far, that society expresses its own internal tensions and contradictions through the medium of everyday relations between women and men.

Women and men occupy different places in the social landscape, and from the moment of birth we are steered towards them. But if this routing of females and males into different spheres and kinds of activity and relationships has effects on individual women and men in the private sphere, it also has the most profound implications for society as a whole. The doctrine of separate spheres not only divides and separates women from men, it divides and separates these *spheres* and the activities and relationships that are housed within them.

A society divided along lines of gender in the particular way that characterizes our own, divides those activities which keep you rooted in the concrete and the immediate from those which depend on being liberated from time and space – with crucial implications for the forms of thought that prevail in and dominate the public world. It is primarily gender that allows the illusion to be sustained that the domestic sphere lies outside and plays no part in 'the economy', when in fact the economic system as a whole depends on and presumes both that the work of reproduction (of keeping people in good repair) can be shut out of the office and the factory, and that individuals will appear in public space each morning ready and able to give over their time and energies to their employer. And if there is not much tenderness in the public world it is because tenderness (in all four senses – the activities of tending to others, relationships of tender to tended, feelings of tenderness and tender qualities) is allocated and confined both to women and to the private sphere. It is gender that thereby ensures that the principal inhabitants and prime movers of the public sphere have the least experience of caring for and paying heed to others. These are the people who sustain the operations of the public world, and who include those who play the most significant role in shaping society as a whole.

Changing the sex of the players would not change the game. Gender, on the other hand, is quite central, necessary and fundamental to the way the game is currently played. The aim of reforming or transforming gender goes far beyond ending 'sex discrimination'. This is not a game of musical chairs.* Gender is inextricably bound up with the relationship between public and private, and changing gender must entail reconstructing this relationship, in some way bringing together the two halves of this divided world. We must try, I think, to have the best of both worlds – but it is by no means obvious what this means or how it might be achieved. First we must grasp the problem, and tenderness is perhaps the clearest illustration.

If there is little tenderness in the public world because tenderness is allocated and confined to women and the private sphere, then the solution might appear to be self-evident: bring it out. But would this mean bringing *women* into the public domain, those *qualities* of tenderness now associated with women, the actual *activities* and *relationships* involved in tending to others now conducted in private (collective child-rearing for example), or a *model* of what it is to tend

---

*The point must not be taken too far, because it is a somewhat abstract way of thinking about it. In imagination we can give half the present occupants of positions generally held by men female bodies, and half of those generally occupied by women male bodies, and it might seem that nothing has changed. But females and males cannot just be substituted for one another except in the imagination. To begin actually to *move* towards such a state of affairs in reality would involve overcoming some formidable obstacles and would have reverberations throughout society which are hard to foresee. If women and men are to make sense of one another this involves participating in each other's worlds, but this would also be a first step towards transforming gender relations in society as a whole.

and be tender based on tenderness in the private sphere? What would it take to achieve each of these things, and what implications would they have for the organization of public life and society as a whole? Would the nature of tenderness have to change in order to become everywhere the order of the day? What would become of men, of masculine qualities, of the kinds of activities and relationships associated with men? Are we talking about a takeover or a merger? Are either of these workable and what would they look like?

We are seriously hampered in trying to get to grips with this (what a masculine way of putting it!) by the 'psychological' forms of thought that abound in modern culture. The most obvious way this shows itself is in the over-emphasis on *personality*. To many, transforming gender is fundamentally to do with changing the personalities of women and men, by recombining in some way feminine and masculine *characteristics*. To some this means combining in each person the 'best' of feminine and masculine 'traits' – perhaps 'nurturance' with 'independence' – to others it means going beyond feminine and masculine as we understand them to a new synthesis which incorporates but transforms and transcends both. Some find it difficult to think of any feminine characteristics that are worth keeping, others feel the same about masculinity. All these ways of thinking share a common potential danger.

Nurturance/tenderness is again the clearest illustration. It is widely held that women are more nurturant than men. Some suggest or imply that this is, in part, rooted in genetic inheritance; others believe this is a characteristic acquired through socialization (the modern heir to genetics). Whatever its alleged origins, the claim is that women possess the qualities of nurturance, of care, empathy and responsiveness to other people's needs, an openness and receptiveness to others. But there is a fundamental ambiguity here. Are these *women's* qualities or values, or are they features of the *activities* to which women are assigned and the *relationships* in which women tend to be involved? The point is crucial because we have to ask whether, perhaps in time, any woman who came to occupy positions now inhabited by men would act any differently by virtue of their being female (and the equivalent applies to men). It is not difficult to think of women who occupy high office and do not appear to be motivated by the principle of care.

The potential danger here lies in detaching the qualities that women and men are said to embody from the activities and relationships in which these are embedded. It is not that there is 'no such thing' as personality, but to say that women 'are nurturant' can be to divert attention away from the context in which nurturing is done, and leave the impression that being nurturant is a kind of movable feast – something you are and hence something you can express wherever you are. Many women are employed in contexts which have some resemblance to domestic life and entail nurturing activities and relationships. But what becomes of these qualities in contexts where they are not called for at all? Sandra Bem, an exponent of the ideal of the 'androgynous personality', is reduced to suggesting that an androgynous manager might sack someone 'nicely'.

It is not just a matter of acquiring or juggling and rearranging personality characteristics, but of changing the kinds of lives that women and men lead. The point is a general one which applies to all aspirations for change which are couched in psychological terms: personal qualities and ways of thinking and feeling are always caught up in activities and relationships, and it is meaningless to hold up a psychological ideal without specifying what form of life is entailed. Without this we end up with a kind of evangelism, a form of preaching that begins by inspiring, but soon leaves you feeling a little ashamed of yourself. You agree that there are higher things to aspire towards – true individuality, a capacity for autonomy, for real love, genuine intimacy – but then it seems it is simply up to you to go ahead and change. If you do not or feel you cannot, then it is your own fault – who or what else can you blame? But it is clearly no good individuals' berating themselves for 'failing' to be autonomous, for lacking individuality or a capacity for intimacy and so on. We must ask: why are these things so hard to achieve in this society? The next step is then to ask: what kind of society would make their realization possible?

Psychological ideals must simultaneously be social ideals. This does *not* mean we should stop talking about ourselves and start talking about society *instead*. Society is not something separate from us. It is as wrong to say that there is nothing we can do about it as it would be to suggest that change could be achieved through some kind of a gender coup d'état. Gender reaches into every corner of human affairs and has to be contended with anywhere and every-where, it is not a matter of waiting for someone else to act – or for change to happen all by itself. What then should we do? We must begin by understanding what it is that we want. What do we want to achieve and why? The best of both worlds, I keep saying, and who could quarrel with that – but what exactly is the best?

It is not out of simple curiosity or a desire to understand that we ask 'what *is*' intimacy, autonomy, individuality and so on. These are *ideals* that people aspire towards and standards by which we measure our own experience. It is not like asking what a pillow is (though even here we are inevitably saying what a pillow *should* be like – a stone is too hard). Such questions demand answers which define, not simply how things are, but how they ought to be, what we should be striving towards. This form of questioning has its roots in what is called 'humanism'.

Humanism has rather faded from public view, even become a little old-fashioned. This is partly because it has been latched on to and distorted out of all recognition by certain groups who claim to fly under its flag (like the so-called 'humanistic psychologist'), partly because it has been drained of any specific content, and partly because of feminist criticism. But the idea must, I think, be clarified and restored to service. The transformation of gender is of the essence, I believe, a humanist project – but gender is as significant to understanding the nature of the humanist project as humanism is to the project of transforming gender.

The word humanism first arose as a positive alternative to the merely negative word atheism. It meant a concern with the human as opposed to the divine. Human-ism is an '-ism' in the same way as femin-ism. As I understand it, the central meaning of feminism is putting women first – in two senses. It means giving priority to women's *interests*, promoting and supporting any cause which seems likely to improve the situation of women, and it means looking at the world first and foremost from the *perspective* of women. Human-ism puts human beings/humanity first in the same two senses: it looks at the world from a human perspective and seeks to promote human interests, to improve the situation of human beings. (Likewise individual-ism puts individuals first, social-ism puts either the social or society first – depending on your conception of each – and so on.)

Humanism is simultaneously an attempt to understand, and a project for the future. It asks: what is it to be human? – in a way which is also to ask: what would it be to *become* human? Here being 'human' is not a factual matter of belonging to the species Homo sapiens, it is not something we already are and cannot help being. Being human is not a fact but a goal, and we cannot set out until we have at least a rough idea of which direction to take. We must have some idea of what being human means. Hence what is probably the best-known line in the humanist manifesto, that of Alexander Pope: 'Know then thyself, presume not God to scan/The proper study of mankind is Man'.* We look in vain for an ultimate authority who can tell us the truth – about what life is or could be, about what we are or might become – we must find this out for ourselves.

The *truth*? Is there such truth? The most important contrast to humanism today is not religion but *relativism*. It is largely because relativism is so widespread that humanism has receded, though many regard relativism as the inevitable consequence of taking humanism seriously, rather than as its opposite. Relativism says there is no truth, it is all relative, it depends on your point of view. There is no singular human perspective, but a plurality of perspectives, and there is no common human interest (hence the connection with the political philosophy of pluralism, with individualist moral philosophy, and their everyday expression in 'everyone is entitled to their own opinion' and 'do whatever you think is right' – and we'll just cross our fingers and hope you don't think exploiting, degrading and inflicting pain on others is right). To put it crudely, the humanist says there is nobody here but us chickens so it's up to us to find out the truth about chickenhood. The relativist insists that when the all-knowing chicken vanished from the sky the idea of truth went with her.

Can there be such a thing as 'real', 'true', 'genuine' intimacy, autonomy, or individuality? A friend of mine bears witness to a recurring quarrel among a group of male manual workers (which inclined towards violence) over the issue of whether a *real* fry-up had to include mushrooms and tomato. Call that a fry-up? Where's the mushrooms and tomato? Is it the same with the things we are talking about here? The question 'do I really love this person' seems to lead naturally to the question 'what is love, I mean *real* love?' Likewise we puzzle over the meaning of true friendship and genuine intimacy – what is it to 'be yourself' or to be 'an individual'? Would we react any

---

*The humanist principle 'know then *thy*self' does not mean your own singular individual self. No-one is an island but a piece of the continent and it is the continent we should seek to grasp – though this is not separate from *us*.

more kindly than these breakfasting labourers to the interjection: excuse me, isn't it a matter of definition?

We are unlikely – and rightly so – to stop being puzzled and confused, and to stop arguing about what these things mean and what they could mean, by being told that it is a matter of definition. But the relativist is surely right on one score. The meaning of such things clearly does vary – there is no single answer to what they mean now. Different societies, and societies within societies, have different ways of understanding the meaning of, say intimacy or friendship, because the people who inhabit them lead different kinds of lives with their own distinctive patterns of relationships. These various ways of understanding and experiencing intimacy and so on are not just influenced by, but inextricably bound up with, the way life is organized and lived. They are rooted in a particular form of social life. But this does not mean that *all* we can ask is what these things mean to me and to you, to us and to other groups or other cultures. It is not like trying to say what a kiss really means when it is obvious to anyone that even in one society it can mean a thousand and one things.

I have suggested that such things tend to mean something different to women and men in this society, and that this is because we tend to live and move in different worlds. But we do not have to conclude that there is no point in arguing about it. Equally, however, there is no point in a shouting match. We cannot both be right, but this does not mean that one of us is right and the other wrong. In fact, *neither* of us can be right, because the feminine and masculine perspectives and principles arise within the same society and are two aspects of the same totality. A society entirely composed of either feminine or masculine people (in the ways these are currently defined) is an impossibility. The feminine arises in the space vacated by men, and the masculine in the space vacated (willingly or otherwise) by women. They imply one another, depend on one another to be what they are. Neither can by itself provide a model of what humanity is or might become.

So what might a model of humanity which went beyond these polarities look like? The remaining chapters are devoted to trying to answer this question. The first step, it seems, would simply be to include both women and men in the category of humanity – but this is not as straightforward as it sounds.

12 · Humanity

The black American writer James Baldwin was once asked what he thought of the famous line in Thomas Jefferson's Declaration of Independence which runs: 'We hold these truths to be self evident, that all men are created equal, that they are endowed by their creator with certain unalienable Rights, that among these are Life, Liberty and the pursuit of happiness.' 'I have one little problem with that', he replied, 'you see – I'm not included.' But at least he was *ostensibly* included: it is all *men* who are said to be created equal. Does it go without saying that women are included? In a sense it does – it has gone without being said for a very long time.

It also went without saying that women were included in that other famous declaration of humanist principles, the rallying cry of the French revolution: 'Liberty, Equality, Fraternity'. *Fraternity*? The idea now sounds decidedly suspect, even rather sinister - a global 'cosa nostra', the ultimate male mafia. Some feminists believe that the Brotherhood of Man is already with us. If such solidarity amongst men is not always apparent, the argument goes, this is for two reasons: firstly because gender relations are to a much greater extent than, say, industrial relations, conducted in private; and secondly because dominant groups generally become visibly united (in spite of what separates them) only when they feel their position is threatened – when they feel that their position is secure they are more conscious of, and more inclined to display, their differences.

The case is considerably overstated, but it is not without substance. There is ample contemporary and historical evidence of such collusion amongst men – with little else in common apart from being men – to perpetuate the subordination of women. And just as tea-drinkers benefit from the exploitation of tea plantation workers in the third world simply because this makes tea cheaper, so there are many ways in which men collectively benefit from the subordination of women regardless of their espoused attitudes towards gender equality.

Baulking at the phrase 'brotherhood of man' is not, then, just a matter of words. Women are half of humanity and no project is humanist which does not explicitly say so. But *saying* so does not get women included in the category. Women cannot be included in the category of humanity merely by an act of thought, by simply striking out man, Man and mankind and substituting person, humanity, humankind and so on. A gap between rhetoric and reality cannot be closed by rewording the rhetoric.

Note that there is resistance even to rewording the rhetoric. One way in which masculine solidarity often does break out and reveal itself is in the jokes men like to make about the use of the word person. Have the dustbinpersons been yet dear? Guffaw. Did you see that programme on the personstory of the Palestinians? Of course such words are silly – the fact that there is no good word for something is part of the process of making change difficult. We generally only have good words for things that are part of the established order. It is not insignificant that there is still no good word that people who live together as unmarried couples can use when referring to each other – partner smacks of a business relationship, cohabitee belongs in the realm of the social security department, boyfriend sounds adolescent, and so on – and that is despite the large number of people who live in this situation.

But words are clearly not enough – what would it take actually to include both women and men in the category of humanity? The answer depends on seeing first that in a very important and particular sense humanity is *not* a category. To see it as a category is in itself profoundly masculine – it is an *abstraction*, and it is rooted in a way of grasping the world in thought that is modelled on *hierarchy*. (Some men have opposed both of these things, but the worlds from which they derive have been and are dominated by men.)

The world does not obligingly carve itself up for us into a tidy system of categories which contain other categories, ever widening and becoming more inclusive. Men classify in order to control or at least feel in control. (Which is why, for example, the psychiatric classification system does for distressed and displaced people what ornithology does for the birds.) Hierarchy is most relevant in this context to the distinctions between brotherhood/sisterhood, friendship, citizenship and so on that we will consider in a moment. It is the *abstract* character of the category of humanity that obscures the gap between rhetoric and reality.

The word humanity today actually has three principal and related meanings. It is the third we are interested in here, but it is important to distinguish it from the other two. The first is acting in a humane or humanitarian way. The second refers neutrally to the set of supposedly shared and distinctively human attributes (synonymous, in other words, with person-ality). The third is as a collective term for human beings (as 'mankind' once claimed to be). Since some believe that humanity expresses its humanity through acting with humanity there is some room for confusion here.

Both the second and the third meanings of humanity lend themselves to the kind of abstraction which allows a gap to open up between rhetoric and reality. I have already referred to the second in Chapter 6: many who profess but corrupt the name of humanism set off in search of that elusive set of qualities that are common to all human beings. It is as if the street beggar shared all the really important things in life with the tourist drinking in a nearby bar, or that you could become his brother or her sister by an act of thought. All human beings may share, for example, a knowledge of certain death, but it makes a difference knowing that it may well be tonight. The 'human condition' includes humans whose conditions can often be described as inhuman.

It is, though, the third meaning I want to take up here: humanity as a 'collective' term for human beings. In what *sense* are human beings a collectivity? Let us leave out the dead and the not yet born and suggest that humanity comprises every human being alive today. In imagination we can roam around the world and in our mind's eye simply add them all together. But this is not how human beings actually live – all added together. We form *actual* collectivities not imaginary ones. We do this by living together in particular ways. Our actual collective existence is characterized by certain kinds of interconnectedness. If humanity means human beings taken collec-tively, then do we mean the imaginary additive collectivity or the actual collectivities we live within? Do we mean human beings 'taken' together, or human beings the way they take themselves to be together?

There is another word to characterize the nature of actual collectivities: society. Human-ity is, in its non-abstract sense, society. This may sound like playing with words but it is a great deal more than that. We are social animals, but that does not simply mean that we are gregarious, that we like or need the company of other human beings. It means that humanity takes the form of society. What matters is not some abstract humanity, human beings combined by the imagination, but human beings actually combining to live together in particular ways. Gender is an absolutely fundamental feature of the ways human beings combine to live together now, and so actually to include women and men in the category of humanity is considerably more than a first step – it would involve transforming these relationships. But how? What humanism aspires towards is the realization of a particular humanity and that means a society in which our interconnectedness takes a particular form. What form? One in which we are *all* included.

What does that mean – to be included? Here there is a dividing of the ways. There are in modern culture two particularly significant visions of including everyone, both of which often fly under the flag of humanism, and both of which are to be found within feminism. Neither takes gender seriously enough, for both in the end simply reproduce the split between public and private.

What is distinctive about modern society is that human beings combine together in two different kinds of ways: the ways of the public and the ways of the private. To understand what these two ways are, it is helpful to use again the distinction between two kinds of interconnectedness proposed by Ferdinand Tonnies: 'community' and 'society'.

'Society' gives rise to a particular idea of what it would be for everyone to be included: the idea of citizenship and of equal rights. Put it like this: in an *abstract* way we are all included already, we are all 'members of society'. But we are not all full members. If we use the analogy of a club, time was, and often still is, when women were not permitted to be full members and so were not allowed to vote or play on the snooker table, and they had to form their own ladies' darts or bowls team. The idea of equal rights as citizens says that we should all be made full members without discrimination, with full voting rights, the liberty to enjoy all the available facilities, and protection from arbitrary expulsion – this is how we will all be included.

There are two fundamental problems with this. Firstly, formal equality is in itself a dubious goal, because if people do not actually live on equal terms then formal equality obscures and in the end legitimizes real inequalities. In Anatole France's famous words: 'the law in its majestic equality forbids the rich as well as the poor to sleep under bridges, to beg in the streets, and to steal bread'. If people do not have equal *reason* to sleep under bridges, steal bread and beg in the streets, then the law can only treat people *as if* they were equal when they are not.

The relationship between gender and class is particularly crucial in this context. There is inequality among men, so if women want equality with men, which men do they want to be equal with? There is a fundamental tension at the heart of equal rights feminism: working-class women are bound to hesitate before uniting in common cause with their middle-class sisters when their middle-class sisters are likely to come out of it a good deal better off than themselves.

But there is another problem too. What is the club? In the main it is not society but 'society', gesellschaft, the public world. The dominant idea of individual rights arises first and foremost in a society where people appear in public space with their own private purposes. The liberty of each to pursue their own purposes is to be regulated in order not to intrude on others' liberty to do likewise. This idea of individual rights is born of an attempt to achieve this balance. But this public arena is only made possible by the work of reproduction being carried on elsewhere. It is the work done behind the scenes that enables, as it were, the play to go on – what happens on the stage is only part of a much wider play. This pursuit of sex equality in the public realm, it turns out, actually helps to obscure the significance of gender.

The most telling expression of this is to be found in the distinctions that have come to be made between 'social', 'economic', and 'political' issues. This is a direct consequence of the doctrine of separate spheres for women and men. With the development of a separate sphere of 'work', men gained a voice outside the parliamentary system: trade unionism. But the concerns of trade unions progressively narrowed to issues focused directly on the workplace, particularly on wages and conditions of work. Any attempt by trade unions to broaden their concerns beyond the workplace are today vigorously resisted, and labelled 'political' and therefore illegitimate. The consequence is that it is now extremely difficult for issues that arise *outside* the workplace – health, housing, education and a whole host of localized neighbourhood concerns – to be expressed directly in the public domain. A crucial part of the reason for this is that it has historically been women and not men who have engaged most directly with these kinds of problems. The marginalizing of women has had the effect of marginalizing such concerns.

It is hard to imagine that people in the pre-industrial household, in arguing about how things were done and life was organized, would have thought of carving up the issues into social, economic and political matters – and in fact they remain as bound up together today as they ever were. It was not simply the removal of production from the household that led to the creation of such distinctions, but the doctrine of separate spheres for women and men. It was this that ensured that one group of workers engaged with issues focused on the industrial workplace, and another with issues outside it. In the process the issues themselves became separated and disconnected. The pursuit of formal equality in the public sphere binds you closer to this established structure, and hence, not only to the doctrine, but also to the reality of separate spheres.

This particular vision of the inclusion of all is rooted in 'society' (gesellschaft). In 'society' people remain separated in spite of what unites them, and in their separateness pursue a concept of justice based on equal rights. It is out of this form of interconnectedness that the morality of rights and abstract principles which Carol Gilligan considers to be masculine emerges. Her feminine morality of responsibility and care emerges out of another form of interconnectedness which has an *affinity* with the alternative vision – rooted in 'community' – of what it would be for us all to be included. But, as we shall see, there are also crucial and decisive differences.

The way that human beings in this society see themselves as relating to one another in private is quite different from their image of 'society'. Here the interconnectedness between people is such that they remain united despite what separates them – the central feature of Tonnies' description of 'community' (gemeinschaft). Being 'included' here means first and foremost a sense of belonging, of being recognized and taken account of. In contrast to the anonymity and indifference of 'society', relationships in the private sphere are felt to be personal and characterized by mutual aid and inter-dependence.

Many, if not most of the compelling visions of a more 'human' society that have taken hold in the popular imagination in the course of this century have been modelled on an idea and ideal of community. The word readily lends itself to rhetoric, of course, and not only when called upon by the powerful. On those rare occasions when people come out of hiding and join with their neighbours to pursue some common cause they often bring the word community out of the cupboard too. It is an insubstantial and short-lived phenomenon in the majority of cases because it is a unity only in the face of some specific threat – a plan for a high speed rail-link, a motorway, a nuclear power station, a toxic waste disposal plant: put it somewhere else. The word community is also routinely called upon when politicians of the right want to give society a more human face, when the police talk about accountability, when politicians of the left want to 'soften' the image of socialism, when the nations of Europe are to become united in spite of what separates them, and so on. All this, however, confirms the point that it speaks to a deeply and widely felt aspiration. But for what exactly?

The alternative humanist ideal to the liberal humanism just discussed is modelled on 'community' rather than 'society'. This is closer to the idea that between friends there is no *need* for justice – or rather between *brothers*, because this alternative has historically gone by the name of fraternity or brotherhood. Everyone is included in fraternity because it is a comm-unity of equals. If justice as the balancing of rights is unnecessary, it is because mutuality is the order of the day. Mutual aid is a central feature of fraternity because the interests of one are so deeply intertwined with those of each of the others that no-one feels they could profit from another's loss.

The word fraternity/brotherhood will no longer do, of course, because of its masculine content. (*Eventually* its direct equivalent – sorority/sisterhood – will have to go too. Very few feminists want to rid the world of males, and this means that most feminists are in fact committed to a project for humanity.) But even allowing for the gender association there are other reasons for looking askance at the words brotherhood and sisterhood.

Why in this form of community were we to regard and act towards one another as brothers/sisters do? First and foremost it was because this was to be a unity among equals and these are taken to be relationships of equality. But the choice of terms rooted in the *family* is highly significant – for two reasons. Firstly, their origins as terms to apply to someone who is not a blood relation are in a context where there is an implied *father*. Fellow members of religious orders were brothers and sisters in Christ, and through him the children of God the father. This was a religious community based on a model of the family, and the members were united in their subordination, and equal only as subordinates. (Those who rejected both hierarchy and monastic seclusion went out into the world with an alternative term and form of address: friend – as in the Quakers, the Society of Friends – which does not imply a higher authority.) The second significance of the family connection is the most important: apart from the fact that people often hate their brothers/sisters, sisters and brothers generally know one another *intimately* and are emotionally involved with one another.

This has implications for the feminist espousal of the value of sisterhood, but that is not the point here. What matters is that *the modelling of community on intimate relationships* has gained a special and increasing significance in modern society. The massive investment of most people in this society in the private sphere of personal life represents a commitment to the basic principles of community – mutual aid and personal(istic) ties. But the modern community of the private has one decisive feature: it is not a community at all. That is because it lacks its *public* character. A community of the private is, in this sense, a contradiction in terms.

In this society, the sense of community has for most people contracted to a small private circle of family and friends. (That the idea of mutual aid has been narrowed to a private core shows perhaps most clearly and vividly in the fact that other people's babies' nappies *smell* worse than your own.) It is among family and friends that people are most likely to feel that they cannot profit from the other's loss, and hence do not feel so much need to devise means for regulating the impulse to exploit one another for their own personal gain. It is within *this* context that Gilligan's feminine morality arises. But this community of the private is defined and defines itself in contrast to the outside world ('society') and in the process develops an ideal of community which can *only* be realized in private – if there. This has a vital bearing on the attempt to create a more human society in which women and men participate as equals.

As the sense of community has contracted to an ever-diminishing private circle, so the idea of a *public* community has become virtually unthinkable. We now find it very difficult to imagine that relationships can be *personal* without being *intimate*, or that mutual aid can possibly flourish in a *public* world. The idea of a public community is even equated with the *worst* not the best of both worlds. We think in contrasts, and if both poles seem undesirable then we tend to be tossed back and forth between the two. People's image of a public community is often an uneasy mixture of the worst of their experience of the private and the public. It seems to combine the claustrophobia and lack of individuation of the private, with the anonymity and indifference of the public. Hence, for example, the alternative to exclusive responsibility for mothering seems to be to pass the child 'from pillar to post'. The idea of a world which involves neither of these things becomes extremely difficult to envisage.

What has happened is that the ideal of community in the modern imagination has become ever increasingly transfigured by the canons of intimacy. Inadvertently, the ideal of a more human world which has more hold than any other in this society has been steeped in and soaked up a model of 'truly human' relationships based on an idealized version of relationships in the private sphere of personal life – to the point that people can scarcely envisage any other kind of world worth trying for. Most give up the public world as a bad job. But the equation of community with intimacy is not confined to those who sound the privatist retreat. Betty Friedan may have urged women to return to an emphasis on the values of community and the interpersonal ties of intimacy, but others who refuse to lock themselves up in this emotional fortress and pull up the drawbridge are nonetheless wedded, however uneasily, to this equation.

The most widely embraced visions of a more human society which have emerged in recent times and which explicitly *challenge* the public/private contrast and refuse to take up the privatist option, demonstrate the same commitment to an ideal of truly human relationships modelled on an idea of what relationships are or can be like in the private sphere of personal life. The fault is seen to lie in the public world and is to be remedied by a sustained intrusion or even invasion of the public by the private. Proponents of these visions echo the feeling that most people in this society have that there is not much humanity in the public world, and so find it difficult to think of anything good to say about it. This is something of a problem if we are to try to combine the best of both worlds. And since men become identified with the public world, it means many find it difficult to think of anything good to say about *men* either, and hence to find anything worth incorporating of the masculine into any new synthesis. The resulting idea of what it would be to 'humanize' society as a whole is fundamentally flawed. It is because people feel that there is not much 'humanity' in the outside world that they attempt to set up pockets of humanity in their homes, with their families, and with their close friends – and the humanity of the closed pocket cannot in principle become the humanity of the entire wardrobe.

In the next chapter we will consider two such visions of a more human society. One of these is based on what I have suggested is a masculine view of the private sphere, the other is based on a feminine view of the same world. Both are impossible projects, but developing a realistic alternative depends on understanding why.

13 · Turning the World In-side Out

The accusation that is levelled and repeated most loudly against the 'outside' world ('society') is that it is an *impersonal* world. But what is to be done about it? In the 1960s an idea took hold that appears superficially to be the very opposite of privatism: be yourself in public. Go public as a self, take it with you when you go out. Don't complain that social life is a masquerade, take the mask off. Do it now. Public space need not be a no-go area for the self – don't desert it, reclaim it. No more role playing, no more donning and doffing of masks – be yourself *always*. Here we have a particular model of community: a community of *selves*.

In the 1980s a new vision of humanizing society has emerged in feminist writing which also consists in a planned invasion of the public by the private. The difference is that the first is based on a masculine view of the private as the realm of freedom, the self, and intimacy between pure selves, and the second is based on a feminine perspective on the same world. Both of these ideals for a more human society oppose privatism in one sense – by refusing to accept that the public world has to be this way – but are profoundly privatist in another. They echo one of the central defining features of modern culture: the tendency to judge all interactions and relationships between people in terms of a model based on an idea of what relationships are or can be like in the private sphere of personal life. It is *inevitable* then that the public world will be tried and found wanting. These two visions of a more human world are both impossible projects because they repudiate the very idea of a public world.

Consider the sixties community of selves first because it came first historically and because the modern resurgence of feminism began in part as a reaction to it. The masculine privatist outlook sees the realm of personal life as an arena in which we can relate on a purely personal level, be ourselves, express ourselves openly and fully, and dissolve the distance that social life normally puts between us. Most conclude that such personal relationships are best conducted far away from society and retreat into the private sphere – and it is only this that the sixties outlook refused to accept. The model of rewarding human relationships is the same, but it was to break out of the cocoon and take over the world.

The best preparation for life became therapy and the encounter group. This is privatism at its most extreme. Therapy must take place somewhere, but it tended (and still does for many) to be thought of as a kind of setting that is not a setting – a kind of pure encounter between persons. This is the stuff of fantasy. It is like the Mills and Boon romantic novel, where the details of the location of the action are simply a backdrop to allow the story to unfold. These are often set in exotic faraway places, but it could just as easily be somewhere else because really it is not anywhere at all. For the sixties therapeutic outlook, however, this was a rehearsal studio. When we have discovered who we really are and how to relate personally to one another we will go forth into the wilderness and transform it into a garden.

Like many apparently radical visions, what is clear in hindsight is how much this one shared with what it sought to oppose. Just as the desire to 'be now', to live in and for the present, were part of the same tendencies which gave us the credit boom and the fading sense of historical time, so going public as a self was little more than a footnote to the growing tendency to personalize public issues and public figures. Anyone who figures in the news now becomes a 'personality'. A Soviet leader is praised for his decision to pander to the western media by putting on a sharp suit and attending to his image on television. The image of Arthur Scargill figures far more vividly in most people's memories of the last miners' strike than what it was about. In a testament to the theatrical quality of so much of public life, Margaret Thatcher and Norman Tebbitt are readily portrayed as wicked stepmother and pantomime ogre. Perhaps most extraordinary of all, it was not very long ago that all most people would have recognized of the Pope was his hat, now I have it on the good authority of the BBC that his favourite watersports are canoeing and water-sking. Personalizing public space is very much the order of the day.

But a public world composed of pure selves interacting with one another is an impossibility. We are never pure selves, not even in private. But even if we were, we gain this idea of self from our experience of personal life in contrast to our experience of public life. An idea which is born in contrast to something else cannot become the whole thing. By analogy (it is more than that), subjective is defined in contrast to objective, and this means that *everything* cannot be either subjective or objective. We can say that this is a false or misleading opposition, but that entails revising both poles of the contrast. To refuse to accept the privatist contrast between self (private) and society (public) is to be committed to rethinking the meaning of *both*.

The distinction between self and role was central here. It seemed that the public world had become a theatre on to which the self would step having put on its social wigs and false beards. We were to take off the disguise, stop playing roles, and be ourselves always. It is most significant that in the arts in this period people sought ways of appearing in public *in person*, as though a public forum – a stage or a book – could cease to be public because you insisted on acting as if it were not.

This outlook is essentially a repudiation of the very idea of society: society is alien and inauthentic, it gets in the way, stops us being ourselves. This is why, for example, the practice of shaking hands fell out of favour. This, it seemed, was purely ritual therefore impersonal and insincere. A practice which used to signify good will, that you meant the other no harm – you could not reach your sword – came to be seen as sabotaging the possibility of a personal encounter, a meeting of selves. The implication is that you could in principle be intimate with everyone you meet. By shaking hands, instead of going forward to greet someone, you were felt to be *withdrawing* from them. (As David Riesman said: 'Etiquette can be at the same time a means of approaching people and staying clear of them.') Similarly, wearing black at funerals could not be genuinely expressive of grief or solidarity precisely because it was a social convention – as if the only way to express yourself was through doing things that nobody else would understand. It was inevitable that, having decried social conventions as insincere, a new set of social conventions should emerge – 'have a nice day now' – which are doubly insincere because they pretend not to be.

Privatism defines rewarding human relationships in a way that ensures that no public world will ever do, and resolves to give it up as a bad job. But like the Cambridge Don in Olivia Manning's *Fortunes of*

War who could never forgive the world outside Cambridge for not being Cambridge, the 1960s outlook could not forgive public life for not being personal life, and proceeded to act as if the whole world *was* Cambridge.

The image of Cambridge, of the private sphere, that was being exported here is the essentially masculine one of the private sphere as a community of selves – the realm of freedom, the self, and intimacy between pure selves. The new vision of humanizing society which has appeared in feminist writing in recent years differs in being based on a woman's perspective on the private sphere, but in other respects it hovers perilously close to being a simple retelling of the same story.

If one form of interconnectedness gives rise to equal rights feminism, the modernized version of the other kind of interconnectedness ('community') gives rise to a quite different kind of project for transforming gender. Here it is not simply a matter of gaining access to the public world, of participating in it on an equal footing with men. There is a fault in the public world and it is to be laid at the door of men. The world is the way it is because it is run by men (we would try to work out quite why men are like they are later). The result is an ideal of *humanizing* the world by *feminizing* it. Thus, in place of violence, competition, calculation and mastery – all those things that set people against one another and which men are seen to stand for – we are to have a world characterized by the essential 'human' qualities of empathy and responsiveness to other people's needs which women represent.

There is the potential for a great deal of romancing in this picture of women, but nevertheless the idea evidently has something compelling about it. For historical reasons, because they have been consigned to the tasks of caring for others, perhaps women have become the carriers of those values which would make for a more human world, and the best way to realize it would simply be to have it run by women or at least according to feminine principles. We considered earlier the problem of whether these are *women's* qualities, values and principles, or those embedded in the activities to which women are assigned and the relationships in which women tend to be involved. It is most significant, then, that many exponents of such a view talk of women's *psychology* as being a model for the truly human. But if psychological ideals must also be social ideals, then in order for such principles to become the order of the day the whole of society must be modelled on these kinds of relationships. This is clearly impossible – public life can never become private life. To charge the public world (now the man's world) with lacking and being in dire need of qualities, values and principles that are rooted in *intimate* relationships is to repudiate *any* kind of public world. If we judge relationships between people in terms of a model based on an idea of what relationships are or can be like in the private sphere of personal life, then the public world is bound to be found wanting, and any kind of public world at all would suffer the same fate.

Here it is helpful to separate the two features of 'community' which have become associated with intimate relations: mutual aid and personal(istic) ties. Consider mutual aid first. The principles of mutual aid as they are currently lived cannot be exported into the public world without being fundamentally transformed, and this entails breaking the link between 'the values of community' and 'the interpersonal ties of intimacy'. This means in some way incorporating the best of the feminine and masculine moralities into a new synthesis which draws on but transcends both. How? First it is crucial to understand what it means to call these moralities 'feminine' and 'masculine'.

It does not mean, as Gilligan has herself made clear, that women and men do not understand each other's moralities or draw on them in their lives. We do, but the point is that women and men tend to participate in different kinds of activities and relationships, and it is in the nature of these that they raise different kinds of issues and pose different kinds of dilemmas. The problems posed by engaging in those kinds of relationships and activities which involve paying heed to others' directly expressed needs in a face-to-face intimate and emotionally involving relationship call for certain kinds of solutions, ones that are quite unlike the dilemmas posed by the experience of life today in the public world. Women and men are generally obliged to find workable solutions to different kinds of problems and these solutions will, in a sense and to a degree, become deeply ingrained. But so-called feminine and masculine values and principles remain as much a feature of the kinds of activities and relationships in which they are embedded as they become personal qualities and ways of thinking and feeling characteristic of women and men. We are all larger than we seem.

So what does a positive synthesis entail? It entails, I believe, developing forms of mutual aid which are compatible with a *public* world. It is most significant that while 'humanity' in the sense of acting in a humane manner is now associated with compassion and hence with feeling, in medieval society it meant to be civil, courteous and polite. I am not, of course, suggesting a return to the Dark Ages, but we pay a high price for this shift towards feeling.

As things stand some notion of human rights may well be essential in order to ensure that paying heed to human need does not depend on the vagaries of feeling. In a society like ours, there are many forms of suffering and deprivation that go unheeded because they are hidden from public view or are depicted in such a way that people do not identify with them – feel them as their own – and this has become for us the precondition of being moved to respond. Building structures to institutionalize care seems to us to be an *impersonal* way of paying heed, and as things stand it often is. But whether or not there will ever come a time when there is no need for justice or indirect forms of care, one thing is for sure: as long as we remain wedded to a conception of 'us' which depends on knowing each of 'us' intimately and being bound together emotionally, we will continue to concentrate our commitment to mutual aid in the private sphere, or build castles of intimacy in the air and leave the public world to look to another principle – mutual exploitation within a system which ensures that some are more exploited than others.

The second feature of 'community' is personalistic ties. That the values of community have become deeply intertwined with intimate relationships shows itself here in the fact that we now find it very difficult to imagine that relationships can be *personal* without being *intimate*. Since men are felt to be rather lacking in the intimacy department, many people now find it very hard to say anything good about the way men relate to other people.

The feminizers, and some who aspire towards synthesis, hold that women have superior 'relational capacities' to men. According to this view, the masculine self is defined in contrast to and over against others, it entails an isolating sense of being distinct and separated from other people. The feminine self, on the other hand, is always a self-in-relation to others. But these relational capacities are clearly, and in the work of Nancy Chodorow explicitly, bound up with intimate relationships. In Chodorow's view, what girls are schooled in from a very early age is a sense of self which provides them with the basis of the relational capacities necessary for *mothering*. In the case of men, the implication often is, not that they have capacities for *other* kinds of relationships, but they are simply lacking in *any* relational capacities. Masculinity becomes a relational *in*capacity. How could humanity have anything to learn about relationships from people like that?

Here again we see how intimacy has become the standard for 'relationships' in general. And so, once again, the question is whether the whole world can be like Cambridge – a different Cambridge, a more realistic vision of it as a society and not a subjective universe, but still Cambridge. And yet the whole world clearly cannot have the character of intimate relationships. You cannot, in any sense of the word, know everyone 'intimately'.

Like the masculine vision of a community of selves, this would appear to be an ideal of community. But it is not – because an essential feature of community is its public character. A community requires people with 'relational capacities' that are compatible with public life. Women and men have both relational capacities (and by implication incapacities) because of the nature of the relationships in which they are caught up. To go beyond gender to a more human society involves drawing on the experience of both.

A model of society based on the private/women's experience can never be anything more than a pipedream. It remains firmly locked into the contrasts we are trying to unmake and remake and leads straight back to the shouting match: girls are better than boys, my world is better than your world. Transforming gender entails rethinking and reliving the contrast between private and public. The outside and the outsiders cannot be included by trying to turn the world in side out. How then? By understanding that public life will never be private life, but it *can* become more personal.

14 · Personal Relationships

In the passage with which Don Bannister prefaced his last novel, Bertrand Russell wrote that love 'is the principle means of escape from the loneliness which affects most men and women throughout the greater part of their lives'. As things stand, our different conceptions and aspirations of intimacy are such that the chances are we will pass each other by like ships in the night and end up, if anything, even lonelier. But why do we take it for granted that only relationships in the private sphere of personal life could ever save us from loneliness? (I am posing the question not saying this is 'wrong'.) Why do we assume that relations in public cannot fulfil our longing for human company?

'Where do you live?' The question asks, of course, where your home is, where you sleep at night. And yet wherever we are we are still living. Another play on words? Not at all. Most people live with home as a constant reference point, which is why the vision of a homeless universe is so unthinkable. Our world has a centre, and it is this that saves us from a permanent sense of being in transit, even if it confines some of us to the point of screaming. But what is distinctive about modern culture is that this small circle of home, family and friends is identified with the *self* in such a way that when you leave the circle, in a sense you leave your self behind you.

Despite gender and social class differences in the meaning and power of the privatist impulse, there is something of a common core: a model of society which places the self at the centre. This self is *significantly* connected to only a handful of others. Beyond the self and its intimates there radiate outwards, like ripples in a pool, kinds of social relationships which become increasingly 'distant' the more 'distant' they are from the private self – the point, as it were, where the stone was dropped into the water. Just as ripples fade the further the circle spreads, so it seems our involvement *must* become less intense. We carry this model about with us, and so as we engage (or rather do not engage) in relationships with others far away from 'home' (the centre of our world and hence the self) it is inevitable that the meeting is not between our selves. Could it be otherwise? Yes it could, and until it is, women and men will continue to talk and live past one another and make impossible demands on their private lives.

The central contrast in this imaginative vision of the world and ourselves is intimacy versus distance. As we saw in Chapter 4, it is by no means self-evident what either of these things mean. I made the point then that pride of place in the privatist mentality tends to be given over to the idea that to be 'intimate' is to be 'close', is to 'confide', is to 'disclose' something of your 'inner self' – in order that nothing be allowed to come between us. What matters here is that both women and men in this society have come to map this contrast on to another one – personal versus impersonal – in such a way that personal relationships must, by definition, be intimate. Indeed I imagine that most people who looked at the title of this chapter without having read the book would simply assume that it was about intimacy in some way. It is this equation of personal with intimate that has to be unmade.

Here I think we can combine something of a feminine and a masculine perspective and arrive at something that is both and neither. Take first a feminine perspective on distance. When women complain of men being 'distant' they tend to refer to three things in particular. We have already considered two of these: men's apparent inability/unwillingess to talk openly about their feelings, and their inability/unwillingness to provide 'support'. But the third is perhaps the most crucial: men, it seems, have a disturbing capacity to 'detach themselves' both from their feelings and from their immediate surroundings. Though men have a tendency to make their presence felt, this presence often feels like a kind of absence – as though he is not really 'there'.

R. D. Laing recounts an incident where a woman psychiatric patient is handed a cup of tea and says: 'thank you. I've never been given a cup of tea before.' Appearances notwithstanding, he suggested, this woman is far from disoriented. What she means is that she has been *handed* cups of tea thousands of times, but this is the first time she can remember being *given* one. (It is presumably 'tea time', time for everyone to have a cup of tea – the prime expression of the bureaucratization of care: routines.) It may be that men are less sensitive to this distinction, feel that they have done what is expected of them, given what was legitimately asked of them, and end up echoing Freud's exasperated cry: what do women *want*? The answer very often is what seems to the woman to be as plain as day: I want you to be *here*.

Men seem only to be *present* on occasions, they seem to dip in and out of the here and now as it suits them. Men of course *have* to do that, it is a precondition of so much of life and work in the public sphere that you not *be* present *in* the present. For women in the domestic sphere the reverse is true – you have to be present all the time. The sixties therapeutic idea of being present in the present was based on the *masculine* contrast. It took one half of the masculine construct and took it to mean being present as a pure self. For women in the private sphere it is quite a different matter. Being here now means being permanently on call to deal with contingencies, with the concrete and the immediate in all its disordered particularities.

Is there perhaps a more positive way of being present in your relationships with others that does not imply intimacy and is compatible with a public world? Consider in this light a proposition about friendship which suggests a possibility. (Remember that 'friend' was an alternative to 'brother' in visions of a non-hierarchical universal community.) The proposition is this: 'Friendship is not the abolishing of distance but the bringing of distance to life.' For many years I attached little significance to the fact that these words were written by a man – Walter Benjamin – but I have since found it productive to ponder whether this might not be an essentially masculine proposition expressing a distinctively masculine senti-ment. (One test of this might be whether a woman reader is less struck by the force of it and promptly loses interest.)

That this is a man speaking is suggested by its style. It is a rhetorical, public form of speech – it is not this, but that – imagine how Winston Churchill might have said it. It is certainly not hedged about with qualifications: in a sense, perhaps, is this right, what do you think? But is the sentiment itself a masculine one? The important meaning of a masculine proposition is one which is made from the vantage point of the social position of men. There is no out-look which does not look-out from somewhere, and an observation is masculine if it is made from the angles of vision afforded to a man by virtue of being male in this society. There is reason to think that this proposition – friendship is not the abolishing of distance, but the bringing of distance to life – is indeed, in this sense, masculine.

In today's climate, to describe an idea, an outlook or a sentiment as masculine is often taken as sufficient grounds to repudiate it. Men have had a lot of bad press in recent years, much of it richly deserved. But not everything masculine is false, ugly or dangerous. I shall not speak here in praise of men or masculinity, but I do want to argue that a constructive resolution of the crisis in relations between women and men today depends on preserving something of the spirit of the masculine perspective that gives rise to this idea of friendship.

As things are, it is men, I think, who are more likely to feel ambivalent about distance, to feel it as both a risk and a potential. If so, it is men who would most prefer to find some resolution of the problem that preserved something of both. Benjamin clearly felt that in some way or other distance *can* stand in the way of friendship, but insisted that these problems posed by distance are not to be resolved by simply going over to the other side, to the abolition of distance. In practice this would probably lead to what the followers of George Kelly (who would almost certainly be asking them to stop following him) call 'slot rattling' – endlessly dashing back and forth between two opposites, never happy to settle for either, forever trapped in the same groove. The hope is to go beyond the opposition to a kind of synthesis which transcends both.

Distance is a problem, but one need not conclude that the essence of friendship must consist in the abolishing of such distance. Instead the problem is a kind of 'dead' distance, the task is somehow to bring it to life. On the face of it this does not succeeed in transcending the opposition between distance and no-distance because it keeps the term 'distance', and takes friendship necessarily to entail distance. But if distance is something that can be alive, something which, far from standing in the way of friendship, is actually an inherent part of it, this changes beyond recognition the meaning of distance. The two terms in the contrast, or 'poles' of the 'construct', are defined in relation to one another, and Benjamin is clearly challenging the construct itself, the way the contrast between friendship and distance is drawn.

A proposition like this invites us to begin by not being sure of what either intimacy or distance actually mean – and that is where we *should* begin. We need to encounter and explore the problems posed by both distance *and* intimacy. (This is not simply a matter of thinking about it, but of actively contending with the issue in our everyday lives.) Benjamin's particular resolution or synthesis clearly does insist on something – but what is it? I take it to have something to do with the *otherness* of other people. Is this a masculine commitment? Are men, by virtue of their experience of living as a man in this society, more likely than women to insist on the otherness of other people? It is difficult enough to call anything feminine or masculine with confidence, and here we are on even less solid ground. Nevertheless I think it is more likely to be men, by virtue of their experience of living as man in this society, who want to find a positive way of affirming this otherness.

What matters here is that we have a possible way of not-being distant without being intimate. People can surely come alive to one another without being familiar, and without confessing their 'innermost' feelings. People come alive as *other* people, but what makes them go dead on you? There are many ways: by regarding them merely as 'other people' (like Norman Normals), as a member of a category and so on – but these are all ways of not engaging with someone and not allowing them to make their presence felt. We already have a way of expressing the opposite of this: being there, and treating someone, 'as a person'.

You cannot begin to bring about change without finding somewhere to start. (You have probably heard the joke about the person who stopped a local to ask for directions only to be told that if that's where *they* wanted to get to, they wouldn't start from here. Many who hope for a better society often give the impression that they would rather not start with this one.) There is, in this idea of 'as a person' already available to us a notion of the personal which need not imply intimacy. Indeed we use it explicitly in the context of relations in public. We *already* make demands of non-intimate relations that they be more personal and there are more occasions when we might. How do you make relationships more personal without being more intimate? Already to a limited degree we break the desired connection, in ways that make it clear that what is valued about personal relationships is often *not* their intimate quality.

The Pope is, of course, a person (one who likes canoeing and waterskiing) – but he is also The Pope. In 'society' (gesellschaft) the person exists independently of the position they occupy. To have a personal relationship with the Pope would mean, as we usually understand it, to see him not 'as the Pope' but 'as himself', probably without the hat. The idea of having a personal relationship with The Pope (with hat) seems incomprehensible. It is easy to conclude that relationships between two people cannot be personal if one or both is occupying a definite social position – but this is misleading.

The relationships that we call personal in the private sphere are social relations which take particular forms. In the family, person and position are conjoined – you are, for instance, Mum. There is no sense in the idea of a child having one kind of relationship with Mum and another with the person who is Mum. With friends it is the idea of having a non-personal relationship that seems incomprehensible. Friendship seems to be a relationship between pure persons, a purely personal relationship in this sense. And yet friendships, too, follow particular patterns in this (or any other) society and we can say things about the kind of relationships they entail. Middle-class people today are inclined to feel, for example, that friends should be invited into the home, and that you should get to know the 'whole person'. For them, people you only meet in specific contexts or do particular things with are acquaintances not friends. But as, for example, Graham Allan has documented, this pattern is by no means universal in our society. Friendships are clearly a particular kind of social relationship, the kind we usually call personal.

If personal relationships are themselves social relationships then how do other social relationships become more personal? Here again it is helpful to turn to the idea of 'community'. Relationships in 'community' are face to face, multi-faceted, and persist over long periods of time (are continuous in some way). The more relationships approach the 'community' type – by combining all three features – the more inclined we are to expect them to be 'personal' and object or become upset if they are not. The more of these features they combine, the more *intimate* they become – you are able to say you know the person 'well'. Mum is all three, sometimes so are our friends. At the other extreme are countless people we are connected with where none of these features apply: tax inspectors, cinema projectionists, the people who made the paper these words are printed on, and so on. But there are many, many cases which fall in between, varying according to which and how many features are present. What matters is that we already object or become upset if these in-between cases seem less than personal.

Health care is a particularly clear example. The complaint levelled most loudly and frequently against the medical profession is the *impersonal* manner in which people often feel they are treated. What do they want? Look at it in terms of the three features (face to face, multi-faceted, and continuous). People value the continuity of the GP in contrast to many hospital outpatient clinics (we talk of 'my GP' like my Mum but not my Pope) – but you can easily be continuously impersonal. There is some ambiguity about whether this is a specific or more diffuse and multi-faceted relationship, because although it is tied to a particular purpose – health matters – the GP may legitimately inquire into intimate details of many areas of your life and circumstances in a way we would not accept from the person who delivers the milk. But the complaint is *not* that doctor and patient should know each other intimately. What upsets people about this relationship is when its face-to-face (or face-to-something-else) character is in some sense illusory. You feel as if you are treated like a lump of meat as opposed to a person, 'as a case' rather than 'as a person'. We believe, in other words, that this relationship *can* be personal without being intimate. What it takes is for you to be recognized, to make your presence felt. You want the doctor to be there, to engage with you 'as a person' not as an object and not as a category.

The doctor's being a doctor and your being a patient is *not* the problem. Relationships can be – and this is the wider point – person to person even where both occupy a definite position, take up a specific role in relation to the other.* What it takes is for people to be engaged in their relations with others with all the concrete particularities that are relevant to the interaction. This means being present *as yourself* in public – but not at all in the sense of the sixties community of selves. This is an idea of humanizing society which is not the exporting of either the masculine or the feminine model of intimate relationships into the public sphere.

We need simply to be engaged in our relations in public. Simply? This entails revising our most fundamental imaginative vision of the world and ourselves and that means changing the *conditions* which lead us to construct it. It means abandoning the model of the ripples in the pool and constructing another in which you are still yourself in

---

*The rotation of roles in the business world is interesting here. Sellers usually seek to establish personal contacts in the firms they sell to, and these firms often respond by constantly changing the buyer in an active effort to prevent the relationship becoming too personal.

the public world. To be a little more concrete, when people want to close the distance between themselves and the people they work with for example, they tend to invite one another to talk about themselves. This usually means talking about your 'personal life' – why does this seem to be talking about yourself? If you talk about the job, it usually means 'stepping out of role' and disclosing your real, inner feelings about what you do. Both assume that you do not do your job as *yourself*, and that you cannot talk *as* yourself without talking *about* yourself.

This model cannot be revised in thought, only by living differently – by asking different questions of the relationships we are involved in and making different demands of them. But if we ask such simple questions of our public lives as: 'why is it difficult to bring this distance to life?', 'what would it be to act here as myself?', we find that there are formidable obstacles in our way, obstacles that run deep into the heart of the structure of modern society. If we did, though, come to feel that we acted in public *as* ourselves, where this did not mean bringing the private out into the public, it would start to matter a great deal what happened there. It would now be happening to *you*, not going over your shoulder. We would no longer tolerate people passing off their impersonal treatment of us with, 'I'm only doing my job' – and others would no longer tolerate it in us. As it stands, people are now prepared to put up with the impersonal character of the public world because they constantly resort to the idea that this is not really *me* here, this is not *my world*. If not, then whose world is it?

(The French social theorist Castoriadis once likened the public world to a huge traffic jam – everyone is trying to vacate public space simultaneously by hurtling through it and out of it as quickly as possible. The problem is that everyone gets in everybody else's way. If only you had a ray gun which could vaporize all the cars in front of you. There is now a product called 'The Revenger' designed to achieve 'in-car sanity'. The advertisement proclaims that with The Revenger you can, 'ZAP road hogs, STUN jaywalkers, BLAST your way through traffic jams. Revenger is attached to your dashboard with self-adhesive fabric. When the tension builds, flip it ON and your Death Ray, Machine Gun and Grenade Launchers light ready for ACTION. (Noise is confined to your car and the satisfaction you obtain is immeasurable.)' Public space is no-one's land. Everyone is going home to say: free at last, free at last, home is the sailor home from the sea, home is the self from society.)

The examples we have considered so far involve face-to-face relationships – but these are not the only kind that can be criticized for being impersonal. Take what is perhaps the most fundamental case, the relationship between producer and consumer. You are connected to whomever made the chair you are sitting on, but they did not make it *for you*. They made it because they were employed to make it, and their employer employed them to make it for 'the market'. There is of course a ferocious and continuing argument between those who believe that the market ensures that only the things that people actually need get produced (otherwise they would not buy them and production would cease) and those who believe that the market makes it impossible for people to communicate their needs to those who produce things, and prevents producers from gaining the satisfaction of knowing they are making something intended specifically to satisfy that need. But what no-one denies is that producers and consumers are currently related indirectly through the mediation of an impersonal co-ordinating mechanism (the market), and it is clearly *conceivable* that this relationship could in principle be more direct, from person to person, without being remotely intimate.

There is also a wider instance of how a relationship can *apparently* be direct, even face to face, without being person to person. This century has witnessed the rise of the ultimate pseudo-community in which everyone is apparently included: the idea of 'the (general) public'. The public here is an anonymous aggregate of individuals taken to be unconnected with one another who are ostensibly addressed as *individuals*. This is the public for the politician and the advertiser. Mass communications are vital in fostering the sense of being addressed directly as an individual – in the case of television, even of listening to, looking at and being looked at by someone who is not there. Everyone knows of course that this is an illusion – they are not talking *to you* at all. The effects of this extend dramatically beyond television to the point where people simply pay no attention to public communications of any kind. I have seen, for instance, a scrapyard bearing a notice on the gate saying in large letters 'Keep Out', and below it in even larger letters 'That Means You'. It seems that you must now act on the assumption that everyone will presume the message is intended for someone else.

None of the features, then, which combine to make relationships *intimate* are actually necessary for a relationship to be *personal* – as we already understand it. This means that we do already know how to make demands of relationships in public that they may be more personal without their losing their public character. But the public world as it is currently constituted relies on the fact that we do not make such demands.

The public world carries on its own sweet way because our hearts and minds are somewhere else. Amongst other things this is very big business. Just as in the early days of mass production, debt had to be redefined as credit and the ethic of thrift and delayed gratification had to go, so now our private fortresses must become units of consumption, providing mass markets for expanding industries which produce things for the household. A work ethic is no longer necessary, it has been replaced by a vicious cycle. Increasing numbers of people are now locked into their jobs by having to pay for all the things they have bought on credit to line their homes with in order to create a comfortable sanctuary to escape to from the emptiness and ugliness of their working lives. Ultimately many become committed to their jobs precisely *because* they hate them.

It is not hard to understand why we go looking for rewarding human relationships in the private sphere of personal life: who in their right minds would go looking for them anywhere else? This could be a long, lonely and unhappy pilgrimage. But change must come from somewhere, and this commitment to the personal may well provide the impulse. Narrow and channel the aspiration for personal relationships into one corner of life and it soon begins to buckle under the strain. If people discover for themselves that the demands they make on their personal lives cannot in principle be realized, and that these arise as a reaction to the emptiness and the ugliness of the public world, they may begin to focus their demands on that world. All of us, individually and collectively, have an interest in broadening the focus of this aspiration. Public life will never be private life, but it *can* become more personal.

Now you might be forgiven for being a little unclear as to how this is part of a solution to the problem of *gender* – I seem to be talking instead of personal relationships. But what we are talking about here is the possibility of a world in which it really *does* go without saying that women and men are included in the category of 'person', a world in which you are neither woman nor man first, but person first. What does that entail? To think of raising women to the same condition as men is to define *person*hood as *man*hood, as it always has been. ('Person' means human being, 'personhood' the condition of being human.) A genuine personhood must incorporate and transcend both womanhood and manhood – or to put it another way, personality must incorporate and transcend both feminin-ity and masculin-ity. This cannot be accomplished in the realm of ideas alone. We can only become persons first by creating a society in which women and men participate in relationships in which *everyone* is regarded as a person first. In other words: *personal relationships*.

It is plainly not at all obvious what that means – indeed by now we should expect to be in the region of barely thinkable thoughts. In a way we will only understand what personal relationships will be, and hence what being 'a person' will mean, in a changed society – if and when it becomes a reality. But we must, of course, begin with the present.

Our current ways of understanding what 'the personal' means arise out of a society divided by gender. The polarities of the feminine and the masculine which we hope to transcend are rooted in a society which insists that a personal life is only possible within the narrow confines of a privileged region cut off and separated from where the main action is, somewhere in the world but not of it. It is here, the story goes, that relationships are personal, here that we are persons first.

Women and men have different tales to tell of this personal life and we must listen to each others' stories. What we both need to understand is that the conflicts and tensions that arise in the private sphere do not have their source within it. The problems people experience in their 'personal lives' derive from the nature of personal life as it is established and defined in this society – defined, that is, in contrast to the public world. But women and men have a different experience of life on either side of this fragile wall and of the relationship between the two worlds it divides. The imaginative visions of the world and ourselves that we construct on the basis of this experience are different and in conflict and both must be reconstructed.

I am not in the business of telling anyone what they *ought* to do, or of trying to paint some utopian vision of how things might be in a genderless world beyond the rainbow. The future is usually a screen on to which people project all the confusions and contradictions of the present. If you listen to all that is written and said about the future, the best you can do is conclude with David Byrne that in the future there will be so much going on that no-one will be able to keep track of it.

The seeds of the future are here in the confusions of the present and that is where we have to begin. We are already confused about most of the polarities in which gender is implicated. Having the best of both worlds, combining and transcending the feminine and the masculine in a new human synthesis, depends on rethinking and reliving the contrasts between private and public as they arise and are felt in the experience of women and men today. To go beyond these to a new synthesis involves unmaking a whole host of oppositions, including the ones I have taken as an illustration and a model (intimacy *versus* distance, and personal *versus* impersonal) but also those between subjective and objective, progress and repetition, nature and culture, and, crucially I think, between psychology and society.

Women and men have a great deal to learn from one another. I said earlier that changing the sex of the players will not change the game, but understanding the position of the other players can help considerably to understand what the game is, how it is played, and how we might rewrite the rules. It is not simply a matter of thinking, but of living differently, and this means participating in each other's worlds – and not just as tourists. I have suggested here that women may have something to learn from men's attempts to contend positively with the experience of distance. But in the end, I believe, it is men who have more to learn from women. It is the *masculine* world view that continues to dominate in this society. It is one which ensures the subordination of women, but men also have an interest in discovering its failings and its consequences.

The belief that women and men are different kinds of people has served historically to divide this society into two apparently distinct and independent realms. That women belong outside society and that the world they inhabit lies outside society have amounted to the same thing, which is why it is *all three* elements of the doctrine of separate spheres which have to be challenged simultaneously: that these are the proper spheres of women and men, that they are in fact separate and must be kept separate, and that one lies outside society. What makes women and men different and unequal is our differing relation to the public/private contrast and so it is this that must be transformed. But it is men who have the greatest investment in the doctrine of separate spheres, and not simply because it enables them to be the prime movers in the sphere in which governing is done and money is made.

Men have hoped to meet women on a terrain that is outside society and women are not having it any longer. But it is not only women who have paid the price or who have an interest in change. Man the builder of dwellings has now built in public space a world in which, and on which, he does not wish to dwell too long. Man the erector of defences against the elements now builds private fortresses to keep his own creation at bay, erecting defences against its intrusions. Homo sapiens has always struggled to survive in an inhospitable world, now the inhospitality is his own creation and hospitality begins and ends at home.

In allowing women, and the concerns that they associate with women, to be cast out of society, men have collaborated in the construction of a public world so devoid of humanity that the need to find humanity in private and with women becomes ever more intense. With it grows the fear of a woman's coldness and indifference, the very things men mete out to one another every day of their lives. Francis Bacon wrote that, 'Wife and Children are a kind of Discipline of Humanity'. If this is how men find it, then they should study this discipline and stop locking its practitioners and their practice away. Humanity confined to the enclave shrivels and becomes exclusive, and these private pools of mutual aid feed vast public oceans of mutual indifference.

More men are troubled by masculinity than is usually acknowledged. Most are simply surviving. But as long as they keep their confused misgivings to themselves and continue to survive as men, the public world which they rebuild every day, and from which they seek refuge in private, will flourish and grow ever more hideous. Men are born into a world that appears to them to be divided along these lines, and so divide their hearts and minds accordingly. They then sustain and rebuild it simply by living as men, by dealing with things in the manner of men. They rebuild it by wanting to be released from or find restored in private what they feel they must endure or ignore in public. They rebuild it every time they fail to smile at or be considerate towards a man where they would have behaved differently towards a woman.

I will not say that women should stop helping men to survive, but men are the carriers of the kinds of polarities that keep apart the two halves of this divided world which we all have an interest in bringing together. Men have come to straddle the public and private worlds in such a way that they hope to be able to turn their backs on the public when they enter the private and their backs on the private when they enter the public. But as the most insightful of proverbs in the folklore of psychotherapy says: whatever you turn your back on will get you in the end.

References

The book draws on a wide range of sources. In order to avoid an unnecessarily lengthy bibliography, only those which are quoted or referred to directly in the text and/or have a significant bearing on its main themes are included below.

Allan, G. (1979): *A Sociology of Friendship and Kinship*. Allen & Unwin.

Bannister, D. (ed.) (1977): *New Perspectives in Personal Construct Theory*. Academic Press.

Bannister, D. (1985): in F. Epting and A. W. Landfield (eds.), *Anticipating Personal Construct Psychology*. University of Nebraska Press.

Berger, J. (1972): *Ways of Seeing*. Penguin Books.

Boulton, M. (1983): *On Being a Mother*. Tavistock Publications.

Brown, G. & Harris, T. (1978): *Social Origins of Depression*. Tavistock Publications.

Brownmiller, S. (1984): *Femininity*. Hamish Hamilton.

Chodorow, N. (1978): *The Reproduction of Mothering*. University of California Press.

De Beauvoir, S. (1974): *The Second Sex*. Penguin Books.

Easthope, A. (1986): *What a Man's Gotta Do*. Paladin.

Friedan, B. (1981): *The Second Stage*. Abacus.

Gilligan, C. (1982): *In a Different Voice*. Harvard University Press.

Goffman, E. (1976): *Gender Advertisements*. Macmillan.

Henry, J. (1972): *Pathways to Madness*. Jonathan Cape.

Kelly, G. (1964): The Language of Hypothesis, in B. Maher (ed.) (1979), *Clinical Psychology and Personality: The Selected Papers of George Kelly*. Krieger.

Lasch, C. (1977): *Haven in a Heartless World*. Basic Books.

Lasch, C. (1980): *The Culture of Narcissism*. Abacus.

Mair, M. (1977): The Community of Self, in D. Bannister (ed.), op. cit.

Oakley, A. (1974): *The Sociology of Housework*. Martin Robertson.

Orbach, S. & Eichenbaum, L. (1984): *What Do Women Want?* Fontana.

Ruskin, J. (1865): Of Queen's Gardens, in *Sesame and Lilies* (quoted in K. Millett (1977), *Sexual Politics*. Virago Press).

Segal, L. (1989): *Is the Future Female?* Virago Press.

Sennett, R. (1977): Destructive Gemeinschaft, in N. Birnbaum (ed.), *Beyond the Crisis*. Oxford University Press.

Sennett, R. (1977): *The Fall of Public Man*. Cambridge University Press.

Smith, D. (1974): Women's Perspective as a Radical Critique of Sociology. *Sociological Inquiry*, 44 (1), 7–13.

Smith, D. (1983): Women, Class and Family, in R. Miliband & J. Saville (eds.), *The Socialist Register*. Merlin Press.

Tonnies, F. (1955): *Community and Association*. Routledge and Kegan Paul.

Vidal, G. (1982): Sex Is Politics, in *Pink Triangle and Yellow Star*. Granada.

Williams, R. (1983): *Keywords*. Flamingo.

Zaretsky, E. (1976): *Capitalism, the Family and Personal Life*. Pluto Press.

Index of Names

Aristotle   75, 129
Aurelius, Marcus   21

Bacon, Francis   172
Baldwin, James   143
Bannister, Don   20, 38, 160
Beauvoir, Simone de   1, 13, 129
Beckett, Samuel   85
Bem, Sandra   139
Benjamin, Walter   162–4
Berger, John   52
Berger, Peter   123
Boulton, Mary   93, 128, 131
Brown, G.   114
Brownmiller, Susan   105, 106
Byron, Lord   4, 27, 35

Castoriadis, Cornelius   167
Chodorow, Nancy   158

Delphy, Christine   15
Donne, John   117

Easthope, Anthony   107
Eichenbaum, L.   100

Fitzgerald, F. Scott   97
France, Anatole   147

Friedan, Betty   32, 151

Gilligan, Carol   76–81, 148, 157
Goffman, Erving   51, 73, 74
Harris, T.   114
Henry, Jules   67–9, 71

James, William   45

Kafka, Franz   12
Kelly, George   38, 163
Kipling, Rudyard   98
Kohlberg, Lawrence   76–81, 121

Laing, R. D.   161
Lasch, Christopher   31–2, 95

Mair, Miller   121
Marx, Karl   21, 32
May, Rollo   88
Morgan, David   14

Oakley, Ann   45, 132
Orbach, S.   100

Pope, Alexander   141
Potter, Dennis   50

Proust, Marcel   21–2

Riesman, David   155
Rogers, Carl   127
Rowe, Dorothy   114
Ruskin, John   26–7, 32, 33,
    39, 83
Russell, Bertrand   160

Segal, Lynne   5
Sennett, Richard   42, 46
Shaw, George Bernard   115

Smith, Dorothy   87
Spence, Janet   59

Thatcher, Margaret   117, 119
Tonnies, Ferdinand   122–4,
    146, 148
Tschudi, Finn   53
Twain, Mark   18

Vidal, Gore   14

Weldon, Fay   86

Index of Subjects

Abstract thought   71, 77, 79,
    81–2, 85–9, 117–19, 127, 136,
    137n, 144–6
Agency/communion   97–9
Androgyny   58–9, 104
Appearance   104–6, 112–13
Autonomy   25, 31, 39, 45,
    98, 99, 100, 115, 128, 132,
    139–42 (*see also* Dependence/
    Independence)

Care   60–1, 64–5, 75, 80 (*see
    also* Love; Nurturance;
    Tenderness)
Character   55–6, 104
Childcare   6, 86–7, 90–5, (*see
    also* Mothers)
Class, social   10, 44–5, 62,
    90–5, 105, 108, 120, 131,
    134, 165
'Community' (gemeinschaft)
    122–5, 133–4, 148–51, 157–8,
    165
Community of selves   121–7
Confidence   106, 111–14
Construct   72

Dennis the Menace   107–10

Dependence/Independence
    97–116
Depression   113–15
Domestic labour (*see*
    Housework)

Economy   25, 28–30, 34, 134,
    136, 147–8, 168
Equality   71, 112, 143–4,
    146–7, 149

Family   32, 34, 119–20, 130,
    133, 149–50
Feminine perspective   9, 12,
    20–2, 65, 81, 110–11, 121,
    134, 142, 153, 156–9, 161, 171
Femininity   5, 18–23, 39, 50–
    52, 54, 58, 103–6, 107–11, 118,
    129, 138, 142, 170
Feminism   2, 11, 26, 33, 39–
    40, 70, 88, 96, 126, 140, 143,
    146–7, 156
Fraternity   143, 149–50
Freedom   34, 36, 44–5, 47
Friendship   25, 37, 40, 162–4,
    165

Housework   6, 29–30, 86–7,
    90–5 (*see also* Work)

Houseworkers 43–5, 83, 114n, 123, 125, 129–32
Human condition 68, 71, 145
Humanism 11–12, 41, 140–2, 143–52
Humanity 26, 32, 68, 100, 142–52, 158, 172

Identity 20, 45–7, 106, 119, 121–7
Ideology 62
Imaginative visions 16, 21, 22, 28, 44, 108, 161, 166, 170
Individual and society 115, 117–18, 132, 139, 145–6, 160
Individualism 132
Individuality 25, 94, 115, 117–35
Individuation 119–121
Intimacy 25, 34, 39–43, 47, 72–5, 139–42, 150–1, 156–9, 161; and distance 41–2, 73, 161–4, 171

Linear thought 98–9; time 89–96
Love 34, 37, 60–1, 64–5, 75, 160 (see also Care; Nurturance; Tenderness)

Masculine perspective 9, 12, 20–2, 27, 32–5, 47–9, 67, 70–71, 75, 81, 110–11, 121, 134, 142, 153–6, 157, 161–4, 171
Masculinity 5, 13, 18–23, 39, 50–2, 54, 58, 68, 97–9, 107–111, 118, 129, 137–8, 142, 144, 159, 162–4, 170, 172
Metaphors 15–16, 20, 28, 41, 44, 46, 52, 59, 91, 108, 109, 117, 120, 121, 136

Mind/body 82, 85–9
Morality 67, 75, 76–81, 148, 157
Mothers 43–5, 65, 70, 90–5, 114n, 123, 125, 128–32 (see also Childcare)
Mutuality/mutual aid 34, 123, 133, 149–51, 157–8
Myths 16–17, 25, 84–5

Natural expression, doctrine of 51–60, 106
Nature/culture 83–5, 95–6, 107
Nurturance 60–1, 64–5, 138–9 (see also Care; Love)

Objective (see Subjective/ Objective)

Person 7, 42, 46, 56, 117–18, 154, 164–6, 169–70 (see also Personal relationships)
Personal life 8–11, 28, 31, 33, 36–8, 42, 43, 47–8, 100, 136, 150–1, 160, 167, 169–70
Personal relationships 30, 31, 42, 47, 48, 133–4, 154, 160–73
Personalistic ties 133–4, 157–8
Personality 22–3, 25, 49, 50–63, 64–5, 97, 102–4, 106, 111, 138–9, 145, 154
Personhood 32, 170
Play 93
Power 70, 72–4, 113, 115
Pre-industrial household 28-31, 40, 48, 133n, 134, 148
Privatism 31–5, 36–49, 95, 100–1, 127, 131, 132, 150–9, 160, 169

Psychoanalysis   28, 107–8
Psychology   9–10, 30, 33, 34,
    39, 43, 49, 60, 61–2, 65, 74,
    97, 101, 106, 111, 113, 115,
    138, 139, 156, 171
Public/Private   3–11, 18–19,
    25–35, 36–7, 44, 48, 75, 76,
    81, 85, 89, 100, 124, 126–7,
    128, 132–3, 136–7, 146, 150–
    159, 162, 170–3

Relational capacities   158–9
Relativism   141–2
Repression   107–9
Reproduction   36, 85, 90, 101,
    147
Ritual   24–5, 47, 121–2, 155
Role (*see* Self and role)
Romanticism   4, 9, 34, 37, 64,
    66, 156

Self   25, 35, 36–49, 77, 121,
    131, 153–5, 158, 160–1, 166–
    167, (*see also* Identity); and
    role   43–5, 48, 130–1, 155;
    and society   37–9
Self-esteem   111–15
Separate spheres, doctrine
    of   5–6, 19, 27, 136, 147–8,
    171–2

Sex and gender   17–18, 50–1,
    137
Sexual orientation   53–4, 126
Sisterhood   149–50
Socialization   51, 138
Society (*see* Individual and
    society)
'Society' (gesellschaft)   122–5,
    146–8, 164
Sociology   30, 34, 39, 43
Subjective   46–9, 60, 70–1, 97,
    106, 111, 112, 114;
    subjective/objective   47–9,
    61, 88–9

Tenderness   37, 64–75, 137–9
    (*see also* Care; Love;
    Nurturance)
Therapeutic outlook   43, 95,
    154, 162
Time   89–96
Trade unionism   147

Vulnerability   67–74, 101

Work   6, 28–30, 34, 86–7,
    132, 147, 169 (*see also*
    Housework)